Finding Summer Happiness

Chris Penhall

Stories that inspire emotions!
www.rubyfiction.com

For Sarah and Hannah

Gareth, Ann, Kevin, Barrie and Sam

and

Jill, Sandra, Sue, Loui, Mark and Mike for the days on the Pembrokeshire Coastal path

Acknowledgements

I had the idea for this novel a few years ago, just before my first novel, *The House That Alice Built*, was published. I wrote it in 2020 and 2021 when all our lives were different for a while.

So, I want to thank all my family, friends, workmates and neighbours for all the Zoom calls, phone calls, texts, messages, walks, kindness and general positivity.

My publishers, Ruby Fiction, for being so supportive and also for wanting to publish the book, and the members of the Tasting Panel who read the manuscript and said "yes": Janice Butler, Carol Botting, Jenny Kinsman, Elisabeth Hall, Jenny Mitchell, Jo Osborne, Alma Hough and Ruth Nägele.

And everyone out there making a difference.

Chapter One

Who is B and what is their relationship to R? wondered Miriam, as she lay under the table, studying the graffiti scratched haphazardly into it. *And is that a heart, which means they were in love, or an apple, which could mean they were just hungry?*

'Miriam?' Someone tapped on the door of the portacabin gently. 'Don't forget you've got that ceremony to go to …'

'Oh.' She closed her eyes and tried to pretend she hadn't heard.

'Hello?' The voice tried again. 'Are you okay?'

'Yes … yes … just give me a few minutes.' She looked up again, longing to stay and follow the trail of letters … *a … n … f …* obviously left there over the years by previous users. Maybe she would make up a story or two about their origins, their lives, their histories. Anything other than roll out from where she was, stand up, put a smile on and open the door.

'Breathe in,' she muttered. 'One, two, three … and breathe out … one, two, three, four, five … and repeat …'

'I'm really sorry,' the voice said again, 'but you'll be late, and I know you won't like that.'

'Okay, it's okay.' Miriam clambered up and brushed the dust from her clothes, the sounds from outside beginning to encroach on her temporarily calm space. Checking her hair in the dirty mirror hanging next to a tatty picture of the Eiffel Tower, she pulled herself up to her full height and walked outside.

Her PA touched her arm and smiled. 'Thank goodness. I thought you were there for the night.'

'It's okay, Justin, it's fine. I just needed to …'

'Hyperventilate and have a panic attack?'

Miriam grabbed the door handle and stopped at the top of the stairs. People were milling around happily, some queuing at the food stalls, others waiting patiently in front of the stage. A woman on stilts was handing out balloons next to a clown throwing buckets of pretend paint over laughing children. 'Is everything all right?' she asked, counting her breaths in her mind.

'Everything is absolutely wonderful. As you knew it would be.'

'No I didn't.' She made her way down onto the field. 'But I'm glad it is.'

Justin squeezed her hand. 'You didn't have to do this, you know? You could have left it to us.'

'Well, if Bethany hadn't let us down at the last minute and decided not to run the event and break her employment contract to boot, I wouldn't have had to. And to go and work for *that* company too? Traitor.'

'Let's not think about *that* company,' he said, his voice calm and soothing. 'And you still could have left it to us.'

Miriam sighed. 'Mum always came to this one though. I wanted it to be perfect, which is why I put Bethany in charge in the first place … *traitor*.'

'There's steam coming out of your ears. Let's not talk about that.'

'But last night when I found out, I thought, "let's make this work". One last time before I officially hand over the reins.' Miriam smiled faintly. 'But I couldn't even do that.'

'Are you feeling okay now?'

'More or less. Is the car ready for me?'

'It's right there.' A sleek black Jaguar was parked just behind the portacabin. 'It'll take you to your hotel where you can put on your glad rags, and then take you to pick up your award.'

Miriam almost winced. 'Business Owner of the Year … well … do I have to go? I'm not sure I can face everyone.'

'You will. You always do.' Justin put his hands on her shoulders and looked at her sternly. 'And you cannot stay in that hotel forever. Can you please let me sort a house rental out for you before I leave the country?'

'I'm quite happy in the hotel. I know where everything is, and I don't have to think.'

'You can't be happy in that hotel. There's no view.' Justin took out his phone and clicked on a photograph. 'And it's also just around the corner from the office, so not healthy at all.' He waved the picture at her. 'Look … see? Isn't it gorgeous?'

'You literally found it an hour ago online.'

'But it's in the place you used to go when you were little for holidays. It'll be lovely. You told me about how your mum talked about that village all the time.'

'But in the hotel people only knock on the door to clean the room or give me food. It's so ordered. No chaos. No one asking me to solve problems, no unexpected visitors … it's so calm.'

Justin held the phone in front of her. 'Personally, I think this looks like a place you could hide away from everyone to your heart's content.'

The car began to rev its engine and Miriam sighed with relief, glad not to have to make a decision there and then. 'I'll think about it.'

'You'd better be quick. As soon as this is finished, I'm heading straight to the airport and on to Brazil.'

'I'll miss you,' she said. 'You're the best PA a girl could ever ask for.'

He blew her a kiss as she closed the door. 'Why you ever sold your house when you've got nowhere to go beats me.'

'It seemed like a good idea at the time,' she shouted, and waved as the car pulled away. 'And so did selling my business. Oh, bloody hell. Into the void I go.' Miriam closed her eyes and practiced the breathing again, trying to pull herself back to "Miriam the MD" of her own company. Miriam the MD who was about to walk away from it all as soon as she'd got this award. Thank goodness nobody had seen her hiding under the table.

Arriving late after getting ready at the hotel, she paused outside the function room, gathering the energy to walk in. Her long red hair was tied up in a sleek, business-like bun, her make-up understated and smart, her plain green designer dress projecting sophistication and elegance. Miriam was ready to convey the persona of a successful, capable woman. This was the last thing she had to do. Pretend all was well – like a swan, gliding effortlessly on top of the water, feet paddling like mad out of sight. Looking up at the ceiling, she took three deep breaths, murmured 'Come on, you can do this,' opened the door, flashed her professional smile and moved towards her seat, nodding at the people she knew. *Confident and in control.*

Somehow over the following hour, she managed to indulge in polite small talk, smile serenely and play the part of Miriam Ryan so well she could have surely been in the running for Best Actress at the Oscars. Once the ceremony got going, she glanced at the clock on the wall, every few minutes mentally calculating how long she had left before she could escape back to her quiet, calm, bland hotel room. By the time the host looked at her and smiled, preparing to call her to the stage, her heart was racing unpleasantly.

'And for our final award, and for the third year in a row, our Business Owner of the Year is Miriam Ryan.' He held up the small glass trophy as Miriam made her way to the stage. All she wanted to do was take it and run, but she forced herself to walk steadily and with dignity around the tables, nodding appreciatively at the applause. 'And we are also saying farewell – not forever, we hope – as today Miriam is stepping down as MD of MR Events.'

'Thank you everyone for this.' Miriam surveyed the room, smiling, still somehow projecting ease, success and contentment. *What an actress I am*, she thought. 'It means a great deal to me. I set up the business with Felix – he's sitting over there – twenty-three years ago, and it's been my passion ever since. Even after we got divorced and I bought him out!' He stood up and bowed to laughing and clapping. 'That meant he was free to set up an award-winning restaurant, and I could concentrate on the events part of the company – although we do *a lot* of cooking. Now I've decided to have another adventure, although I've no idea what it is yet.' She laughed. 'But I'm so pleased that Felix is the person who will be at the helm from now on.' She raised her glass. 'To Felix, and to you my friends and colleagues. Thank you for voting me Business Owner of the Year!' She took a sip of her drink. 'And now I have a car waiting to whisk me away. Enjoy the rest of the party.' She shot off stage, grabbed her bag, waved at everyone and hurried towards the exit.

And that's when she saw him out of the corner of her eye, sitting at a table in the corner and watching her as she called the lift. She looked at the door, pretending she hadn't noticed, fighting the wave of nausea that came with the sudden memory of the same event last year.

Bloody Artie Morgan. As if things weren't bad enough before she'd met him.

Miriam pressed the lift button again, desperate to get away, and took her phone out of her bag, bringing up Justin's details.

Hi. I'll take the house. Just send me whatever I need to sign. As long as it's a long way from here. She pressed send and got into the lift. 'Maybe it'll help me remember happier times,' she said to herself.

The doors opened on the ground floor and she walked out, attempting to look like someone who'd just won another award. Not someone who'd had a panic attack at an event just four hours ago and was hiding from a man.

Her phoned pinged and she read the message. *Leave it to me, almost ex-boss. Your wish is my command. J x*

Climbing into the car, she stared out at the streets as it began to move through the traffic, trying not to think about last year, concentrating on the names of the shops, the people walking past, buses, motorbikes and cars, all merging into a stream of colours and noise. But there he was in her mind's eye. *Artie Morgan.* Standing next to one of the food trucks at the repurposed fashionable warehouse venue that last year's awards ceremony had been held in. She'd rushed there after a visit to her mother at the nursing home, her decision made to sell the company. She'd also decided that she might, eventually, buy a food truck of her own. Artie Morgan was an expert in this, it transpired. Charming, funny, warm Artie Morgan. Her knight in shining armour.

Although it turned out his armour had turned to rust a long time ago.

'More like, "come into my web said the spider to the fly",' she muttered.

The blast of a car horn pushed the image away, just as she arrived at the hotel.

But now I'm gone, she thought. *Free of all of it. And that is a good thing, isn't it?*

One week later, Miriam closed the hotel room door behind her and watched her luggage being pulled along the corridor by the porter. Taking her phone out of her bag, she opened the last message from Justin. *I just managed to get this done before I disappear up the Amazon! They didn't confirm until I got off the plane from Rio. Attached is the contract, directions and contact details of the letting agent. All done within a week with very little internet. I'm waiting for a round of applause here. Not a raise, obviously, as I don't work for you any more. I demand champagne for finding this when I come to visit you though. Anyhow, enjoy whatever it is you decide to do next. And I'll be in touch when I'm back from South America.*

PS: I think this was meant to be. Finding that house. It all happened so quickly, like it was waiting for you.

'Don't get all mystical on me, Justin.' She sighed. 'Nothing is meant to be. It's all down to us.'

Miriam opened the document and checked the address. Then she clicked on a photo and smiled. Two weeks ago she'd had no plan but now, thanks to Justin, she had one.

It was to go and stay in a house by the sea for a while. That was it.

She gazed outside, waiting for the lift to arrive. The early summer sunshine reflected off the office blocks opposite so the windows looked like giant cubes of ice, and she shivered involuntarily. She remembered hurriedly reading the paperwork Justin had sent from Brazil as soon as he'd arrived, signing it and sending it back as quickly as possible. Her mind had begun to fuzz by that point, fraying at the edges after years of precise, focused thought, and she was grateful he had organised it all for her.

The lift arrived and she stepped in. 'Time to go,' she said to no one as the doors closed. 'Time for a long break. Away from people, responsibilities and watching the clock.'

Her car was waiting for her outside after she had checked out, her luggage already safely stowed away in the boot. Climbing in, she waved goodbye to the concierge and drove out into the London traffic, heading towards her last farewell before she left the city.

Pushing the door of The Croft open, Miriam's stomach filled with nervous butterflies. She put the bunch of flowers and a basket of cupcakes and muffins on the reception desk, and rang the bell, the background aroma of sandalwood and bleach making her heart beat uncomfortably fast. *I don't want to ever smell that again. Ever*, she thought as Val, who was stationed at the desk that day, walked over from the café.

'Hello, Miriam,' she said warmly. How lovely to see you. It's been a while.'

Miriam smiled. 'I'm ashamed to say it's been months. I've been very busy sorting out my life. As you do.'

'Well, that sounds exciting.' Val looked at her expectantly

'Yes, I've sold my house, sold the business and I'm heading to Wales for a little while.'

'Goodness me, that's huge.' Val hugged her and suddenly, out of nowhere, Miriam wanted to cry. 'Oh, yes, that reminds me – the pictures,' said Val gently, stepping back and squeezing her hand comfortingly. 'You said you were going to pick them up.'

'Sorry it's taken so long. I …' Miriam was too ashamed to explain she couldn't face a box of family photographs. 'I had a lot on.'

'I understand. It's quite common. Now, we put them in the safe under the desk when you rang to tell us you were coming.' Val walked behind the table and keyed a code in. 'Here you are.'

She handed over a jiffy bag. 'We didn't have space for the cardboard box, I'm afraid.'

'That's fine. This is easier to carry.' Miriam put it in her bag without looking at it. 'I wanted to say thank you to everyone for how they looked after Mum, how you all look after everyone. It was a difficult time, but you all made it almost bearable.'

'Oh, that's very kind. We do our best.'

Miriam looked at the floor and tried to gather her strength. 'So, I've made a donation – the management team know about that – and I've got you all these.' She pointed at the gifts she'd left on the desk.

'How very thoughtful.' Val hugged her again, and this time Miriam allowed the tears to come. 'It's okay, it's all right,' murmured Val. 'We understand. We get fond of people – our residents and their families – and we think it's important to cry.'

But I don't cry, thought Miriam. *I just don't.*

She stood back and held out her hand. 'I have to go. I've got a long drive ahead of me. But I couldn't leave without stopping in.'

'Keep in touch,' said Val as Miriam turned towards the exit.

She waved before heading outside and getting back into the car, checking her make-up in the mirror to make sure the tears hadn't smudged it. Then she took a brush out of her bag and tidied up her hair before she switched on the engine and pushed back out into the London traffic.

As she drove over the Severn crossing, the early afternoon sun illuminated the greens and browns on the hills on the other side of the river, and she glanced left, smiling at the cloudless blue sky shining along the coastline. It made her feel lighter somehow, as if she'd physically left the last few years behind somewhere in London in storage.

'This is all about me,' she said to the empty passenger seat. 'No one to worry about. No one.'

Pausing to buy supplies from a supermarket just off the motorway in Cardiff, she continued along past Swansea and down towards Carmarthen, stopping briefly for another break at the end of the M4.

Nearly there, she thought, starting the car up again and studying the sat nav. 'Surely not,' she muttered irritably, double checking the arrival time on the screen. '*Two* more hours?' Reaching inside her bag on the passenger seat for a mint, she accidentally knocked it over, spilling her purse, phone, make-up and diary on the floor. Gathering it all up, she rifled through the diary until she found the date – June 1st – and smiled at what she'd written. *Freedom*, it said. Then underneath, *do whatever you want*. She laughed. *Was it normal to remind yourself to relax by writing it in a diary?* she wondered, then drove out towards the exit as a scruffy green Jeep suddenly veered in front of her, nearly clipping the side of the car.

'Oi!' she screamed, swerving around it, scraping along the side of a fence before managing to put the brakes on. An arm waved apologetically from the driver's window of the Jeep, apparently oblivious to the destruction as it drove off along the main road.

Miriam jumped out to check for any damage, seething. The vehicle appeared unharmed, although her heart was still racing when she set off west again, only calming down as the roads eventually quietened and the landscape changed.

She stopped at a lay-by on the brow of a hill which swept down towards the sea and texted the contact at the letting agents so they could meet her at the house. Allowing herself to rest for a few moments, she gazed at the gentle curve of the shore which sloped upwards to dramatic cliffs in the distance. The sun was slowly setting in the west, the sky a heady mixture of orange, blue and almost black, the darkening waves breaking powerfully on the beach below. For a moment, she felt peaceful. Then the buzz of a motorbike speeding past brought her back to the present, so she stretched, checked her sat nav and began the last part of her journey. She navigated the increasingly narrow roads, which were dotted alongside with cottages, luscious hedgerows, and protected by high, bowing trees. The sea glittered in the distance as the lanes swept up over the hills, disappearing again when the car dipped into a valley.

It was almost dark when she pulled off the tiny village road onto the driveway of the house, and she was too tired to feel anything but relief at her arrival. A small figure with long, dark, wavy hair and a kind, smiling face, climbed out of the car parked in front of her and waved.

Miriam got out wearily. 'Hello,' she said.

'Hiya. It's Miriam, is it? I'm Rhiannon. The letting agent.' She shook Miriam's hand, still smiling. 'Of course I'm the letting agent. You'll have worked that out! Why else would I be here? I'm really an estate agent, I am, but I'm covering someone else who's the letting agent, and I have to keep saying it so I remember. I didn't know when I accepted the job …' Her voice trailed off and she looked at Miriam expectantly.

Miriam smiled. 'Good to meet you,' she said.

'You too. Lovely house, this. Apparently.' Rhiannon took a key out of her bag and put it in the lock. 'Not been in myself though, to be honest. I'm new, you see. Just moved down from the Cardiff office. Broken heart I had, so had to get away. Fresh start and all of that.' She pushed the door open. 'Ta dah! Welcome to The Grange!'

They both stepped into the hallway and Rhiannon switched on the light. The walls were striped with yellow and white, with a light slate-grey floor and an elegant stairway to the side.

'Oh, there's lovely,' squealed Rhiannon. 'I could live here myself. Aren't you lucky!'

Miriam smiled. 'It seems I am by the looks of it.'

'It was all very last minute, wasn't it?' Rhiannon pushed the nearest door open. 'Now, *that's* what I call a kitchen. Look at the range over there. You can get very creative culinary-wise.'

'I plan to live on ready meals, dips and takeaways.' Miriam laughed. 'So, no creativity here.'

'Oh. Pity that. It looks like it likes to be cooked in. You know what I mean, don't you?'

'Oh, I do.' Miriam peered out of the doors into the garden. 'I used to own an events company and we mainly did our own catering, so I've spent a lot of time in kitchens over the years.'

'Well, you can use this one to sit down and enjoy the view in, then.' Rhiannon picked up a large file from next to the sink, scattering several pieces of paper on the floor. 'Oops …' She gathered them up and put them back. 'The owner seems to have left you a few recipes. That's kind.'

Miriam opened the fridge door in the hope that some kind soul had left some chilling wine in it, but there was nothing there.

'The owner went away in a bit of a hurry, apparently,' said Rhiannon 'But she's left a list of instructions here too by the looks of it.'

'I think I'll look at that tomorrow. I've been driving all day, and I just fancy a glass or two of wine. Then I'll head to bed.'

'Would you like me to give you a quick tour of the place?' Rhiannon looked hopeful.

'No thanks. I'll be fine. But could you help me bring my cases and bags of food in?'

'Pity. I'd love a look around myself.'

'Well, you can pop over sometime and I can show you.'

Rhiannon laughed. 'That's a deal then. Come on, let's get you settled in. I'm sure you'll be very happy here.'

I'm just looking for some peace and quiet, thought Miriam. *Not sure I can stretch to happy.*

Once all the bags were put in the hallway and Rhiannon had noisily left, Miriam couldn't even summon up the energy to put wine in the fridge, let alone drink it. So, she ate a couple of breadsticks and went upstairs to locate the master bedroom. And when she found it, she unpacked the overnight bag she always kept in the car just in case, placed her slippers carefully by the bed, put the jiffy bag containing the photographs in the bedside drawer, climbed under the duvet and enjoyed the deepest sleep she had had for many years.

Chapter Two

Miriam woke up. A shaft of sunlight beamed from a crack between the curtains, warming her shoulders, and she stretched, her ears searching for the familiar London traffic noise. Opening her eyes, she remembered that this was not a smart, generic hotel room in the city, but a cosy retreat by the sea. And that today was the first day of a very long, very empty, very quiet break.

'What shall I do today?' she mumbled. 'That's right. Anything I want. Or nothing.'

Stepping onto the floor, her feet instinctively searched for her slippers, which she always left neatly next to her bed so she could put them on without looking and thus start her day efficiently. She slipped them on and stood up, enjoying the silence punctuated by the sound of the sea far in the distance.

'Ten a.m.,' she muttered,' glancing at her mobile phone to check the time, 'I haven't slept till 10 a.m. since … since …' An image of her lounging in bed in her last student house drifted into her mind, then disappeared. 'Since then.'

Grabbing her overnight bag, Miriam took out her emergency cardigan and put it on, then opened the curtains and gasped. Beyond the tangle of rosebushes and rhododendrons, the sea glistened a bright blue under a sky dappled with white clouds. Seagulls swooped and glided on the breeze as a yacht bobbed in the distance.

'Hello, view!' she said. 'I'm here!' Her phone rang, puncturing the peace, and she picked it up, remembering she'd arranged a call for this time. She couldn't help being slightly irritated she'd forgotten. Miriam Ryan never forgot an appointment, whether it was work or pleasure.

'Hello. Fiona?'

'Yes, it's me. How are things today?'

'I'm here.'

'At your new home? What's it like?'

'The view from the bedroom is beautiful. It's all sea and sky and flowers and …'

'Not raining?'

'Not raining. But I think it will be a different kind of gorgeous when it is.'

'What's the house like though?'

Miriam spun around. 'Actually, I went straight to bed. The kitchen looked nice … big … and this room is very lovely. All floral and homely, and the en-suite is very impressive.'

Fiona laughed. 'That is Miriam I'm talking to, isn't it? I mean it is after ten, and you seem to have just got up!'

Miriam giggled. 'Maybe it's the sea air. Or probably the long drive.'

'How did you feel when you arrived? Did anything seem familiar?'

Miriam looked out of the window. 'I don't know. I can't see anything.'

'You'll have to explore and let me know.'

Miriam paused. 'I don't really want to see anyone though. Not yet. I want to be a bit solitary. You know – wander along the beach unnoticed. I've got enough ready meals and dips to last weeks.'

'Well good luck with that … and Miriam?'

'Yes?'

'Have a think about that solitary thing. Consider how good it is for you. Remember when we talked about the reasons you felt like that?'

'I know. Caring fatigue, if that's a thing.'

15

'If that's how you feel, then it is a thing.' Fiona's voice was gentle and calm.

'I'll be fine. I'm going to unpack, roam around the house and have a walk – alone – seeing as it's such a lovely sunny day.'

'Go for it. And enjoy. Speak soon.'

'Bye.' Miriam put the phone down and sighed. *Solitude at last*, she thought, walking down the stairs and making herself a bowl of cornflakes. She sat at the kitchen table, listening to the comforting ticking of the clock in the hallway. 'I could go back to bed,' she said out loud. 'I could have a bath ... I could watch television … I could explore the village—no, I don't want to explore the village as there will be people there. For a while, this will be me, myself and I.'

Then the doorbell rang, and she almost jumped with surprise. Then it rang again. She crept over to the wall next to the window in the living room and peered out. A curly-haired, bearded man stepped backwards into the driveway and looked around, then up. She put a hand to her unwashed, unbrushed hair, looked down at her emergency cardigan and decided to stay where she was.

'Joanna?' he shouted at the house. 'Joanna?' His voice trailed off as he walked around the side, and Miriam heard him try the gate. Then he reappeared again, looking confused and stared at her car for a few moments, until he turned around and sauntered off down the road towards the village.

Who's Joanna? she wondered. Then made her way to the en-suite so she could start her day feeling clean.

After a shower, she looked at the suitcases and bags left at the bottom of the stairs that needed to be unpacked, before glancing outside at the blue sky. She gave in to the blue sky, grabbed her jacket, put on her sunglasses and stepped outside to birdsong and the sound of children playing in the distance. Walking to the road, she stood for a moment, trying to get her bearings. The village was to her left, and in the other direction was a public footpath snaking across a field towards the sea, so she crossed over and began to walk, putting her headphones on so she could pretend to be listening to music if she encountered any other human beings.

As Miriam moved closer to the coast through the yellow gorse, the smell of salt, sand and seaweed lifted her spirits. Walking down the rocky steps to the beach, she strode towards the sea, pausing to take off her shoes and socks, enjoying the sensation of the warm, wet sand on her feet. Then she stepped into the cold, fresh water, which sent a pleasant shiver around her body. A ball bounced close to her, then into the surf, followed by a Labrador who picked it up and ran back along the shore. Miriam watched as it dropped the ball in front of its owner, who had curly hair and a beard. Assuming it was the same man who had been looking for Joanna – whoever Joanna was – she decided to walk in the opposite direction.

On the west side of the beach were rocks and boulders, and she sat on them for a while, listening to the sound of the waves, allowing them to slow her thoughts until the shouts of a family nearby roused her, and she made her way back to the house.

After feasting on cheese on toast, Miriam dragged her suitcases upstairs and began to unpack. When the silence became deafening, she went downstairs to switch on the radio she'd discovered in the kitchen at breakfast. Returning to her work after she'd turned the music up so loudly she could hear it in the bedroom, Miriam carried on hanging up her clothes to 'The Power of Love' by Huey Lewis and The News and 'Galway Girl' by Ed Sheeran. It was during Little Mix singing 'Break Up Song' that she heard the doorbell ring, and then ring again repeatedly, followed by a very loud knocking.

Peering outside, she saw the same bearded man with his dog, and decided that this time she couldn't hide. She sighed and opened the window.

'Hello. Can I help you?' she shouted.

He looked up. 'Hello. Who are you?' he said, smiling.

'Who are you?' she replied, trying to sound upbeat rather than irritated, and only half succeeding.

'Where's Joanna?'

'I don't know,' she answered. 'Can you tell me who you are?'

'I'm Jim. I'm the landlord of the pub down the road and, as I said, who are you?'

'I'm Miriam.'

He looked at her expectantly. 'And …?'

'And what?' Miriam couldn't help herself. She just wanted to be left alone. She didn't want to get involved in any conversations about anything. And he was beginning to sound rather rude. 'I'm unpacking at the moment.'

'Staying with Joanna, are you?'

'No ... is Joanna the owner?'

He looked at her, confused. 'Well, yes.'

Miriam took a deep breath. He wasn't going to go away. 'I'll come down,' she said. She closed the window, hurried downstairs and opened the door.

'So …' He smiled again. 'I went on holiday and Joanna wasn't here when I got back. That was a couple of weeks ago. I saw your car on the driveway and thought she may have bought a new one, but … very nice by the way! The car, I mean.'

'No. I'm renting the house for six months, so I don't know anything about Joanna.'

He peered around her into the hallway as if he was looking for signs of his missing friend. His dog flopped down onto the gravel and sighed. 'What?' said Jim eventually.

'I'm renting the house. I arrived yesterday.'

He frowned slightly and was silent for a moment, then said slowly, 'Six months? But what about Joanna?'

'I don't know. This was all very last minute.'

'She's gone?'

'Apparently. For six months. Look, Jim, I had a long day yesterday and I'm in the middle of unpacking, so I'd best get on.'

He smiled again. 'I'm sorry. This is a bad start, isn't it? Joanna's a good mate and it isn't like her to, you know? Just disappear … her texts have been bouncing back and, well … good to meet you.' He held his hand out and Miriam shook it.

'Oh. Well ... nice to meet you too, Jim.' Taking note of his confusion, she softened a little. 'I'm sure she's fine. I mean, she managed to sort out letting out this place, so hopefully she didn't leave for a bad reason.'

'Yeah, you're probably right.' Jim didn't look entirely convinced, but he hesitated then stepped back. 'The pub is just down there. The Whippet, it's called. Pop in for a chat when you're settled. One free drink to make up for this strange welcome.'

Miriam nodded. 'I will, thanks. So nice to meet you.'

He walked away slowly, and as she began to shut the door, he turned back. 'So you're going to be doing all the—?'

But Miriam had already gone.

After the unpacking was done, Miriam decided to sit in the garden and enjoy the sunshine, so she made herself a cup of tea, took the set of keys hanging on a peg next to the cooker and unlocked the kitchen doors that led out to the decking. Placing the cup on a table, she stood for a moment and smiled. *Well done, Justin*, she thought. *This is wonderful*. The lawn sloped down towards a bank of trees, with borders bursting with colourful blooms and plant pots full of greenery. In one corner was a two-storey outbuilding, with bright floral curtains and a ceramic gnome with a fishing rod on the step. Picking up her drink, Miriam walked over to it and tried to open the door. It was locked, so she rummaged through the key ring and tried each one in turn until finally she got inside. The room had a sofa, table, two chairs and a small kitchenette, and there was a wide flat-screen TV on one of the walls. She took a sip of the tea, put it on the sink draining board and climbed the spiral stairs to a mezzanine where there was a double bed, an en-suite and a telescope trained on a window in the eves, with a pile of books on astronomy stacked on the floor next to it.

'Interesting,' she said, sitting on the floor and looking through it. 'You'd love this dad, wouldn't you? If you were here. All those nights gazing at the stars round your mates' houses as you couldn't afford a telescope of your own.' She smiled at the memory and continued to study the horizon, but all she could see was the bright blue sky. She tapped the telescope. 'I'll come back later,' she said, then went back to the decking to finish her drink.

After washing up her cup, she browsed through the file of instructions that Rhiannon had noticed the previous day. There was a list of emergency contacts, information about the area and food deliveries from local farms, a photocopied spreadsheet and a lot of recipes.

'Don't need the recipes, but thank you anyway … Joanna?' she said. 'The list of takeaways will do very nicely though.'

Miriam sat at the table for a moment, listening to the breeze rustle through the trees. The thought of looking at the night sky through the telescope was very tantalising, so she decided to fill the time until it got dark by having a long soak in the big, beautiful bath.

Grabbing a bottle of wine from the fridge, Miriam picked up a glass and carried them both to the summerhouse. Turning the light on, she poured herself a drink and climbed the stairs to the telescope, keen to gaze at the night sky, even though she had no idea what she would be looking at. Sitting on the floor, she checked through the books to see if any of them had titles like *Astronomy for Beginners* or *Astronomy for People Who Don't Know Anything About Astronomy*.

But all she found was *Astronomy Today*, *The Complete Dictionary of Astronomy*, *Turn Left at the Sun* and *Stargazing*, all written by someone called Alan B. Thomas. At the bottom of the pile was *The Novice Astronomer*.

'That's me,' mumbled Miriam, taking a gulp of wine. She turned to the first chapter. "Before you download a stargazing app, it's worth reading through the first chapter so you can understand the basics of what you're looking at," it said.

An app? I could do all this on an app? she thought, then decided she couldn't be bothered to walk back to the house to get her phone, so simply peered through the telescope into complete darkness, not having the energy to concentrate on reading a book. There was a wheel attached to the side of it, and she considered adjusting it to see if it would make any difference, but then remembered it wasn't her telescope. It looked expensive, and she didn't want to break it, so she just moved it around gently, trying to find a constellation instead. Even though she hardly knew what one of those actually was.

She moved back and took a sip of wine, staring out of the window at the stars spotting the sky, then she looked through the telescope again, adjusting the position slightly. And there they were – hundreds of thousands of stars and planets, like fireworks hanging silently in the air. It was so beautiful she didn't want to move so she sat for a while, mesmerised, as if she was studying a painting.

Eventually the night clouds gathered together, finally obscuring the tiny glimmering pinpricks of light, and Miriam glanced at her watch. 'It's nearly half ten. How have I been here for so long?' She stretched and considered just crawling onto the bed rather than making her way back to the house, but then she remembered that the doors were unlocked. 'I may be in deepest Wales,' she said to the telescope. 'But I think not securing my property would still be very … unsensible …' So, she pulled herself to her feet, grabbed the bottle of wine, locked the door and walked across the grass, glad the garden was illuminated by the light she had left on in the kitchen as everything else around her was pitch black. She stopped to pour herself another glass of wine, holding it up to the sky. 'A toast to you, lovely house, and you, gorgeous stars.' She listened for a moment. All she could hear was the hooting of an owl and the distant murmur of the sea. 'And to some well-deserved seclusion.' She took a sip, made her way to the kitchen, then up the stairs and straight to bed.

Chapter Three

'Can we talk about the business?' Artie handed her his card, brushing her hand as he did. 'Over dinner? I could be exactly what you need.'

'Ah, really ...' Miriam smiled. 'I've only just made the decision to sell. There's a lot to think about before I do anything about it.'

'Well, I could be exactly what you need – whether you decide to sell the business or not,' he said quietly.

Miriam tried to wake up. Even though it was almost black, the dark shadows seemed to jump and swirl from the walls over the bed and along the ceiling. She tried to find the light, any light, just a glimmer, but she couldn't. It was like she was drowning in the darkness. She shouted and shouted but no one came. So she lay there and screamed until tears ran down her cheeks, along her arms and to the tips of her fingers.

And then she woke up, her hair matted to her head, her breathing anxious and short. She fumbled for the button on the bedside lamp, but the room was still unfamiliar and she couldn't find it, so she rolled out of bed onto the floor, desperate to find a chink of light in the darkness, then pulled herself up against the wall, moving along it until she felt the switch.

The room was flooded with brightness – warm and welcoming and kind – and she sank to the floor until her breathing returned to normal and she could climb back into bed, wondering why, after so long, the sickening fear of the dark had returned.

The pitter-patter of the morning rain roused her from her restless sleep, the wind whipping up in the background. Climbing out of bed, Miriam pulled back the curtains and watched dark grey clouds sweeping across the bay, the waves angrily crashing into the surf and droplets of rain slipping down the window. *This is the day for an exhilarating walk*, she thought. *It'll blow away the demons from last night.* After grabbing a bowl of cereal for breakfast, she dressed in her wet weather walking gear and stepped outside.

As she got to the gate, she glanced towards the village. The sound of the sea booming onto the sand pulled her the other way, and she set off across the road towards the footpath.

The rain dappled Miriam's face as she paced along the beach, the breeze whipping up the waves as the birds hovered and danced along the currents and a group of surfers prepared to stride into the sea in the distance. She felt invigorated and free, swept along by the surroundings. When it got too wet to be comfortable, she took a different path back to the road and found herself next to the pub, which looked invitingly dry and welcoming.

Shall I? she wondered, pausing by the open door. *If I go in, I'll have to speak to someone…*

The sound of an espresso machine fizzing into life made her turn almost involuntarily, and she was coaxed inside by the smell of freshly brewed coffee.

Taking off her raincoat, she walked over to the bar, deliberately not making eye contact with anyone in the room.

Jim waved. 'Hello there,' he said, carrying a tray of drinks over to a table by the window. 'I'll be with you now in a minute.'

'Hi.' Miriam perched on a bar stool and studied the menu.

'We do a lovely brunch, we do.' Jim walked back towards her and smiled.

'Oh, it's just a drink for me today. I'm just having a look for future reference.' Miriam looked up. 'I'll have a latte, please.'

'Can I tempt you to something sweet?' He waved towards a shelf piled with fresh Victoria sponge and chocolate cake.

'Looks delicious and, actually, if I wasn't so damp, I would. But I think I just need a bit of caffeine to get me through five more minutes in the rain before I get to the house.' She laughed.

'There is quite a lot of precipitation out there this morning.' He scratched his beard. 'But it means the coast path walkers spend more time in here than out there. So every cloud, you know, quite literally has a silver lining.' He made her latte and placed it in front of her. 'On the house. To make up for our very odd first meeting.'

'That's okay. You caught me by surprise, that's all.'

'It's not like Joanna to be so mysterious.' Jim absentmindedly scratched his beard again. 'This thing is driving me round the bend,' he said irritably. 'I grew it to give me a bit of gravitas. The problem with inheriting a pub from your dad when you're only twenty-seven is no one takes you seriously enough. I thought this would help, but it just itches all day long.'

'Oh, dear,' said Miriam, not sure what to say next.

'Sorry, too much information!' He smiled. 'Back to the matter in hand ... Joanna. I've tried phoning her a few times but it doesn't connect, and the texts just keep bouncing back.'

Miriam put her hands around the tall glass, enjoying the heat, then took a sip. 'Just what I needed.'

'I hope she's okay,' said Jim.

'I'm sure she is.' Miriam looked at him and decided that her "as little human contact as possible" philosophy wouldn't be harmed by being just slightly helpful. 'I'll definitely ask the letting agent if she knows anything.'

'I'd be very grateful. So you enjoy cooking then?'

Miriam took another sip of her drink. 'Usually, yes. But ...'

'If you need any help—' A group of people tumbled in through the door and bustled to the bar, and his attention turned to them. 'Hello. Refreshing weather out there!'

What does he mean, "if you need any help"? wondered Miriam, watching him deal with his new customers. Then she gazed out of the windows at the sky, heavy with rain, and forgot about it immediately. She finished her coffee, put on her raincoat and slipped out of the pub unnoticed.

The rain had temporarily stopped so she ambled along the road, trying to find a connection to the childhood holidays her mother had talked about in the cottages and little shops on the main street, but she couldn't quite place anything, apart from a sensation of vague familiarity. Turning the corner to the house, she noticed two hunched figures standing underneath a huge green and white golfing umbrella. They were ringing the doorbell and knocking on the door with some urgency.

Miriam hurried towards them. 'Can I help?' she said. 'Is everything all right?'

The elderly woman, who was wearing a bright blue rain cap and long orange mac, looked at her anxiously. 'We're looking for Joanna.'

Miriam inwardly sighed. *This again?* she thought.

'Joanna's not here. For six months.' The pair looked at her blankly. 'She's gone away … somewhere …' Miriam trailed off.

The man stepped forward. He was draped in a see-through mac with "Adventurous Island Adventures – You Won't Regret Taking the Plunge!" written on it in big black lettering. 'No, she can't have,' he said with completely certainty.

'Yes, she has.' Miriam tried to sound kind. They were soaked, and she didn't want to keep them standing outside for long. 'I'm renting the house for six months. It was all rather last minute though.' They continued to stare, wordlessly. 'Jim in the pub didn't know either, so ...' She rummaged around in her bag and took out her keys. 'It's very wet, so I'd best get inside.'

'Oh,' the woman said eventually. 'So, you'll be doing it then ...?'

Miriam opened the door. 'Doing what?'

'Our food ... the cooking ... the meals, you know?' The woman didn't look too happy. 'I mean Joanna always does it, and she wouldn't leave without making sure someone did it.'

'I'm sorry, I'm not sure what you mean.' Miriam stepped inside the house in the hope they may take the hint and leave.

'What my wife is trying to say,' said the man, sternly, 'is where is our food? We are here waiting for our lunch. We come on this day every year for our lunch. And then, of course, all the other dinners and such too ... until the end of September.'

'And such too,' repeated the woman. 'Been doing it for fifteen years. Regular as clockwork. All through the summer.'

Miriam could feel her stomach churn. What could they possibly mean? Did they expect her to feed them? Who were they? Surely they wanted to see Joanna, not a random stranger like her?

'But you want to see Joanna for the meal?' she said. 'You don't know me.'

The woman looked stricken. 'But this is what we *do*.'

'We haven't got any food,' said the man. 'It's all in the book ... look.' He took a small A5 diary out his pocket and waved it in front of her. 'All there!'

It began to rain again, and Miriam gave in. She couldn't leave them on the drive in the wet. And they obviously had no intention of returning to wherever they were staying.

'Why don't you come in and we can sort it out somewhere dry?' She pulled the door open wide.

'This is very irregular,' said the woman, shaking the umbrella violently, scattering rain over Miriam, who thankfully still had her raincoat on. 'Very unlike Joanna. Very.'

'Never happened in fifteen years,' muttered the man, taking off his walking boots and putting them under the handstand. 'Julie. Take off your boots, please.'

'Oh ... yes,' the woman said irritably. 'It's the hunger. Makes me forgetful.'

Miriam walked through to the kitchen, a fixed smile on her face. 'Would you like a cup of tea?' she said.

'As long as there's a nice hot meal to follow.' Julie sighed.

Miriam turned to the kettle and took four deep breaths whilst looking at the wall. *This is strange*, she thought. *Very strange.* 'So, can you explain what Joanna does exactly?' She turned to find them sitting at the kitchen table. Julie was drumming her fingers.

The man nodded helpfully. 'Well, we book in at the end of the summer for the next year. Then pay Joanna in three instalments.'

'You pay?'

'Milk and three sugars for me,' said Julie. 'Henry will have semi-skimmed milk and no sugar ... he's on a diet.'

Miriam took the tea bags out of their container and started to rummage in the cupboard for the sugar. 'I've not had to use this yet,' she muttered.

'Have you got anything to eat at all?' Julie glanced at her watch. 'It is quite late.'

Henry put his hand on her arm. 'Julie, you're getting hangry, aren't you? Let's give this nice lady a few minutes to get herself organised.'

Miriam poured the boiling water into the mugs and stirred the tea aggressively. *I'll just give them a ready meal*, she thought.

Repay them all the money, then find out what on earth is going on. I need to text Rhiannon immediately.

She picked up her phone. Then put it down again as her guests stared silently and expectantly at her.

'I've only got ready meals and dips.' Miriam placed the mugs of hot, steaming tea in front of them. 'There you are. That should warm you up.'

'Well, I could do that.' Henry's voice rose at the end irritably.

'But I wasn't expecting anyone.' Miriam pulled out her stash of microwavable food and lay the boxes out in front of them.

Julie looked up at her pityingly. 'No, this won't do.'

'Is that all you have?' Henry seemed almost angry with her. 'You need to look after yourself a bit better. You are what you eat after all.'

Miriam stared at them. 'I'm just having a rest.' She glanced out of the window, then back at them and panicked. She really didn't want to deal with anyone at the moment and could feel her heart beginning to race. 'How about a nice takeaway?' She smiled brightly. 'I've got a list. I could order one to be delivered.'

'Oh, now that's a treat!' Julie's face lit up. 'A nice drive into town, and we could collect it.'

'Ah, okay. Well, that's excellent. Do you want me to order online or ring for you in advance?'

'In advance? No, you can drive us in and we'll browse when we're there. I'm nearly out of petrol and my next scheduled trip to fill her up is—' Henry rifled through his diary ' —the day after tomorrow.' He stood up. 'It will be a treat for you too.'

Miriam watched helplessly as they bustled to the hall and put on their wet weather gear. Julie opened the front door and turned back. 'Come on, chop chop. You've not even told us your name. They'll all be closed if we don't get a move on.'

'Miriam,' Miriam said quietly. 'Miriam …' Then she put her coat back on, grabbed her car keys and drove them into town.

Chapter Four

Miriam lurked around the house and gardens for two days after Henry and Julie left, the rain almost hemming her in, alert to the possibility they may turn up again unannounced. They had eventually settled on a Chinese takeaway which had been eaten rapidly at her kitchen table, the only conversation between them speculation as to what had happened to Joanna.

Then they had left, said they would see her next time, even though Miriam had assured them she would find out what was going on and arrange for their money to be refunded. Then she'd left a voicemail message for Rhiannon, who hadn't got back to her yet, and Miriam cautiously downgraded the alert level to "They may not come back".

Waking up on the third day to breaks of blue in the grey sky and a watery sunlight shining on the grass outside, she decided that getting out of the house was a good idea. So, she mapped out a circular route along the coastal path, packed some dips, breadsticks and a bottle of water, and set off, watching the clouds slowly disappear east and the dullness lift as she climbed the cliff steps at the west side of the beach. Sitting on a bench at the top, Miriam watched four birds with black heads and orange beaks swoop down towards the sea, then up, over and over again. She made a mental note to look up what they were.

Her phone began to ring, so she took it out of her backpack. 'Hello, Fiona. Guess where I am?' she said.

'Judging by the outdoorsy noise, I'd say you were outdoors.'

'Well, as you're not going to guess – I'm on the headland at the end of the beach, looking out at the sea.'

'You mean the headland you talked about – the one your mother told you about? The one you were dragged up all those years ago?'

'… and I'd moan and moan and cry – that's what she said anyway. I have no memory of it. It is absolutely gorgeous up here, to be honest.'

'Well, you were only young ...'

'… and had very small legs.' They both laughed at the same time.

'So, are you all settled in yet?'

'Yes, sort of, but …'

'But?'

Miriam kicked a stone onto the gorse. 'No, nothing. It's lovely. I'm keeping myself to myself … met the pub landlord … my landlady has disappeared without telling anyone. Oh, and I found a telescope.'

'A telescope!'

'Don't say it like that. I've always liked looking at the stars. You know, just looking up at them … and there's a summerhouse too.'

'A summerhouse. That does sound gorgeous.'

'It is rather lovely, to be honest.'

'Quiet?'

'Exactly what I need.' Miriam almost mentioned Julie and Henry but decided it was too odd and too complicated. 'Just me, birdsong and the roar of the sea,' is what she said instead.

'Well, it sounds blissful. Sorry, I've got to go. Speak soon.'

'Bye. I appreciate you checking in on me, Fiona.'

'It's fine, I want to. Bye then.' The phone went dead and Miriam put it back in her rucksack, watching the birds for a few more moments before the distant hum of human voices drove her onto her feet and pushed her west along the path.

The wind whipped up around her with only the chattering of the birds to accompany it as the whites of the waves cascaded into the sea. A field of cows watched her calmly as she strode.

Eventually, she walked back along the road to the house, invigorated and refreshed, and found a parcel propped up behind a pot plant on the doorstep. Expecting it to be for Joanna, she picked it up and checked the label. It was addressed to Miriam but with no surname 'Oh. For me?' she said to herself. 'Must be from Fiona ... she must have been so busy she forgot to write my name down properly.' She unlocked the door, took off her jacket and boots, and walked to the kitchen to put the kettle on. Opening the package, Miriam pulled out a string of small round fairy lights and stared at them, bewildered. 'Nice, thank you … but fairy lights?'

She made herself a cup of tea and sent a text. *Thanks for the fairy lights, Fiona. They're lovely. Any significance?*

The reply came immediately. *Nothing to do with me ...!*

Miriam took a sip of her tea, her mind beginning to click, click, click. *Who on earth would send me fairy lights? Is it something to do with Joanna?* She remembered Julie and Henry and their regular bookings – now hopefully to stop – at the house. *Maybe it's something to do with that ... from Rhiannon.*

She checked her phone again to see if Rhiannon had actually responded to the message she'd left a few days earlier. She hadn't, but just as Miriam was about to message her again, she put the phone down.

'Nope. Too much like work,' she said to a robin which had flitted onto the table on the decking outside.

She took her drink to the garden and sat for a while, listening to the birds and the sea, and the occasional car thrumming past on the road outside. Checking her phone again to see what the weather would be like overnight, she smiled – an almost clear sky.

33

'Stargazing time again,' she said to the robin, which had hopped up to the tree in the corner. She downloaded a podcast called *Astronomy For the Complete and Utter Beginner: An Idiot's Guide*. Then she went inside, lay on the sofa and began to listen.

It was early evening when she suddenly woke to the sound of the doorbell ringing repeatedly. Trying to gather her thoughts for a moment, she sighed. 'People,' she muttered. 'I only want them when I'm ready for them. I don't want spontaneous visits for goodness sake.' Rolling onto the floor, Miriam furtively crawled to the window and peered out through the curtains. Two men and two women were huddled around one mobile phone. 'It's not connecting,' said the taller of the women. 'Ring the bell again.'

Miriam sighed. More of Joanna's friends. More questions. *But at least they won't be demanding food*, she thought, shuffling to the hallway on her hands and knees in an attempt to pretend she hadn't been spying on them from underneath the window. Then she stood up and walked casually to the front door.

She took a deep breath, opened it with a flourish and smiled widely. 'Hello. Can I help?'

'Is Joanna there?' said the woman with the phone. 'She's expecting us.'

'Oh. I'm renting the house for a few months. Joanna's gone away for a while.'

After a moment's stunned silence, they all began talking over each other. 'What do you mean?' 'Where's she gone?' 'Is she all right?' 'Why didn't she let us know?' 'This is really strange.' 'I was so looking forward to it.' They all stopped at once and looked at Miriam expectantly.

'I honestly don't know where she is.' Miriam smiled again. 'I'm sure she's all right. This was only organised a couple of weeks ago. Very last minute. I'm sure she'll be in touch.' She

34

began to close the door. 'I'm sorry – I was in the middle of something. Nice to have met you.'

And then she heard someone say 'But what about our meal?', and her heart began to pound. *Not this again*, she thought, realising she really would need to give Rhiannon another ring to find out what was going on.

'Meal, what meal?' She decided to feign ignorance.

'Our annual meal. We've been coming for the past ten years,' said the woman with the phone. 'We hadn't ordered anything in particular this time, just sent a list of things to avoid and went for her pot-luck option.'

Miriam glanced up at the sky to see a solitary star already twinkling invitingly. 'I honestly have no idea about any meal,' she said. 'But I'm sure they do some lovely stuff at the pub.'

'But we've paid in advance.' The woman with the phone had stopped smiling.

'I'm not a cook,' Miriam said, exasperated – although, actually, she was, or had been many years before. 'And I only have ready meals, and I haven't been paid anything. I'm sure we can sort it out. Why don't you leave me a name and number and I'll contact the letting agents to see if they know anything?'

The woman nodded and smiled again. 'That's a good idea.' She scrawled a number onto the back of an envelope she'd pulled from her coat pocket and handed it to Miriam. 'Sorry to have bothered you.'

'Not at all. Enjoy your meal at the pub.' She waved at them as they walked towards the road, then closed the door, put the envelope in the kitchen, grabbed a bottle of wine and a glass from the fridge, and made her way to the summerhouse, trying to ignore the tiny pricks of anxiety stabbing at her. 'I just want a holiday,' she muttered. 'Not to sort someone else's problems out …'

She walked into the summerhouse, switched the light on, opened the bottle of wine and poured herself a glass. As she was opening the fridge, she heard a quiet, unidentifiable noise – it sounded like a grunt, and she paused for a moment, listening, but the room remained silent. *Must have been some animal outside. This is the countryside after all*, she thought. *Not London.*

But as she turned towards the sofa, she noticed a pair of feet in mismatched socks peeping over the top of the arms. Suppressing a scream, she backed towards the sink, her heart racing, and slowly opened the drawer. All she could find was a spatula, but she picked it up and looked towards the sofa. A man lay spreadeagled on it, snoring softly. He was wearing only a pair of boxer shorts and a grubby Cardiff City sweatshirt, and a can of lager sat unopened on the coffee table next to him.

Miriam stood there, unsure what to do. *Who the hell is this?* she thought. Her heart began to beat even faster and her breathing started to quicken *Flight or fight. Flight or fight?* She decided on flight. Slowly.

She tentatively moved towards the door but managed to knock a pot plant off the windowsill as she did, which clattered noisily to the floor. Miriam watched, holding her breath, as the man snorted then opened his eyes slightly. He stared at Miriam, obviously confused, then, after a moment, he clambered up to his feet and stood behind a chair.

'Who the hell are you?' he said loudly.

'Who the hell are you?' shouted Miriam, waving the spatula in front of her like a sword.

'What are you doing in my summerhouse?' he countered.

'What are you doing in *my* summerhouse?' said Miriam.

He stared at her for a minute. 'This isn't your summerhouse,' he said. 'It's my aunt's summerhouse.'

'It's my summerhouse for the next six months.' Miriam was still pointing the spatula at him, her mind racing.

'What?'

'I'm renting the house.'

'But where's my aunt?'

'Joanna?'

'Yes,' he said, his voice rising again.

'I don't know,' said Miriam firmly. 'And I am fed up of having this conversation with everyone I meet.'

'She didn't tell me she wouldn't be here.'

'Well, I'm sorry. I've just had a group of people at the door expecting to be fed, and as for Julie and Henry …'

He stepped back again, and Miriam noticed his long, muscular, slightly hairy legs.

'Oh, Jesus,' he mumbled. 'If I'd known I'd have uninvited company I'd have put some bloody clothes on.'

Miriam involuntarily glanced at his long, muscular, slightly hairy legs again, then at his unshaven face and his tousled hair, and felt an unwanted flutter in her stomach. Their eyes locked for a moment, and then they both looked away.

'If you're renting the house, why have you decided to drink a bottle of wine in the summerhouse?'

Miriam picked up her glass and took a swig of wine. 'Because I wanted to.' She knew she was being childish, but she couldn't stop herself.

'Well, there's plenty of room in the house for you and your wine, so if you would be so kind as to return there.'

Miriam glanced upstairs, where she could see the telescope on the mezzanine tantalisingly pointing at the night sky.

'Ah, you found the telescope,' he said, as if that explained everything.

'I was interested in looking at the stars,' she said.

37

'I would like to put some trousers on.'

'Ah, yes, of course.' She picked up the wine bottle and opened the door. 'How long are you here for? The weekend? A week?'

'About six months off and on,' he said.

'You're going to be living in my summerhouse for six months?'

'My aunt's summerhouse, actually.'

Miriam inwardly stamped her feet. *I just wanted some peace and quiet*, she almost screamed to herself. *Some peace and bloody quiet. Away from people. And all I seem to have got is ... bloody people*!

'Right,' she said out loud, striding across the lawn and back to the kitchen. Back to her phone.

She dialled Rhiannon's number and left a voicemail. 'It's Miriam. I left a message a couple of days ago about some people wanting to be fed and saying they have paid money. Today, I've had four people on my doorstep asking for food, and I've just found a man in his underpants in an outbuilding. Could you please ring me back?'

The curtains were now closed in the summerhouse. 'Rude man,' Miriam said out loud, pouring herself another glass of wine. Then she walked to the living room, where she switched on the television, found *Bridget Jones' Diary* on Netflix and sang along to 'All By Myself'. Except she changed the words to "wanna be" instead of "don't wanna be", and tried to forget both her unwelcome guest and the starlit night she could now not enjoy.

The following morning, she put on her dressing-gown and slippers, brushed her hair, cleaned her teeth and padded downstairs, her head a little woozy after consuming the entire bottle of wine the previous evening.

She turned on the kettle, put on Radio 2 and took a couple of headache tablets. The fairy lights were still on the kitchen table looking for a home. So, she filled the cafetière with coffee, put the milk in the frother to warm and took the lights upstairs, where she placed them on the windowsill of her bedroom, so it felt like there were stars even if the weather was dull and unfriendly.

When she walked back down the stairs and opened the door of the kitchen, he was there, wearing a pink fluffy dressing-gown and rooting around in the fridge. *And drinking most of her coffee.* Miriam felt that unwanted flutter and a stab of anxiety at the same time, and took a deep breath to try to cancel them out.

'Where's all the food?' he said grumpily.

Miriam wordlessly poured the rest of the coffee into a cup and scraped out the remnants of her frothy milk on top of it, trying not to look at his muscular forearms stretching out from the too-short sleeves.

'Nice dressing-gown,' she said, sitting at the kitchen table.

He looked down at it. 'Oh. It belongs to an … ex.'

'Oh.' Miriam took a sip of her coffee.

'Seriously. Where's the food? Aunt Joanna always has food in the house.'

She looked at him. 'Seriously. I'm not Aunt Joanna. I'm here for a rest. Not to look after you, or anyone else who may be knocking at the door. And you really should ask before you come into my kitchen. If I had known you'd be here, I would have been wearing something more appropriate.'

'Actually, technically, it is also my kitchen. I divide my time between my property over there.' He indicated the summerhouse. 'And some of the rooms in here. Particularly this room. I would assume it would all be in any contract you may have signed.' He took some bread out of the breadbin and put it in the toaster. 'This is our shared space. I won't just walk into the rest of the house while you're here. Normally I do. But, for the time being, because of this – how can I put it? – situation, I'll make some concessions.' He opened the fridge. 'At least you've got butter,' he muttered. 'No one warned me about this. I've got a deadline. I can't be doing with this.'

Miriam's phone rang loudly at the same time as the doorbell went. 'Justin! You're in Brazil … aren't you?' she said as she opened the door to Rhiannon.

'Houston, we have a problem,' he said.

'There's a bit of an issue,' said Rhiannon at the same time, rushing past her into the kitchen.

'I've found some missing paperwork,' they said almost in unison.

'Who are you?' Joanna's nephew said.

Rhiannon seemed to forget there was a problem for a moment and smiled coquettishly. 'Rhiannon Jones. Letting agent extraordinaire. Well, quite new to this office … supposed to look after the sales side, but someone took a career break without much notice … had to leave Cardiff quickly … broken heart.' She looked him up and down and batted her eyelashes.

'At last! Someone who may know what's happened to my aunt.'

'Rhiannon, this is ...' Miriam looked at him. 'Your name? I don't know your name.'

'Alan,' he said, sitting opposite Miriam.

'Miriam …' Justin was shouting down the phone. 'I'm phoning from South America. This needs to be quick – the wi-fi is going to disappear soon. I'm about to get a canoe from the Amazon back to civilisation.'

'Sorry. Go on.'

'I'm going to say this quickly – there was a page missing on the contract which I didn't notice. It must have been because the signal was so bad ... well, it *was* there. I just didn't see it.'

'Go on …' Miriam could feel her heart beginning to sink.

'It was the one about the supper club-stroke dinner club-stroke events club-stroke cooking commitments.'

Miriam looked at the phone.

'Are you still there?' He sounded nervous.

'Yes.' Miriam didn't really want to know what he was about to tell her.

'I'm so sorry. I'd had two caiparinhas in quick succession … they're deadly. Taste all nice and non-alcoholy, even though there's loads of alcohol in them. Liars, they are.'

'Caiparinhas … what were you doing sorting out contracts whilst drinking cocktails?' Miriam tried to sound calm, but she could sense the volume of her voice rising.

'Caiparinhas are rather deceiving as far as their effect is concerned, to be fair …' Rhiannon trailed off.

Justin's line began to crackle. 'It looks like some numbers were missing on the paperwork … well, they weren't missing. I sort of saw some figures and just assumed they were connected to the rent … but it turns out … they were for an allowance for you. There is no rent … because of this … you've signed a contract which means you're going to have to—' The phone crackled more loudly and the line went dead.

'Justin? What do you mean?' She looked up at Rhiannon. 'Would you care to continue?' She sounded much calmer than she felt.

'So, the thing is this – and don't blame me – the guy looking after this went on holiday, and no one told me because I'm new and ... well … he's right. You've got to take over the running of Joanna's events and meals.' She handed Miriam a large folder.

'There's a budget, and there are funds which will be transferred to your bank account … and there's the dates and names. Most of them are meals, you know, but there's the Look-alike Festival run by the landlord of The Whippet pub you help out with, and a big event just after that ... Star something or other.'

'Stargazing and Sandcastles,' Alan said flatly. 'That's mine.'

Miriam took the folder silently, then looked at them both. 'But I came here to get away from all of that,' she said. *I came here so I didn't have to have responsibilities or care about anything or anyone for a while*, she thought. *I can't do this.*

'Sorry.' Rhiannon looked stricken.

Miriam sadly gazed outside at the sloping green garden surrounded by rose bushes. 'It's a pity. It would have been a lovely summer. You can find someone else, can't you?'

Rhiannon looked at the floor. 'Um … no. There's a clause in it that says you can't get out of it. My colleague says they accepted you because they looked up your name on the internet, and you're obviously experienced. No one else applied, you see. That's why they did it so quickly. Didn't ask for references or anything.'

Miriam felt a surge of annoyance. 'That can't be right. It's just cooking, it's not a prison sentence.'

'That's what my colleague said.' Rhiannon began to back towards the door. 'He said it was weird and irregular, but Joanna's solicitors had put it all into place.'

'So that'll force you to get some proper food in, at least,' said Alan. 'I'll write a list of what I need. Don't look at me like that – I've paid Aunt Joanna in advance.'

She could see he was biting his lip and assumed it was to stop himself laughing. Miriam threw the folder onto the table. 'I'm going to speak to my solicitor,' she said sternly. 'I am not spending my summer cooking for people I don't know … or anyone. I mean I don't even want to cook for myself.' She took her phone and walked upstairs 'Now, excuse me. I'm sorting this out.'

Sitting by the bedroom window, she took a few deep breaths, then called her solicitor. 'Hello. It's Miriam Ryan here. Can I speak to Jeffrey Goldstock, please?'

The deep breaths weren't helping though, and she could feel her heart pounding as the receptionist put her through.

'Hi, Jeffrey. How are you? No, there's nothing wrong with the sale of the business. It's all going through … no, it's something else. You won't believe what's happened. I'm renting a house in south west Wales for a few months, to have a rest after everything, and due to an administrative error I seem to have signed a contract which means I have to … work. Yes, I seem to have a job. Which is exactly the opposite of what I wanted to do …'

Miriam sat on the bed feeling extremely irritated. Jeffrey's response hadn't been as cut and dried as she'd expected.

'My advice is to fulfil your obligations whilst we look at what you've signed,' he'd said. 'Strictly off the record – after his behaviour, it's not out of the realms of possibility that Mr Morgan, should he find out about this, will try to make something out of the fact that you are not adhering to your contract. He could go to any trade publication and cause you some embarrassment.'

'But I didn't sign a contract with him,' Miriam had said, trying not to raise her voice. 'I know I changed my mind at the last minute – entirely his fault – but there was no contract. And I can't think of any publication that would be interested in anything I'd done.'

'I believe he's not happy about the money he spent preparing for the sale. And my sources tell me he isn't a good loser. If you

43

decide to start another company, you don't want your reputation already tarnished by rumours spread by him.'

'So, you're saying I actually have to work?'

'Send me the details and I'll have a look through it. But if I were you, I'd just say yes for the time being.'

'Right … right. Thank you, Jeffrey. As you know I'm a stickler for fulfilling my obligations. Even though, in my opinion, Mr Morgan was *not* going to fulfil his after he had signed. If I'd given him the opportunity.' She'd put the phone down and was now staring out of the window, trying not to scream.

Her stomach lurched uncomfortably. 'Nope, not thinking about that. Stop thinking about it,' she said to the wall and stood up restlessly, walking onto the landing. She could hear Rhiannon and Alan chatting in the kitchen, so decided to go up the set of stairs leading towards an attic room to explore and check out the view instead of going back downstairs.

The door creaked noisily as she pushed it open into a big, bright space with wooden floors and a wide window overlooking the sea. Several chests of drawers stood against the walls close to a pile of boxes, stacked haphazardly next to the door. And in the middle, pointing towards the sky, was an old brass telescope. Miriam clapped her hands with excitement and knelt on the floor to look through it, almost knocking over a pile of books next to her. She picked them up and looked at the titles – they were mostly the same as the ones in the summerhouse, *Astronomy Today*, *The Complete Dictionary of Astronomy*, *Turn Left at the Sun*, *Stargazing* and *So You Want To Be an Astronomer?*

'Miriam. Miriam?' Rhiannon's voice interrupted her thoughts, and she pulled herself to her feet. 'It's just, I know this is all a bit … unusual,' she shouted. 'But until it's sorted out, we sort of need to, well, you know … well, *you* need to ... and I can help you, although, to be fair, I'm a letting agent – although I'm supposed to be an estate agent, so how I've got involved is well ... irregular, but at the end of the day …'

'Yes, yes. I understand that.' Miriam walked back down the stairs to find Rhiannon hovering by the front door, looking awkward.

'It's just till it's sorted out. Only, you've got some bookings over the next few weeks, and it would be really helpful if—'

'You are legally obliged after all,' Alan shouted from the kitchen. 'Not that I care. All of that entertaining gets on my nerves, I'm not going to lie.'

Miriam sighed, feeling trapped. Despite her general unwillingness to get involved with anyone at all, Rhiannon did look very stressed, and there was something in the way she spoke that reminded Miriam of herself only a few months ago. She couldn't do that to anyone – even if she was annoyed. *Very* annoyed. And exasperated. Plus Jeffrey had told her she couldn't walk away for the time being.

'I'll do the bare minimum,' she said finally. 'But I'll do it. Can you send me the full contract? I think its best to start again. My solicitor is going to go through it with a fine tooth comb.'

'Of course. And in the meantime, I'll help. I really will.' Rhiannon looked relieved. 'It's not my fault though. I feel trapped, to be honest. By decency.'

Miriam looked at her and burst out laughing. 'By decency. I like it. I mean, its not funny generally but ...'

'I heard something creak very loudly upstairs.' Alan poked his head round the kitchen door.

'Yes. I went into the attic room.'

'Ah,' he said, giving her a look she couldn't work out, then he went back into the kitchen.

'He's very attractive,' murmured Rhiannon. 'For an older man, that is. Looks a bit like Hugh Jackman, doesn't he?'

45

'Hadn't noticed,' said Miriam, who had been trying to work out who he reminded her of.

'I'll pop back this evening, shall I? We can work out a plan of action. I'll let myself out.'

'Okay. Bye, Rhiannon.' Miriam went into the kitchen to make herself a cup of tea, but Alan was already heading back to the summerhouse.

'Thank goodness,' she muttered, watching his long, muscular, slightly hairy legs as he went.

'Hiya!' Rhiannon beamed as Miriam let her in later. 'To be honest, I'm a bit nervous about being with you, because if I were you, I would be very, very, *very* cheesed off about all of this.'

'I am,' said Miriam sharply. She had just got off the phone with Jeffrey Goldstock. Apparently, the contract was watertight and she needed to wait a while before she tried to get out of it. Her mind clicked back to the moment she'd signed and sent it electronically, desperate not to think or concentrate, allowing someone else to go through the fine-print for the first time in her life. It was a pity cocktails had got in the way. So, she was stuck. For the time being, at least.

Making a mental note to check her bank account to make sure the rent she'd paid in error had been sent back, she sighed. *I haven't looked at my accounts for a month. Deliberately. And now I have to. Because of work.*

Rhiannon's face fell and Miriam softened. 'Not your fault though,' she said, more gently this time. 'We seem to have been caught in a series of unfortunate events.'

'You could just go, and I wouldn't blame you.'

'Well, I'm a bit of a stickler for fulfilling commitments, and my solicitor has told me I can't just flounce off, no matter how much I want to. I'm fighting with myself about this a bit though.'

Miriam pulled out a chair and sat down. 'Sit down. I promise I won't bite.'

Rhiannon sat at the opposite end of the table and smiled slightly less widely. 'Well, I'm happy to help. I feel responsible. Even though I'm not …'

Miriam picked up one of the folders that Joanna had left. 'To be honest, I want to make this as easy as possible. I'm supposed to be having a break.'

'Fair play. I'm supposed to be climbing the heady heights of estate agency and earning huge amounts of commission, rather than being a letting agent and sorting out catering. I am a dab hand with colour-coded cards and post-its though.'

'Just as well.' Miriam pushed a stationery box towards her. 'I found this next to the folders and spreadsheets. You can be in charge of that bit.' She ran her hand down the page. 'I don't really want to do this. It feels too much like work … like the past.'

'Tell you what, I'll gift you this stationery box with all the pretty cards and highlighter pens, and I'll take on the much more responsible task of going through all the information about the bookings.'

'That's very kind of you.' Miriam smiled. 'I generally like to organise everything – I'm a control freak. And I'm having an argument with myself about that too.'

'We have a deal. But only on the condition you put the kettle on.' Rhiannon pushed the box back along the table.

'Okay. That's a good deal.' Miriam stood up and began to make the tea. 'There's not too many, are there? Meals, I mean?'

'No ... no ... don't worry. Not too many. And by the time that Stargazing event happens, I'm sure you'll have sorted something out.'

The thought of organising a big event made Miriam feel slightly sick for a moment. 'Definitely. I won't be involved in that at all,' she said firmly, handing a mug to Rhiannon. 'Let's get this done as quickly as possible, and then move on.'

Rhiannon looked up. 'Maybe this is all for a reason, you know? Us getting caught like this. I mean …' She took a sip of her drink. 'I came here for a fresh start. My mum said it would do me good to get away from Cardiff. I fall in love a lot, you see. She says I'm addicted to it. She thought that if I came to this part of the world, where people are more spread out, it would be more difficult.'

'Spread out?' Miriam wished she could fall in love more easily.

'In Cardiff, you can go for a night out … suitable men everywhere. Positively dripping with them, it is … but here … well, she says it could make me more discerning.' Rhiannon thought for a moment. 'She said it's like I'm in a pinball machine, pinging from one man to another. I quite like it, to be honest, but she said it was exhausting to watch and I needed some space between love affairs …'

'Ah, well. I'm not really one for fate, or things happening for a reason.'

'Because you're a control freak and that would mean you're not in control?'

'Oh, well …' Miriam laughed. 'I hadn't thought of it like that.' She put her mug down on the table and picked up a pen. 'I find lime-green highlighter is an excellent way of taking over the world one list at a time, although I'm not exactly sure what I need to highlight?'

'No idea either.' Rhiannon smiled. 'But I'm sure we'll find something.'

Chapter Five

'You could just walk away.' Fiona sounded like she was in a supermarket.

'Are you shopping?' Miriam was flicking through the folder without really looking at any of its contents.

'Yep – I had to rush out between appointments.' Miriam heard the clatter of a basket and the ping of a self-service till. 'Explain again. What's making it difficult for you to leave?'

'My huge and unremitting sense of responsibility.'

'Oh yes, that. The thing that made you feel so …'

'Trapped. Yep, that's the one.' Miriam looked out of the window as Alan put a backpack in the scruffy Jeep parked almost out of sight behind the summerhouse. 'And I've been advised that if I don't stay, my past – Mr Morgan, that is – God, he was in my life so briefly but caused so much havoc – could decide to cause me some problems. Oh, remind me. Did I say I wanted to be alone?'

'Yes, that's why you sold your house, sold your business and cleared off to Wales for a while.'

Miriam looked at the calendar hanging under the clock on the wall. 'I'm going to do what I have to, and then get my legal people to contact Joanna's solicitor and tell them it's not working. So at least it will look as if I've given it a go.' She took a carton of pineapple juice out of the fridge. 'Although Rhiannon is worried that this contract won't allow me to get out of it. I told her it was a really strange contract if it didn't.' She poured herself a glass and put the juice back in the fridge.

'How do you really feel about that?'

49

'I really plan on doing the bare minimum, don't you worry. And there's something about this house. It's in the village my mum used to talk about. Under normal circumstances, it would be perfect. I'm reluctant to leave, to be honest. I will. But—'

'Got to rush. Speak soon!'

'Bye. Thanks for fitting me in at such short notice,' Miriam muttered and put her phone down before unfolding the spreadsheet on the table. She felt the familiar nausea when she did it, unable to focus on the names and dates or the menu choices. *Get a grip*, she thought. *It's just cooking. It's what you do … what you used to do. Doesn't have to be complicated. And you don't have to entertain or anything. Just* get *a grip*.

Seeing Alan walk across the lawn towards the kitchen, she instinctively darted towards the living room but got her cardigan caught on the kitchen door handle and was unable to move.

'All right?' he said, putting some keys on the worktop.

'Yes, thank you,' she muttered, holding a glass in one hand whilst attempting to release the fabric from the door with the other.

'Need some help?'

'No, it's fine.'

'Hmmm,' he said, walking over and unhitching the cardigan from the handle.

'Thank you.' Miriam stepped back and looked steadily at the window beyond his shoulder in an effort to avoid his gaze.

'Well, I'm off for a few days. Couldn't leave you there like that. Who knows what I'd have found when I got back?'

She nodded. 'Have a nice time.'

'As you no doubt noticed, I've put the spare keys back on the table, just in case. But just for emergencies. It's not carte blanche to go and use my telescope.'

She thought she could see the shadow of a smile as he turned towards the door.

'I've no intention of doing anything of the sort,' she said primly. 'I won't go near your summerhouse.'

'Good to know,' he said, walking back to the garden. Miriam followed him outside and sat down at the table.

'How did you get your Jeep over there without me noticing it?'

'There's a little lane further down the road that just leads here.' Alan picked up a bag he'd left next to the car and opened the door.

A flicker of recognition fluttered into Miriam's mind. 'Hang on! Were you at the services at Carmarthen last week?' she said. 'Because a Jeep very like yours cut me up!'

He paused, then frowned. 'This isn't mine. Belongs to a friend. My car decided to die a couple of weeks ago, so he's very kindly lent it to me.' He smiled. 'Delivered it to St Dogmaels where I was staying, so I'm not saying this isn't the vehicle in question, just that I wasn't in charge of it at the time.'

'Oh.' Miriam sipped her drink.

He climbed into the Jeep and closed the door. 'Take care,' he said, before driving off.

I'm usually quite nice, thought Miriam. *I don't know why I'm being like this. Or maybe I do.*

Putting the glass on the table, she stretched her arms over her head. 'I just don't want to care about anyone for a while,' she said to herself, and sighed. 'Just for a while ...'

The first group of official guests was for that evening and, according to the spreadsheet, the booking was for six people who wanted a delicious Thai meal. There was a number next to the entry which cross referenced with some pieces of paper in the folder detailing various recipes. Miriam examined them with interest. They looked delicious, but she had no intention of cooking any of them. Instead, she drove to the nearest supermarket where she threw in a large selection of ready meals, some puddings, plus several bottles of wine.

Gliding by the fresh food section, she began to feel guilty. *Oh no … oh no*, she thought. *I can't just give them ready meals. I've signed that contract.* Pausing next to the fresh chillies, her hand reached towards a packet. 'No. Don't,' she muttered to herself. *But I've signed a contract. A contract. I've signed a contract.* The words rang around in her head. *And I can* cook. *I ran an events company. I can't pretend …*

'Are you all right?' A woman was watching her from behind a shelf of coriander.

Miriam looked up, startled. 'Oh, yes, thanks. Just having a bit of a conundrum about a meal I'm cooking tonight.'

The woman leaned towards her. 'I may be wrong, but from what you've got in your trolley I think you probably have a lot of people coming to eat with you tonight? Don't tell anyone, but sometimes I get ready meals and pass them off as my own recipes. Ply everyone with wine – they never notice. It's all about confidence.' Then she grabbed two pots of herbs and walked towards the fish counter, turned around, came back and said quickly, 'I chuck in extra chillies and such, and give the food made up names and everything! That means I'm less likely to get caught out. Oh, I feel better for telling someone that. I feel cleansed.' She waved and walked away again.

Thank you, thank you, my guardian angel, thought Miriam. *Although I don't believe in any of that, so you're not. No, you're like my cooking twin. It's a sign. A definite sign. Although I don't believe in signs. What the hell's the matter with me!* Picking up four packets of ready chopped chillies, garlic, ginger, basil and coriander, she decided to Google some lesser-known Thai dishes just in case she decided to go the whole hog and give her ready meals new identities. She felt quite naughty. And it felt good.

Miriam forced herself into work mode that afternoon, dressed the table, got all the crockery ready, put the wine and beer in the fridge, and then had a long soak in the bath.

She put the ready meals in the oven, plus one in a saucepan to give off some enticing spicy curry aroma, and placed some chillies and coriander artistically on a plate in case anyone wandered into the kitchen. By the time the doorbell rang, she was reluctantly ready to briefly revisit her life before she was the MD of a successful events company.

Smoothing down her dress, she felt a sudden surge of anxiety. *Pretend, pretend, pretend*, she thought. *It's not important. Just pretend.* Taking a deep breath, Miriam opened the door, her well-practised smile ready and waiting, only to find a stressed looking woman holding a harp on the doorstep.

'Oh, I'm so sorry I'm late. I've tried messaging Joanna, but it kept bouncing back, and so did the voicemails.' She picked up the instrument and hurried into the dining room. 'Thank goodness they're not here yet.' She began setting up her harp by the fireplace. 'I couldn't have a cup of tea, could I? I'm sorry, I didn't catch your name.'

'Miriam. I'm Miriam, and you're here to eat and you also happen to have brought a harp?' She knew she was clutching at straws.

The woman looked at her, confused. 'No, I'm the entertainment. Although, if you've got any spare food, I wouldn't mind. Fed the kids and no time for me.'

'I'm sure I've—'

'Where is Joanna? She all right?'

Miriam took a deep breath. *Here we go with the well-rehearsed speech ready prepared for the dinner guests*, she thought. 'Joanna is taking a rest for a few months, and I'm renting the house while she's gone. I'm afraid I don't know where she is or what she's doing. But she is very well, I believe.'

'What, you're doing all the cooking and stuff?'

'Yes.'

'Are you being paid?'

'It's a bit complicated.'

'So, you're renting a house and cooking for people?'

'Sort of yes and sort of no.'

'Oh.'

'Oh, indeed.'

The woman pushed her long grey hair behind her ears. 'Must get it cut.' She smiled. 'But with the kids, the day job and this job, I just never seem to find the time.'

'So, do you take sugar in your tea … you didn't tell me your name?'

'Sorry, you did ask. It's Mary. Joanna books me a few times a year when there's a Welsh theme to the cooking.'

'Welsh? Um ... excuse me.' Miriam rushed to the kitchen and checked the spreadsheet. It definitely said a Thai evening, and there was an *M* written next to it.

She put the kettle on and opened a bottle of wine. 'Well, if they want Thai food and a Welsh harpist, that's odd but up to them,' she said to the oven.

Mary wandered into the kitchen. 'Is everything all right?'

Miriam poured herself a glass of wine. 'Yes, yes. It appears they opted for Thai food with Welsh entertainment.' She waved the bottle at Mary. 'Would you like a glass?'

'Go on then. Just one shouldn't interfere with my – what shall I call it? – art!' Miriam handed her the drink and Mary took a long gulp. She looked around the kitchen. 'It's very tidy in here. Usually when Joanna cooks, there's pots and pans everywhere.'

'I wash up as I go,' Miriam said quickly. 'I find it easier.'

'Funny that Joanna went and never told me though.'

'She didn't tell anyone apart from her solicitors and the letting agents, apparently.'

'That's odd. Mind, I only see her about four times a year these days.' The doorbell went. 'Right, I'm on.' Mary finished her wine then rushed back into the dining room. 'Let me start playing and then open the door. I'm starting with "Ar Lan Y Mor".'

Miriam smoothed down her dress, her heart racing again, but as soon as the haunting sound of the harp floated through the house it seemed to flick a switch in her brain, and she moved almost serenely to the door.

'Welcome, welcome.'

The guests all murmured hello. 'Good evening,' said the man who stood at the front of the group. 'Nice to meet you. I'm Graham. We're really looking forward to our meal. Joanna excelled herself with her Cantonese feast last year.'

Miriam waved them in, smiling, despite wanting to run away. 'We've had a good day's walking,' said the woman behind him. 'Love this part of the coast, don't we?'

The others nodded in agreement and went into the dining room. 'Beautiful music again, Mary,' said Graham. 'Where's Joanna?'

'Joanna is taking a rest for a few months, and I'm renting the house while she's gone,' said Miriam, automatically delivering the speech again. 'I'm afraid I don't know where she is or what she's doing. But she is very well, I believe.'

'Goodness me,' said the woman. 'I hope she's all right. She never messaged us or anything.'

'It was all rather last minute.' Miriam tried to sound upbeat. 'Now, would you like some drinks? Joanna's booking form said you wanted a Thai meal with Welsh entertainment?'

'Oh, yes.' A tall, wiry man pulled out a chair. 'Like to mix it up. Love a harp, don't we?'

The others nodded and sat down around the table. 'We do this every year. Same part of the coastal path for a walk, then come to Joanna's for a feast. Then we drive off somewhere new. But we always start here.'

'It's nice to come back to places you love,' said Miriam, clicking into efficiency mode. 'So, do you want me to pour your drinks or leave them on the table and sideboard?' She wasn't sure she was up to playing the hostess role properly.

'Joanna just piles it all on the table, and when we run out she brings us more.' Graham laughed. 'Means she's not to-ing and fro-ing all the time.'

'Right, I'll bring it all in.' Miriam grabbed three bottles of wine and carried them in for her guests.

'*Waaay*,' they all shouted as she put them on the table. 'Drinks!'

'*Waaay*,' they all shouted again when she arrived with the beers, then 'Oooooh,' when she brought in the water.

'Okay then. I'll bring in the food and leave you to it.' Miriam hoped they'd be this easy to please all evening.

'Aren't you joining us? Joanna always does. Fills us in on what she's been up to in the past twelve months.'

'I haven't been up to much, to be honest,' said Miriam evenly, wishing she could just go and look at the stars in the quiet as Mary began to play 'Crocodile Rock'.

One of the women stood up and began to dance, so Miriam slipped out to the kitchen and took another slug of wine. *Never knew a harp could sound so raucous*, she thought, spooning out the ready meals into some serving dishes. Then she took another gulp of wine and carried the first lot through, and another slug when she took in the rest to find the party jumping around the dining room to 'We Are the Champions'.

'So ...' She smiled. 'We have traditional Gaeng Keow Wan Gai, Pad Sataw, spicy beef salad ...' She watched as they continued to dance. 'Plus … this …' She pointed limply at a dish of egg-fried rice. 'These …' She indicated a plate of noodles. 'And … everything else … enjoy.'

She backed towards the door and hid in the kitchen, pouring herself another glass of wine whilst wondering why she'd even bothered to Google Thai recipe names to cover up her ready meal deception. Then she began to take more bottles of alcohol out of the fridge ready to take in.

'Hello. Graham and his gang are in full swing by the sounds of it.' Alan was standing at the door leading into the garden.

Miriam stepped back, surprised. 'Oh, I didn't see you there. I thought you'd gone off for a few days?' His face was unshaven, his light brown wavy hair flecked with grey, and he was smiling. She looked at the floor, confused and annoyed that she was pleased to see him.

'I had.' He walked over to the counter and took one of the bottles of beer. 'But then I realised what the date was. Graham and his friends always have this date. And normally I'm on hand to help entertain them.'

'Do they need much entertainment? They seem to be doing pretty well already.' Miriam took another sip of wine.

'I normally go in and chat after they've finished their food.'

'Are they interested in the food?'

He smiled. 'Yes and no.' He pulled the top off the bottle and opened the lid of the bin before she had time to protest. He looked up at her. 'I see you've been slaving over a hot stove then.' He pulled out the sleeve for the microwaveable Thai green chicken curry and held it up.

Miriam bit her lip. *I'm not going to feel guilty about this*, she thought, *seeing as I'm supposed to be on holiday and this is a big mistake. Although I do feel guilty because I'm a perfectionist and this is deceitful. And I've signed a contract. And I don't break contracts. But I'm on holiday and I don't want to cook.* Can't *cook at the moment.*

Alan took a gulp of the beer. 'Your expression keeps changing. You're having conflicting thoughts, aren't you?'

'No, I'm not.' Miriam bristled.

'You feel guilty,' he said.

'No, I don't.'

He smiled. 'I won't tell them. Honestly.'

'Nothing to tell.'

'But you owe me.'

Miriam picked up her glass and took another drink. 'I had some difficulty sourcing the ingredients due to limited time,' she said.

'Bold move. But not true. I'll go in and keep them entertained as it can get messy. When Mary the Harp goes rogue the drink really flows. And she's started early by the sounds of it.'

Miriam listened. 'Is that "Ace of Spades"?' she said faintly. 'On a harp?'

'Impressive, isn't it?' He laughed, opening the door. 'See you on the other side.'

Miriam watched him go, both relieved he was taking over and annoyed as she really did owe him now. She looked longingly outside as the stars twinkled in the black sky. 'I just want to have a long, long rest,' she said to herself. 'And I seem to have somehow gone back to cooking for people. Well ... not cooking. Microwaving. Which is bad in itself.' She took another sip of the wine. 'But *I* had to choose the bloody meals and heat them up.' Opening the door, she put on a coat, grabbed a blanket, took the wine and sat outside in the dark, enjoying the distant sound of laughter and harp for a while. The stars seemed to multiply, glistening comfortingly above her, and she wrapped herself in the blanket then lay down on the decking, staring at the sky, her anxiety slowly dissipating until she fell into a deep sleep.

'Miriam ... Miriam? Are you all right?' She woke with a start. Alan was kneeling down next to her, touching her hand gently. 'Miriam,' he said quietly again.

'Oh.' She struggled up, tangled in the blanket, stumbling into a chair. 'I must have dozed off. What time is it?'

'Just after midnight.' He held his hand out. 'Hold onto me while you get out of that.'

'I don't know how I got wrapped up in it like this,' she muttered, trying to grab a table. 'It seems to be attached to me.'

Alan took her hand firmly. 'Here.'

He held her gaze for a moment, his eyes warm and kind. Miriam tried to say something but couldn't formulate the words.

'If you stand still now, you can unravel yourself,' he said eventually.

'Ah yes ...' She managed to shed the blanket and stood back, still holding his hand.

'Alan? Al ... and—!' Graham appeared in the doorway, swaying a little. 'What are you up to, eh?'

They let go of each other's hands and almost jumped apart.

'All ready to go then?' Alan walked into the house.

'Yes, taxi's here. The others are all outside.'

Miriam followed them through to the front door.

'Great night, Al,' shouted Graham as he clambered into his seat. 'Thank you very much ... sorry, I've forgotten your name ... *not* Joanna. That'll do! The food was amazing!'

59

Mary had decided to hitch a lift home with the revellers rather than call her husband and was trying to fit herself and the harp into the back seat of the second cab, until someone pulled her inside, the harp bursting into a tuneless melody as she fell along its strings.

The drivers hooted their horns as they drove away, and suddenly there was just Miriam and Alan and the silence.

'I'll help you clear up,' he said. Miriam looked at him woozily, the wine wearing off and being replaced by weariness.

'No, it's fine. I'll do it in the morning.'

'It'll take five minutes,' he said briskly. 'Just loading the dishwasher, it is. I think your morning hangover headache won't thank you for the mess if you leave it.'

Miriam sighed. 'Okay, thank you.' But at the back of her mind rang the words, *don't forget you owe him now – and what was* that *earlier in the garden, that moment?*

Whatever it was, she didn't want it. Didn't want anyone. Not now. It was too difficult.

Chapter Six

Miriam blearily woke up to birdsong and the distant crashing of the waves, her head fuzzy from the night before. *Yet again*, she thought. *Don't make it a habit.* Rolling over, she looked at her phone to check the time and sighed. 'Seven o'clock in the morning? For goodness sake. I don't need to be awake this early.'

Then she lay back and stared at the ceiling. 'And I'm talking to myself too much.'

The morning light shone through a chink in the curtains as if it was waving at her, so she got up, had a shower, packed some bread and juice, and walked to the beach to eat her breakfast.

The breeze slowly soothed her aching head, and as she sat on the sand, she breathed in slowly, enjoying the fresh, salty air. *This is what I came here for*, she thought. Taking a sip of her drink, she gazed at the waves gently breaking on the shore and began to relax, only a couple walking their barking dogs in the distance breaking the silence.

As she stood up, Miriam glanced along the beach at an oystercatcher swooping towards the water and noticed a man striding purposefully out of the sea, his skin glistening with water. He pushed his hand through his wet hair, seemingly oblivious to his surroundings. Miriam was transfixed as she watched him walk through the shallows onto the sand and along to the dunes. Then she looked away, embarrassed, as she realised that the figure was Alan.

Sitting down again abruptly, she diverted her gaze towards the opposite end of the beach, then took out her phone and checked the weather forecast for the following day, hoping he wouldn't notice her. *Not in the mood to talk to anyone*, she thought.

Especially not half-naked men who ... She wouldn't allow herself to think the thought she knew was hovering in the air, despite noticing him rubbing his chest with a towel out of the corner of her eye. Studying her phone with deep concentration, she scrolled along the screen, as sun after sun after sun appeared.

'Oh, lovely,' she said out loud. 'I'll have a day on the coastal path.' Then she remembered she needed to check the diary to make sure there was no catering to be done, and sighed, irritated. *Not how it's supposed to be*, she thought.

'All right there, Miriam?' Alan's voice carried along the breeze from the other end of the beach. She winced, embarrassed he'd noticed her, then stood up to see him waving at her. 'You should have come in for a swim with me instead of just sitting there. The water's lovely.'

Miriam nodded, glad he was too far away to see her face redden. 'Headache!' she shouted, tapping the top of her head. She imagined him smiling to himself at her discomfort. She just knew he'd know – just *knew* it – and rolled her eyes. *So much for peace and quiet and not wanting anything from anyone*, she thought, suppressing the image of him striding out of the sea which had popped back into her mind.

When she eventually arrived home, Alan was in the kitchen filling up a rucksack with food.

'Um …' Miriam stood in the doorway. 'Why are you emptying the fridge?'

He shoved some apples into a bag and smiled. 'Just going on that site visit for a few days. The one I came back from to help out.'

'But ... that's my food.' Miriam folded her arms in front of her then realised what she was doing and leaned against the door frame instead, trying to look relaxed.

'Aunt Joanna always gets my food in. So, technically, it's mine too as I've paid for it.'

'Money's not in my account yet.'

'It will be.' He took two boxes of breadsticks from the counter. 'Not much here though.'

'But … I …' Miriam couldn't speak properly again. She was very annoyed – he was very irritating, and he was taking *her* food. But given the fact she had only just stopped being a highly successful businesswoman, she should be able to at least confront him effectively. It didn't help that all she could think of were the chest hairs peeping over the top of his sweatshirt …

'Technically,' she said eventually.

Alan zipped up the rucksack. 'Yes?'

'It's my food. I went out and bought it. I had no idea you were going to steal it.'

'I'm not stealing it.'

'What am I supposed to eat?'

'Well …' He smiled again. 'To be honest, you've got hardly anything in anyway, and you need to go shopping. Plus, Julie and Henry are booked in again tomorrow. So, I'm just hastening your visit to the supermarket.'

Miriam looked up at the ceiling and took a couple of deep breaths. 'I was planning a day out tomorrow,' she said. 'This is not what this break is supposed to be. Commitments and looking after people.'

'Well, best get going.' Alan opened the back door. 'See you in a few days.'

'Bye.' Miriam couldn't decide whether she was pleased he was going or disappointed.

'Oh,' he said turning back. 'Breadsticks, dips and apples are a bit limited as supplies go, so I think you need to up your game a bit.' Then he closed the door behind him, laughing at his own joke.

Miriam tried to think of something clever to say as she watched him walk across the garden to his Jeep, but nothing came. 'I can make my own home-baked breadsticks and fresh dips if I want to,' she said to the door. 'I'm very good. I just don't want to. Because I'm supposed to be having a rest!'

Picking up the phone, she scrolled through to Fiona's number then looked at it for a moment. Fiona would calm her down and make sense of this. Not Alan. She had no idea why Alan affected her the way he did. Well, she did know, but she didn't want to deal with it. She was trapped in something that she had been trying to get away from. And she was furious.

Then she put the phone down. 'Not supposed to be speaking to Fiona till tomorrow,' she said to the clock. 'Can't keep just picking up the phone when I get a little wobble.'

So, she checked the diary and spreadsheet. 'Ah, Pie Night. No entertainment. Easy.' Grabbing her car keys, Miriam headed towards the nearby town to stock up on food. And when she got back, she packed a rucksack ready for a morning's walk along the coastal path.

The sun peeped through the curtains and Miriam stretched, looking forward to her adventure. She showered, dressed in the clothes she'd laid out the night before, ate the planned breakfast of fruit and yoghurt, and made herself a cup of tea. Opening the back door, she took out her map and sat outside, listening to the birdsong and the distant roar of the sea. She studied the terrain and worked out where to park, found a path that took her on a circular route inland and made a mental note to take her pocket book, *Birds for Beginners*, so she could enjoy a spot of birdwatching.

As she stood up, Miriam noticed that Alan had left the summerhouse window open, so she grabbed the spare keys from the kitchen and walked across the garden towards it.

Inside, three sweatshirts had been discarded untidily on the sofa, some socks lay on the floor and a pair of walking boots sat muddily on the draining board. Miriam twitched, fighting the need to tidy everything up, and pulled the window closed hurriedly, almost slamming the door behind her before locking it.

'Not my mess,' she almost chanted. 'Not my mess. It's his mess. What a surprise.'

Out of the corner of her eye, she noticed something move nearby and peered into the greenery to check what it was. What looked like a hare hopped through a gap between the hedges at what she had assumed was the end of the garden.

A hare? Intrigued, Miriam followed it into a large orchard and found herself amongst the trees. In the middle was a little bench, so she sat down, beaming happily inside. *This is the place I can hide*, she thought, *away from the guests. I can retreat until they need me*. Moving her arm, she saw something scratched on the back of the seat and looked closer. *To J, this is where you punched me when I told you I loved you. Yours forever and ever. H xxx*

She smiled. 'That's romantic,' she said to the hare, which had paused under a tree. 'I wonder who they are.' Then she got up and walked back to the house to collect her things for a walk on the cliff path.

Parking the car at the top of the headland, Miriam climbed out and put on her walking boots. She grabbed her rucksack, locked the door and turned westward towards the silvery, calm sea. Two other walkers a few hundred metres ahead slowly disappeared around the headland, and she sighed with relief that she would be enjoying the scenery without having to make brief small-talk with anyone at all. As she got further from the car park, she began to feel part of the landscape. She moved steadily, the sun warming her shoulders, the salt in the air taking her back again towards childhood holidays, her mind searching for the images, still just out of reach. But the rhythmic crashing of the waves punctuated by the warbling of linnets and calls of the gulls gradually weaved their magic, and her mind emptied of everything apart from what was around her.

Eventually, the path took her downwards towards some rocks, where she sat for a while, her eyes closed, just listening to the ebb and flow of the tide.

Exactly what I need, she thought. *Exactly.*

'Miriam! ... Miriam!'

She almost jumped, shocked by another human voice, especially one that knew her name.

'Well, I never! What brings you here?' Rhiannon stood in front of her, holding a flag and a shopping trolley full of small bottles of water. 'If I'd have known how difficult dragging this down that track was going to be, I'd never have said I'd help.' She sat down and grabbed a bottle for herself. 'Fancy one?'

'No, no thanks.' Miriam looked at her. 'Where did you appear from?' she asked, confused. 'I didn't see anyone when I was walking down the path.'

'Over by there.' Rhiannon waved her arms in the general direction of some gorse behind them. 'Parked the car a couple of miles away. Nice day for it though.'

'Nice day for what?'

'The Fun Run. And Walk. And Amble. Didn't you know?'

'No.' Miriam sighed and almost laughed. *Not alone at all*, she thought.

'They'll be here any minute. The first ones anyway. The front runners.' Rhiannon stood up and planted the flag in the ground. 'They have to go round this, I give them some water and then they carry on up over there.' She pointed at the path Miriam was planning to take.

'May have to go back the way I came,' she said.

'Yes, well, you may get knocked over by some of the more competitive runners stroke walkers stroke amblers.' Rhiannon laughed and, as she did, the pounding of feet rumbled in the distance, getting louder and louder as they got closer and closer. 'Here we go.' She giggled. 'I thought this would help me get more involved in the community, you know. Meet more people.'

'Well, I'd best get out of the way, then. Nice to see you. Quite a surprise as it's in the middle of nowhere.'

'Miriam! Hello,' Jim the landlord shouted breathlessly, pausing to take a bottle of water from Rhiannon.

'Oh, who's this?' Rhiannon smiled.

'Jim. This is Rhiannon.' Miriam picked up her rucksack.

'Lovely to meet you.' Rhiannon flicked her hair and watched him as he continued running.

'Huw, Joe, Philippa … that's Miriam,' he shouted at a group heading their way. 'That's Miriam, you know. Looking after Joanna's place.'

They all waved. 'Helloooooooo.' As they ran, she heard them shouting to another group behind them and began to walk more quickly as she realised they were speaking about her. 'Oh, that's her, is it … what's happened to Joanna? Funny if you ask me.'

She put her head down and focused on climbing up the path back to the cliff as the beach filled up with runners.

'Well, if it isn't Miriam.'

She stopped and looked up.

Julie and Henry were sitting on two rocks in front of her.

'Oh,' she said. 'Where did you come from?'

'Over there.' Julie waved at yet another path meandering through the buttercups to a narrow road. 'We like to walk over here and watch the Fun Run from a distance. We come every year. Henry makes sure he puts it in his diary.'

'Why didn't you take part?' Henry sounded almost annoyed. 'It would help you meet people and be part of the community.'

'I'm only passing through.' Miriam smiled. She wanted to say, *I came not to meet people and not to be part of the community, but it's proving more difficult than I expected.*

'Looking forward to our meal tonight. Hope it's home cooked this time.'

'Oh, yes. Pie night. Heading back to sort it out now. See you later.'

That is only half a lie, muttered Miriam to herself guiltily as she headed east, back to the birds and the waves and away from the people.

She drove home, her head a cacophony of conflicting emotions. *I don't have to do it. Yes, I do. I've signed a contract. But I'm on holiday. A long holiday. An important long holiday. But I can't let them down. You're putting pies in an oven, Miriam!*

When she arrived, she turned the oven on, rushed up the stairs, and grabbed her journal and a pen.

She inscribed on the front, *The Diary of Miriam Ryan, aged 45 and three quarters*, laughed hollowly at her own joke and then wrote on a fresh page:

I was supposed to start this journal months ago to help with the anxiety. However, this is the first entry.

All I can write is that I cannot believe
A – that I am in this mess and

B – I should walk away and could walk away, but, actually, for some reason, I can't walk away.

C – I feel guilty about serving ready-made pies when I shouldn't really be doing this anyway.

Although one brownie point here – I haven't made a list of things to do! Well done, Miriam.

Miriam closed the journal and put her pen down. As she placed it back in the drawer, she picked up the jiffy bag with her family photographs and sat for a few seconds with it in her lap. Deciding not to deal with the pictures and all the memories they would bring, she began to put it away, but, as she did, she felt something hard through the bubble wrap and reached in to find out what it was. Pulling out a silver necklace with a blue gemstone hanging from it, she looked at it for a few moments, almost stunned. It had belonged to her mother, but Miriam hadn't seen it for many years. She held her breath as the tears began to cascade silently down her cheeks, trying to create an image in her mind of her mother wearing it. But she just couldn't summon up any kind of image and sat in frustrated silence, waiting for the feeling to go. Then she took a few deep breaths, dabbed her face with a hankie, put the necklace on and walked downstairs, anticipating the comforting smell of freshly baking pastry that was about to fill the house.

Smoothing down her dress as the doorbell rang, she took another deep breath. *At least it's just Julie and Henry*, she thought. *Just two people. Pretend they're your friends and not customers.* She opened the door with a flourish.

'Hello,' she said as her guests walked past her.

'Good to see you've made an effort this time.' Julie took off her coat and handed it to Miriam.

'Well, you did catch me by surprise last time.' Miriam hung up the coat and waited for Henry to take his off.

'Keeping it on for a while. We've been out all day and it's got very cold.'

They walked through to the dining room and sat down. 'Looks better than it did on our last visit too,' huffed Julie.

Miriam smiled, having made a decision not to get irritated. 'Like I said. It was all a bit of a surprise. But I've got all of Joanna's information now, so I'm more prepared. Wine, beer or a soft drink?'

'She's only winding you up, Miriam.' Henry laughed. 'We think it's very, very funny.'

Julie beamed. 'It is. It is! And it's certainly confused Henry. He didn't write this in his diary list of things to do and places to see. He does love a list!'

'I have a photographic memory, but I like writing things down too.' He patted the chair next to him. 'I think you should tell us all about yourself. Don't worry, I won't be taking notes!'

'That does smell very nice.' Julie looked towards the kitchen. 'Homemade, I hope?'

Miriam nodded, feeling even more guilty.

'Well?' Henry leaned forward.

'Wine or beer?'

'He'll have a beer, and I'll have a glass of red wine.'

Miriam walked into the kitchen, followed by her guests, and opened the oven door to inspect the food. 'I've done roasted vegetables and gravy,' she said, relieved she'd hidden the pie boxes out of sight in the bin – by the side of the house this time.

'What brings you here?' Henry persisted. 'You've got a story, I can tell.'

Miriam poured their drinks, thinking about what she would say. 'Here you are.' She gave them the glasses and poured some water for herself. 'I sold my business and I'm having a break.'

'What sort of business?' Julie sat down on one of the kitchen chairs.

'An events company. Built it up from a small catering company. Originally a food truck …' Miriam bit her lip. She didn't want to say any more, feeling unable to deal with the anxiety that came with the longer version.

'That's exciting.' Henry took a long gulp of beer. 'Sold it for a lot of money, did you?'

'Henry!' Julie said. 'None of your business.'

'It's okay. I'm financially fine, Henry. Thank you for asking.' Miriam smiled and took another sip of water. 'Food will be ten minutes.'

'But why here? It's the back of beyond. We love it, come every year. But it's very quiet.'

'I used to come here when I was a very little girl with my parents,' Miriam touched the necklace around her neck. 'And … I thought it would be nice to see it again.'

'Ahh.'

She noticed Henry studying her curiously, so she opened the oven again to check the food. 'And you? Why do you come back every year?'

'It's our calm place,' Julie said. 'Since we retired, we've been all over. Just got back from Buenos Aires last month. Off to Cambodia in November. But … well, we love it.'

'We rent the same cottage for a few months and escape our routine. Not that we have one now.' Henry laughed.

'Although we do have to go home every couple of weeks to make sure the plants don't die … even though we installed a system at great expense to water them when we're away.' Julie rolled her eyes at her husband.

'I don't trust the thing,' he muttered.

'It was your idea!' Julie laughed. 'It's okay. I still love you, dear.'

'I know you do.' Henry smiled and blew his wife a kiss. He turned back to Miriam. 'We sold our business too,' he said. 'We know what it's like to let go of something like that.'

'Oh, what was it?' Miriam asked, just as the doorbell rang. 'Excuse me. I wasn't expecting anyone.' She smoothed her dress and opened the front door.

'Have you got a minute?' Jim stood on the path looking flustered. 'I was taking the dog for a walk and I couldn't go by without … it's worrying me more and more to be honest.'

'I've actually got—'

'Oh, Jim. Hello.' Henry walked up behind her. 'Come in. Haven't had a proper catch up yet. Too many people on the fun Fun Run stroke Walk stroke Amble earlier.'

Jim walked in and sat down, the dog laying at his feet with a sigh.

'I'm afraid I haven't got enough food for everyone.' Miriam sensed the evening was about to slip out of her control again.

'Just eaten. Don't worry. Go ahead.'

'We'll eat in here, shall we?' Julie went to the dining room and began to collect the cutlery. 'Cosier.'

'Drink?' Miriam opened the fridge door, thinking about the orchard at the end of the garden and wondering whether anyone would notice if she hid there for a while.

'Oh, beer thanks.'

'So, what's the problem?' Henry asked as Miriam gave Jim his drink and began to get the food out of the oven.

'Joanna. All these people at the Fun Run stroke Walk stroke Amble today asking where she was and all. And I thought, she's my friend, you know? I need to know she's all right.'

They all looked at Miriam. 'Are you sure you don't know anything?' Julie put the plates on the table and sat down.

'I really don't know anything at all. I've asked the letting agents. It's nothing to do with me, to be honest.'

The doorbell went again, and Miriam managed not to roll her eyes. 'Wonder who that could be,' she said, trying to sound cheerful.

'Hiya!' Rhiannon was standing at the door, smiling nervously. 'I was just passing and …' She lowered her voice. 'I saw Jim walking this way, and so I got to the end of the village and thought I'd pop in.'

'To say hello? To me or to Jim?' She stood back from the door so that Rhiannon could come in.

Rhiannon followed Miriam through to the kitchen and waved at everyone.

'Hiya!' she said. 'I'm Rhiannon.' She flashed a smile at Jim and flicked her long, curly hair. 'I was helping at the Fun Run stroke Walk stroke Amble earlier.'

'Oh, yes.'

'By the rocks I was, with the flag and the water.'

'Yes, I remember you.' Jim smiled at her. 'Sit down then, Rhiannon. This is Henry and this is Julie, and we're trying to work out what's happened to Joanna who owns this house.'

Miriam opened the fridge door. 'Wine or beer?' she asked.

'Half a glass of wine, please. I'm driving.'

Miriam poured the glass and handed it to her. 'Rhiannon works for the letting agents, actually.'

'Oh, yes. I did ask my colleagues. I'm new, you see, so sort of just got dropped in all of this …'

'Much like me.' Miriam took a long swig of her drink, visualising herself laying on the decking and staring at the stars.

'And, well, nothing to report really. Sorry.' Rhiannon looked at her glass, clearly embarrassed.

'Nothing at all?' Jim leaned forward and smiled at her again.

'Well, I asked, and we've contacted her solicitors because they sorted everything out – they said she didn't want to be contacted. Unless there was an emergency.'

'An emergency?' Julie looked confused.

'Someone dying, basically. A relative.'

'That's bleak.' Henry sighed.

'It's very odd though. She was such a part of the community … just disappearing off like that without telling anyone. Very out of character.' Jim scratched his beard thoughtfully. 'She's been like a very kindly aunt to me. Kept an eye when my parents decided to open that bar in Spain and leave me to run the pub. Don't know what I'd have done without her.'

'Maybe there are clues around somewhere?' Rhiannon said, sounding doubtful.

'What kind of clues?' asked Julie.

'I don't know… photos, letters … strange messages in odd places …'

Miriam took another long gulp of her drink. 'Speaking of which, does anyone know what that writing on the bench in the orchard is all about?'

They all looked up at her and she regretted opening her mouth immediately.

'What bench?' said Jim.

'There's a bench and someone scratched something on it – "this is where you punched me when I told you I loved you", or something like that.'

'That's a clue. It's a clue!' Henry almost jumped to his feet.

Rhiannon clapped her hands together. 'This is very exciting. I mean, I don't know her or anything …'

'But it might not be.' Miriam looked at them, surprised at their reaction.

'It might be though.' Julie went to the hallway to get her coat. 'Come on. Let's go and look.'

Miriam put the food back in the oven.

'Have you got a torch?' Jim had started rummaging through the kitchen drawers. 'We need to see it properly.'

Miriam watched the hive of activity and turned the oven down, deciding that ready meals or not, she wasn't going to be accused of burning the pies to a crisp. She did still have some professional pride.

'Here we are,' said Jim, holding a torch aloft. 'Come on then, Miriam. Where's this bench?'

Grabbing her emergency cardigan from the hallway, she opened the back door and guided them across the garden to the orchard, with Jim just behind her illuminating the way.

'Here we are,' said Miriam, pointing at the scratched inscription as everyone crowded around the bench.

'Oooooh, now, that's interesting,' said Julie.

'J must stand for Joanna,' said Jim

'Not necessarily – probably – but not necessarily …' Henry said thoughtfully.

'Romantic though.' Rhiannon sighed.

They stood and stared at it for a while in silence.

A car door slammed nearby. 'What are you doing in the garden in the dark?' Alan's voice got louder as he walked towards them.

'Alan!' Jim shook his hand. 'Good to see you. We're trying to work out what's happened to your Aunt Joanna and Miriam found this.'

'I thought you were away?' Miriam said sharply, pleased to see him and irritated at exactly the same time.

'It was too misty for my needs.'

'Oh, what exactly is it you do again?' Miriam was drowned out by everyone talking at the same time.

'We're worried about her ...'

'Joanna is so reliable...'

'... doesn't want anyone to contact her.'

'Well, I want to know where she is too. I'm frankly a bit put out she didn't let me know. I'm her only living relative, after all.'

Miriam stood aside, watching them all caring so much about this woman she had never met, feeling suddenly claustrophobic and unable to explain why. She backed away slowly and went back to the house, leaving them to their mystery. Then she walked up to the attic room where she sat for a few minutes, staring at the darkening sky.

When she went back downstairs to the kitchen, Alan was drinking a bottle of beer.

'Glad you've got more provisions in,' he said.

'You're welcome.' Miriam opened the oven and prodded the pies to check they hadn't dried out.

'You disappeared very suddenly,' he said.

'Wanted to keep an eye on the food.' Miriam poured herself a glass of water.

'Right ...' he said quietly as the rest of the group hurried back into the room.

'Well, that was interesting,' said Jim.

'I'm hungry!' Henry sat down at the table.

'Pie time!' Julie laughed.

'Right, I'm off. So, I've set up a WhatsApp group so we can share ideas and information.' Jim walked towards the door. 'Why don't you give me your number, Rhiannon, so I can include you in case the letting agency gets more correspondence from Joanna?'

'Very exciting,' she squeaked, following him and his dog out of the house.

'Oh, and Miriam, I need to talk to you about the Look-Alike Festival too. Just pop in and we'll get something in the diary.'

Look-Alike Festival? she thought. *I'll be gone by then. Won't I?*

Chapter Seven

'So.' Fiona's voice sounded calm and comforting. 'How's the journal going? Do you think it's helping?'

Miriam sat on the window seat in her bedroom, watching the clouds stream across the sky and the angry white-cropped waves far in the distance.

'To be honest, I wrote my first entry very, very recently. And it's quite hard not making it a list of to-do's. You know, if I write "I wanted to run away", my instinct is to write "don't run away next time" – and put a tick box next to it!'

Fiona laughed. 'Well, you have had a life of making lists. We have talked about it a lot, so it's understandable that it's a hard habit to break.'

'I think I'm confused about why I'm getting those feelings, to be honest. I mean, I know why I get stressed. But the anxiety comes when I least expect it. When my guard is down.'

'Understandable.'

'Yes. But irritating!' Miriam stood up and began to pace around the room. 'This was supposed to be a complete break, but because of this contract, there are all these people to deal with. They *are* nice. Very nice. And, normally, I might think it was fun. But I feel trapped … and that's how I felt before …'

'How would you feel if you walked away?'

Miriam almost laughed. 'I signed a contract. I've spent my life signing contracts and getting other people to sign contracts, trusting people to do what they're supposed to do, and then ...' Her voice broke unexpectedly. 'After what happened with ... you know, *the* contract, and the timing of it …'

'Are you trying to say that you can't leave because of what happened to you?'

'I can leave any time. But I'll be breaking a contract. And because it's me I can't leave until someone else can take over. It's just the way I am.'

'Do you think you can try and enjoy it?'

Miriam watched Jim walk down the road past the house with his dog as Alan pulled out in a camper van.

'I thought he drove a Jeep?' she said.

'Sorry?'

'Nothing. I didn't mean to say that out loud.'

She saw them wave and chat for a moment, then they both went their separate ways.

'I don't want to feel anything for anyone at the moment,' she said quietly.

'How easy do you think that will be?'

'I can try!'

'You can!' Fiona laughed. 'It's nearly half past ten. I'll have to leave you in a moment. But, what about the past... ?'

'My parents?' finished Miriam. 'The memories are so vague, I don't seem to have connected to anything.'

'Maybe you should stop trying – it will happen when you're not expecting it.'

'Maybe.'

'I'm away next week. So we'll catch up the week after?'

'Yes. Enjoy your break. Bye.'

Miriam put the phone down and glanced out of the window again, searching for something that would capture the memory of her parents somehow, as she absentmindedly watched a food truck drive past towards the beach.

'Fish and chips,' she muttered. 'We used to eat fish and chips and go and sit on the sea wall. Mum was always talking about it.' Her mother's necklace lay on the bedside table, and she picked it up. 'Lucky charm?' she whispered, putting it on, then almost laughed. 'Although I don't believe in any of that. I really don't! This place is really getting to me.' Grabbing her coat, she opened the front door of the house and walked to the gate. Instead of turning right towards the beach and away from people, she turned left towards the village to see if she could find her past. *Maybe this will work better than looking at old photographs*, she thought.

The narrow streets were busy with tourists, the clear skies bringing them to the coast despite the wind, and she managed to lose herself amongst them as she paused, admiring the window display in a craft shop, full of brightly coloured pots and mugs with sea-themed paintings hanging above them. To the side were some books next to a notice about some 'Dark Sky Astronomy' events. As she stared, someone picked one of them from the display and began to read through it, turning the back of it towards the window. Miriam looked closer, then almost laughed as she realised the photo of the author facing her from the book was Alan. Camper van Alan. Or was it a Jeep Alan? Alan, who had a telescope in his summerhouse, and whose missing aunt had an even better one in her attic.

Maybe I can ask him to teach me the astronomy basics, she thought, walking down the street to the sea wall. *No. Not a good idea. I don't want to make friends or have connections.* A seagull landed on top of a bin, then swooped up to sit on a nearby roof. *I want to be as free as a bird ... like you.*

Standing in front of the fish and chip shop, Miriam tried to summon up a memory. She knew she'd been here before with her parents – they used to talk about it all the time. How they'd treat themselves after a long, lazy day on the beach, or stop off after a drive further west. She knew she had been here, but she didn't recognise it. Frustrated, she bought herself a bag of chips and some cod in batter, smothered it with salt and vinegar, then walked to the sea wall and sat down. She watched the parents and children on the beach below building sandcastles and running at the sea, laughing and screaming excitedly.

A little boy put up a wicket and picked up a plastic cricket bat, then waited for his father to begin the game. A couple of other children were standing nearby to act as fielders. His father threw the ball, and the little boy hit it high into the air. Instead of running, he watched, mesmerised, as it landed with a plop in the sea, then laughed at his father rushing to retrieve it. And whilst Miriam sat, she felt a flicker of something, like a tiny fragment of an old film, a half-formed image of her on the beach, running towards her parents as she threw a plastic cricket ball in the air. But she couldn't see them. She knew they were there, but she just couldn't picture them.

Miriam finished her food, put the empty paper in a nearby bin and walked back to the house. Pausing outside Jim's pub, she decided the meeting about the Look-Alike Festival could wait – instead, she decided to investigate the telescope upstairs in the attic room.

As she turned the key in the lock, Alan's van sped past, pulling into the little lane further down from the house. She looked at the sky, now almost cloudless, the wind having blown it clear from the west, and imagined a crisp black night sky full of bright, twinkling stars. Then she thought about the first time she'd used the telescope in the summerhouse, admiring the bright lights of the stars but having no clue what they were called or how they connected, despite rifling impatiently through the pile of books.

Taking her coat off, she looked up at the landing. The door to the attic stairs was firmly closed. 'Think this should be my hobby,' she muttered. 'Stargazing. Like my dad. Something completely different. Only I mustn't work too hard at it. Remember that …' Walking through to the kitchen, she saw Alan getting out of the camper van, talking animatedly on his phone as he did.

Putting the kettle on, she took a mug out of the cupboard and grabbed a tea bag from the jar. Alan was standing in the garden, still talking, but definitely not smiling. Miriam took the teapot off the shelf and put it next to the mug, then grabbed another one from the cupboard. She thought for a second and put them both back again. Alan had stopped talking and appeared to be staring at the sky just as the kettle came to the boil.

Miriam! she inwardly chastised herself. *Making someone a cup of tea does not mean you're going to be anything but someone who makes them a cup of tea. Jesus!*

Smoothing down her jumper, she opened the kitchen door.

'Fancy a hot drink?' she said loudly.

Alan looked at her, unsmiling. 'No,' he said abruptly.

'Oh.' Miriam almost jumped back inside as he slammed the summerhouse door behind him. 'Bloody rude man.' She poured the boiling water over the tea bag and almost threw in some milk. 'Rude,' she muttered again and went to the sitting room so she could find a podcast on her phone to teach her more about the night sky.

'Um … excuse me.'

Miriam felt herself grunt as she woke up suddenly. Her headphones were on the floor next to the sofa, her mobile phone still in her hand.

'Miriam … sorry to disturb.'

She sat up woozily. 'I must have fallen asleep,' she said quietly.

'Yes ...' Alan stood awkwardly in the doorway. 'I wanted to apologise. For earlier on.'

'Ah … yes. You were very rude.' Miriam picked up her headphones.

'It wasn't anything to do with you.' He took a step into the room, then stopped. 'I had been having a – how can I put it? – difficult conversation with someone.'

'Well, that isn't my fault.' Miriam deliberately didn't look at him, concentrating on re-attaching the headphones to the mobile phone.

'I'm trying to apologise,' he said irritably.

She stood up. 'Well, I'm going to have a cup of chamomile tea. So, if you want to make amends, you can put the kettle on.'

'Right …okay.' He walked ahead of her to the kitchen. 'I'm going to have something stronger,' he said and opened the fridge.

'Do you ever replenish your own fridge?' she muttered.

'Sometimes,' he said, taking out a bottle of beer and turning the kettle on. 'I'll actually pour the water over the tea bag for you, to make sure you know I'm serious about the apology.'

Miriam tried not to smile. 'That's something, I suppose.'

'This is a very strange situation we find ourselves in.' Alan made the tea and handed her the mug.

'It is a bit. I'm here to get away from it all, but this is anything but.'

'What is it that you're getting away from?' He sat down at the kitchen table. 'As we are almost sharing a house, it would be nice to know.'

Miriam looked at him, not sure how much to say, then was distracted by the chest hairs peeping over his sweatshirt again.

'Miriam, are you all right?'

'Yes, yes.' She sat down. 'I sold my business, which I loved very much, but I wanted a break … *needed* a break from all of that. Had no idea where to go, but had this idea that spending time in this part of Wales for a while would be nice.'

'It is very beautiful, so I get that.'

'But there was a lot going on, and organising somewhere to stay just kept getting pushed further and further back. And one of the things I'm trying to do is not be so very organised, so I really bought into it.'

Alan laughed. 'So you were very organised about being disorganised?'

Miriam laughed too. 'Oh, yes. I'm very committed to to-do lists, you know.'

'So you wrote "be less organised" on a list of to-do's!'

'And I moved into a hotel round the corner from my office after I sold my house and put all my belongings in storage. I was quite enjoying it. The order, not having to think. But my PA decided that it wasn't good for me and found this place. I'd mentioned the village as I spent time here with my parents when I was very young, and my mum talked about it a lot.'

'Ah, revisiting your childhood …'

Miriam sighed. 'I was so young when I came here. I don't remember any of it. All of what I know is from what she told me … through her eyes. And after she died, I wanted to reconnect to it …' She trailed off, not sure how to explain why.

'That's understandable.'

'But Justin – my PA – he found the house for let when he was about to go on a trip along the Amazon ...'

Alan stood up and went to the fridge. 'Are you sure you wouldn't prefer a beer to chamomile tea?' he asked, waving a bottle at her.

'I don't normally drink alcohol until after six.'

'That sounds very organised and like the kind of thing you'd write on a list.' He pointed at the clock on the wall. 'It is nearly five though.'

Miriam laughed. 'I'll let myself be edged out of my comfort zone.'

Alan opened the bottle. 'Glass or au natural?'

'Straight from the source is fine by me.'

He put it on the table in front of her. 'So, Justin was off up the Amazon ...?'

'And things were a bit fraught. The sale of the business had been delayed ...' She took a gulp of her drink. 'Lots of things to sort out, and I was tired and stressed and didn't read the paperwork properly.'

'You've had a very busy few months by the sound of it.'

'Yes, for all sorts of reasons.' Miriam sighed. 'And now, as you know, I've accidentally signed a very tight contract to take over your aunt's strange catering venture.' She took another gulp of beer. 'I have to admire whoever drew that up. Full marks to them.'

'I can see that would be problematic.'

'Well, it's a pity. My solicitors are looking into how I can get out of it, and once that's done and we find someone else, I'll be off.'

Alan stood up. 'May as well make the most of it in the meantime though.'

'Actually ...' Miriam took another sip. 'You're an expert on astronomy?'

'Yes ...' he said slowly.

'Would you give me some pointers on how to use a telescope?'

'I normally charge for that,' he said, deadpan.

'Do you? Oh, sorry, I—'

'But, as you've been dropped in it a bit, thanks to my aunt, I feel a bit responsible ... so yes, of course. And I was joking – I'm always helping people out with their stargazing for free. When were you thinking?'

'Tonight.'

'Tonight?' He looked at his watch. 'I've got a thing I've got to sort out – to do with what happened earlier.'

'Oh, okay.'

'But I will. On the next clear night, I promise.' He finished his drink quickly. 'And on that note, I'd better be off.'

He closed the door behind him, and Miriam sat watching him walk across the garden, wondering how she'd let her guard down and told him so much about herself. 'I was going to be a closed book when I came here,' she said to the spider plant on the windowsill. 'But I'm acting like a leaky information tap. Twit.'

Rummaging through the cupboards, she found a tin of soup and heated it up whilst trying to listen to the astronomy podcast she'd fallen asleep to earlier. Then, as darkness eventually fell, she scrolled through her music collection, chose a David Bowie playlist and switched it on through the speakers very loudly. Then she made her way up to the attic room accompanied by 'Starman'.

Managing to focus the telescope quite quickly, she hoped to identify the shapes in the sky, trying to remember some of the podcast. 'Celestial sphere,' she said a few times, as if by saying it she would work out what it meant. She also remembered the words "pinpoint" and "position" too. But they didn't mean anything either. She stared at the patterns dotting across the sky, glimmering and twinkling like fairy lights, and let herself get carried away by the beauty sweeping across the bay and into the distance.

After a while, her legs began to ache so she stood up, knocking one of the boxes over onto the floor. A pile of papers spilled out, and she began to gather them up. 'You idiot!' she muttered.

'Sorry?'

She looked up. Alan was standing in the doorway, holding two mugs.

'Oh, I thought you were out?'

'Chamomile?' he said, handing her the tea. 'My appointment finished earlier than expected.'

'Ah … you don't look very happy about it.'

He smiled faintly. 'It didn't go according to plan. Never mix business with pleasure.'

'Amen to that,' muttered Miriam.

Alan looked at her surprised. 'Story to tell?'

'Do *you* have a story to tell?'

'Best not.'

'No, quite.' Miriam took a sip of her tea. 'I knocked these over,' she said, sitting down amongst the bits of paper and beginning to gather them.

Alan kneeled down next to her. 'My aunt is a real hoarder.' He sighed.

'Are these recipes?' Miriam looked more closely. 'Glamorgan sausages. My mum used to make them. Bara brith! She taught me how to make that. How funny.'

Alan looked at her. 'Why don't you bring them downstairs? It may inspire you to cook. Isn't there a note in the file saying you should help yourself?'

Miriam laughed thinly. 'Oh, no … not interested. I'm having a break from all of that.'

As they finished putting the paperwork back in the box, Miriam's stargazing playlist clicked onto 'I Only Have Eyes For You', the first few notes hanging in the air, unsettling and seductive. Their eyes locked for just a moment, then they both looked away.

Alan coughed, 'Great version, this,' he said, eventually.

'The Flamingos, isn't it?' Miriam looked out of the window.

'Art Garfunkel,' Alan said after a pause. 'That was a good take on it. Although, you know, Carly Simon sang it beautifully.'

There was a key change as a cloud drifted across the sky, casting a shadow on the shaft of moonlight illuminating the floor.

Miriam searched her mind for something to say, staring steadily ahead, unable to look at him. She realised she was fighting something she didn't want to acknowledge.

'Michael Bublé,' she said suddenly.

'What about him?'

'I heard him sing it. Once.'

'Ah.'

They both fell into silence, Miriam still tidying the box, Alan apparently concentrating hard on the song.

'Do you always have a playlist to your hobbies?' Alan smiled as the last few chords melted away.

'Oh, well, I used to put them on when I was working at home. I'm just trying to create the right atmosphere, that kind of thing.'

He stood up and held his hand out. 'Need some help to get up, Miriam?'

'No,' she muttered. 'I'm fine.' Then she rolled onto her knees, eventually holding her hand up to him. 'This time, maybe.' She stumbled into him as he pulled her up, and for a millisecond their eyes met again. Her heart began to race, her stomach fluttering like a schoolgirl's with a first crush. She stepped back and turned towards the window, sensing his gaze following her.

She forced herself to look ahead, fighting the urge to turn back. She could feel herself being pulled towards him but made herself check her phone instead, pushing away the hint of the something that was hanging in the air between them. 'Oh, look at the time. I didn't realise ...'

'Next time there's a clear night,' he murmured. 'Like I promised. I'll help.'

'Thanks.'

'Night then,' he said, walking down the stairs.

Miriam bit her lip. *What was that?* She thought. *No, I know what it was, but, remember, don't let anyone too close*. An image of the chest hairs peeping over his sweatshirt popped into her mind. 'Miriam!' she said out loud. 'Stop! It! Think. Of. Something. Else.'

A stray piece of paper was tucked under the windowsill, so she gathered it up and put it back in the box. Under it was a recipe for Welsh onion cake.

She looked at it. Her mother used to make something very much like it, but she'd always just called it her "onion and potato thing". It looked very easy, didn't have many ingredients. Miriam's hand hovered over it uncertainly for a second, then she took it, went down the attic stairs to her bedroom and put it in her bag.

Chapter Eight

The pinks, blues and yellows of the houses by the harbour in Tenby shone, reflecting the bright sunlight and the sparkling sheen of the water. People bustled around and paused to chat, sat at the cafés and browsed around the narrow streets.

The town had been one of the places Miriam's mother had talked about, so she'd decided to drive there. She felt she needed a change of scene, and wanted to be around people but not be *with* them – craved their energy, but not *them*. She pottered around the shops, examining knick-knacks, then joined a queue to buy an ice cream which she ate whilst paddling through the shallows on the beach. After that, she found a café, ordered lunch and sat for a while reading a book she'd found in the house about the area.

Eventually, she stood up and walked back to the car, passing a busy farmers' market which spilled out onto the pavement. The colourful fruits and vegetables mingled with cheese stalls and tables full of cured meats and chutneys. She took the recipe out of her bag and checked it. *Buying some onions and potatoes won't do any harm*, she thought. *I could just bake those anyway. It's not like cooking.* She stepped in and felt a flutter of happiness, remembering the early days of the food truck she and her ex-husband, Felix, had run, and their early morning visits to the markets to see what was there so they could decide on their menus for the day.

Moving through the stalls, Miriam relaxed and allowed herself to enjoy the colours and shapes of the food around her. The fragrance of fresh herbs mixed with the strong aroma of brewing coffee, combined with the sweetness of sizzling onions, reminded her of meals, and events and parties she'd catered for.

Images of people laughing and talking and eating appeared in her mind, filed away from a happy past a long time ago.

She was glad that the last two years didn't appear in her mental film.

Pausing by a stall overflowing with vegetables, she assessed the spring onions, new potatoes, spinach and carrots, instinctively putting her hand down to pick up a big red pepper. But as she did, someone dropped something behind her, and she came to, her hand hovering mid-air. *No, no, no*, she thought. *No cooking.* The panic appeared from nowhere, surprising her with its intensity. She hurried to a stall selling takeaway paella and bought that instead to eat at home.

Waiting on the doorstep when she got there was a parcel addressed to her – first name only, just like the last one. Miriam picked it up and carried it to the kitchen, tearing it open to find three lights in the shape of flowers, with the batteries already in them. Switching them on, she smiled as they flashed red, then blue, then red again, and rifled through the jiffy bag to see if there was any clue about who they were from.

'Well, mystery giver of light, thank you,' she muttered, and carried them up to her bedroom where she found space for them on the dressing table. Then, taking out her journal, she wrote, *I had a near-miss with a red pepper today.*

She closed it, then opened it up again.

Look – no list of to-do's!

As she stood up, she noticed Rhiannon parking outside the house and went downstairs to open the door.

'Hiya!' Rhiannon slammed the car door behind her. 'I've got something for you.' She was waving a piece of paper above her head triumphantly.

'Fancy a cup of tea?' Miriam walked to the kitchen and switched the kettle on.

'Please. Common or garden variety English Breakfast if you've got it.'

'I'll join you.' Miriam got out a teapot. 'I've got biscuits too.'

'That's impressive.'

'Not homemade.' She smiled. 'I just bought some because Alan seems to spend a lot of time eating my food.'

'If it gets him in the house, I can think of worse things.'

'It's like having a hungry teenager grazing from the fridge.' Miriam put the tea and biscuits on the table and sat down. 'So, what have you got for me?'

Rhiannon handed her a flyer. 'Outside caterers,' she said excitedly.

'Ahhh … interesting.' Miriam looked at it. 'I have got a couple of meals for about ten people in the next few weeks.'

'You could keep it hush hush, you know.' Rhiannon tapped the side of her nose conspiratorially. 'I know the guy who runs it from my Cardiff past – don't ask. They're setting up a branch round here to see how it goes for the summer.'

Miriam stood up and checked the spreadsheet. 'Actually, the first one is on Sunday. It says here they want a seafood feast. Not sure ready meals could cover that ... and it says "TJ" next to it.' She looked at Rhiannon. 'Any ideas what that means?'

Rhiannon looked at her blankly. 'Nope. Sorry!'

'Do you think they could come up with something at short notice? Seafood themed?' She looked at the spreadsheet again to check how much the guests had paid, then shut it dramatically.

'What's up?' Rhiannon was in the middle of chewing a biscuit.

'I'm supposed to be having a long break away from budgets, amongst other things, that's what's up.' Miriam sat down and took a sip of tea. 'Just get them to do something reasonable. But we need them to get the food here without anyone noticing.'

'Ooooh. Interesting.' Rhiannon looked serious. 'I do like a challenge.'

Miriam got up and checked the spreadsheet again. 'The following one is a curry night a few days after. That's easy. For the caterers, not me.' She ran her fingers down the list. 'And there's that Look-Alike Festival. Oh …' She sighed and sat down again.

'What's up?' Rhiannon smiled. 'That sigh seemed very despondent.'

'It is. Even thinking about all of this is like working. Caring about it …'

'I've got an idea.' Rhiannon took a long gulp of tea, placed the mug firmly on the table and stood up. 'Let's go to the pub.'

'I'm not sure I— '

'I've got the hots for Jim the Landlord, so you'd be helping.'

'True love?'

'Not exactly.' Rhiannon giggled. 'Come on. As you're here, you may as well enjoy the bits of it you can.'

'Oh, why not?' Miriam got up. 'Give me five minutes to change and I'll be with you.'

'It's just the pub, come on.' Rhiannon took her hand. 'Honestly. You look fabulous as you are, and you'll change your mind in between going upstairs and coming back down again.' She pulled her towards the door. 'Get your jacket.'

Miriam smiled and took it from the hook next to the door. 'Just for ten minutes though. You can stay as long as you want …'

The lights of the pub glowed welcomingly as they walked towards it, the happy chatter from inside spilling out into the street when they opened the door.

'Hello, ladies. Welcome to Gin Night.' Jim waved at them from the bar and pointed at an assortment of bottles on a shelf behind him. 'We've got someone from a local distillery over by there if you want to improve your knowledge of the beverage. Or, if you just want to drink gin, our selection is printed on this.' He handed them a laminated list with a dramatic flourish.

'I'll have that one please.' Rhiannon pointed at the one at the top of the paper and looked into Jim's eyes, flicking her hair back elegantly as she did.

'Of course, madam.'

'Rhiannon.'

'Rhiannon., of course. I do remember.' He reciprocated the gaze for a few moments longer than necessary, then smiled at Miriam.

'Can I have a cocktail? An Elderflower Collins?' She sat down on the bar stool.

'A cocktail. You and your sophisticated city ways.' He laughed. 'I'll Google it. Unless you want a Negroni, or a Gin Fizz? I know them off by heart.'

'It's easy, honestly. You'll have all the ingredients.' Miriam watched the gin expert chatting to a group of people at the far end of the room. Part of her wanted to go over and find out more, but she wouldn't do it because that was what she would have done a couple of years ago. *And that would be another thing that would remind me of work*, she thought. So, she averted her gaze and watched Rhiannon and Jim flirt for a while until Jim had to serve another customer.

'It's lovely here, isn't it?' Rhiannon sighed. 'Doing me good, it is, being away from Cardiff. Meeting new people.'

'It is very nice.'

'Still definitely planning on leaving if you can?'

94

'Yes.' The word got caught in her throat, along with a brief prick of unexpected sadness. 'I really need a break and this isn't it.'

'Pity.' Rhiannon smiled at her. 'I think it would be fun.'

'It is fun. Hard work though. But fun. But …' Miriam paused, the reasons why there was a "but" on the tip of her tongue.

'But. I get it.' Rhiannon looked over at the gin expert. 'I'm going to go and improve my knowledge,' she said. 'Back in a bit.'

Miriam relaxed for a moment, enjoying the low buzz of conversation and laughter around the room. 'This is a very nice pub,' she said to Jim as he put some money in the till. 'The view of the sea from here is gorgeous.'

'Thank you. I try hard to make it welcoming. You should see it during the Look-Alike Festival. Mad, it is. Talking of which, we need to organise that meeting.'

'Can we do it next week? I've got a few things to sort out, but next week would be okay.'

'Tell you what, we can talk here over a lovely brunch, is it? What about next Wednesday at eleven?'

Miriam took out her phone and put the date in her diary, uncomfortable she was being sucked back into the thing she was trying to get away from, but guilty enough not to say no. 'Done.'

'We can have another chat about Joanna's whereabouts too.' Jim took a diary out from under the counter and wrote the date down. 'Known her long?' He nodded over at Rhiannon who was giggling at something the gin expert was saying.

'She's the letting agent for the house. We only met on the day I arrived.'

'She seeing anyone?'

'Not sure, to be honest. Think you should definitely ask her.' Miriam smiled and finished her drink. 'Anyway. I'm off. I'll see you on Wednesday.'

She waved at Rhiannon. 'I'm heading home,' she mouthed. 'See you soon.' Stepping out into the cool evening, Miriam took a deep breath, enjoying the fresh, salty sea air, and walked back along the empty road to her very temporary home.

It was Sunday, and Miriam glanced out of the kitchen window to check that Alan's Jeep, or camper van, or whatever he was driving wasn't there. He was supposed to be away, but she felt so on-edge that she didn't trust anyone.

'Can you come in an unmarked vehicle?' she whispered at the phone, feeling like she was in some kind of reality crime programme. 'It's just that no one can know that I've got caterers in.'

'Of course,' the person she was speaking to whispered back. 'I'll be there shortly.'

Putting her phone down, she began to move chairs from the garage into the dining room, opening the adjoining doors to the living room to give more space. For a while she forgot that this was not her job and she didn't want to do it, until the doorbell rang.

'Please don't be anyone who knows me,' she muttered, looking at the clock. 'The undercover caterers will be here soon.'

'Miriam … Miriam?' Rhiannon was hissing loudly on the doorstep. 'It's only me!'

Miriam opened the door.

Rhiannon tiptoed in. 'You're smiling,' she said very quietly. 'That's a surprise.'

'I'm pleased to see you. I was worried it would be someone else and I'd get found out.'

'This is quite exciting, isn't it?'

'No. It's quite stressful, and you don't have to whisper.'

'*You're* whispering,' Rhiannon whispered.

'Oh. Oh?' Miriam laughed.

They walked through to the kitchen. Piles of serving dishes were on the table, along with napkins and glasses.

'I finished work early so I can help out.' Rhiannon put her jacket over a chair.

'Thank you. I really appreciate it.' Miriam opened the fridge door and pulled out a bottle of wine. 'Can I tempt you?'

'Surely you're not drinking on the job?' Rhiannon giggled.

'I haven't got a job ... so no.'

'Go on then.'

Miriam poured them both a glass and held hers aloft. 'Thank you, Rhiannon, for saving the day.'

'You are very welcome. I'm not gonna lie, it makes a nice change.'

The doorbell rang again.

Miriam looked at the clock. 'That will be the caterers. I hope.' She rushed to open it.

A young man with a goatee beard smiled at her. He was wearing a T-shirt, jacket and a hat, all with Limoncello Caterers emblazoned across them.

'Hi. I'm Pedro.'

Miriam held out her hand and almost dragged him inside. 'Not quite as discreet as I'd hoped,' she said, panicked. 'Let's talk in here.'

'Oh, okay.'

'You need to move the van,' she hissed.

'I will, but you've just asked me in ...' Pedro looked confused.

'Yes, sorry. You can do it in a minute. That *is* unmarked, isn't it?'

'Yes, like you asked.'

97

'Pedro … is that you?' Rhiannon rushed out of the kitchen. 'I thought you'd send someone else.'

'Rhi! You look gorgeous as always.' He pulled her into a hug. 'Couldn't miss a chance to say hello. And thank you for recommending us for this job.'

'No probs. I know you'll be great.'

'Now ...' Miriam was beginning to feel very anxious. 'There's a lane just down the road to the right which leads to a parking space by the summerhouse. If you park there, I'll help you get all the food inside.'

'Right, will do.' Pedro turned to go.

'Remember, if anyone asks – which they may around here – you're a gardener.' Miriam looked at his clothes and sighed. 'Can you hide your jacket and hat? You could say you're wearing the T-shirt for a friend?'

'Fine.' Pedro looked confused again. 'I'll do it now.' He almost ran back to the car.

'I hope I haven't frightened him.' Miriam looked at Rhiannon. 'I just have professional pride ... and ready meals are bad enough.'

'I thought you didn't want to cook?' Rhiannon went to open the patio door.

'I don't.'

'So, professional pride is something you can't afford to have in this situation.'

Miriam sighed. 'You're right.'

As the van parked up at the end of the garden, they both hurried out and waited while Pedro opened the door. He began to unload the food, passing it on to Miriam and Rhiannon, then carrying the larger items in himself.

When it was done, Miriam shut the kitchen door firmly behind them.

'So, what have we got?' she asked, examining the collection of dishes on the table, then she glanced out of the window. 'If Alan comes back, you'll have to run outside and make sure he goes straight into the summerhouse,' she said to Rhiannon quietly.

'He's not supposed to be here though, is he?' Rhiannon followed her gaze.

'No, but he never is. And yet, somehow, he is here a lot.'

Pedro looked at them both. 'Shall we get on then? Seeing as this is a bit more cloak and dagger than I expected.'

'Of course, go on,' whispered Miriam.

'Still whispering.' Rhiannon giggled.

'I'll explain what we've got then,' said Pedro.

'Sorry,' whispered Miriam. 'Carry on.'

'We've got mussels with clams, cream and samphire, cockles in vinegar, smoked mackerel and stuffed aubergine as a vegetarian option. That's the starters.'

Miriam opened the lid, the aroma of shellfish, vinegar and samphire making her mouth water. 'These look and smell delicious.' She smiled at Pedro. 'I don't think I could have done better myself.'

Pedro beamed. 'Thank you. We aim to please. Then, we've got sea bream, cod, sea trout and langoustines, with laver bread, French fries, green beans in garlic and lemon, and a tomato and mozzarella salad.'

'Excellent. And for dessert?'

'Lemon meringue pie, strawberries and cream, and a selection of Welsh cheese and biscuits.'

'Very impressive.' Miriam nodded, then noticed the time. 'But you have to go ... now!'

Rhiannon smiled apologetically. 'Sorry, Peds. One day I'll explain, but she's right.'

'I'll be back first thing in the morning,' he said, backing towards the door. 'I hope it goes well. Normally I give out my card but—'

'As it's on the quiet, you can't,' said Miriam firmly. 'But I'll make sure word somehow gets around about your company. Don't worry. I've been there myself – now, run!'

He hurried back to the van and turned the engine on.

Miriam sighed as she watched him pull away. 'Do you think I frightened him?'

Rhiannon laughed. 'You were very assertive. I can't lie.'

Miriam smiled. 'I think, until quite recently, I was like that rather a lot.' She took a sip of wine, looked at the trays and plates on the kitchen table, took a longer glug, and said, 'Right, let's get to it. Can you finish laying the table? I'll get all the booze ready.'

Rhiannon finished her drink and saluted Miriam. 'Yes sir!' Then she clicked her heels, collected the cutlery and went to the dining room just as the doorbell rang again.

Smoothing down her dress, Miriam rehearsed a smile and opened the door.

A silver-haired man with a goatee beard pushed past. 'Late, late. Sorry I'm late, love. Got a bit delayed at the surgery. A doctor's work is never done.'

'Hello. The rest of the guests haven't arrived yet. You're a bit earlier than we were expecting.' Miriam watched him as he opened the door of the downstairs toilet.

'I'll change in here,' he said, ignoring her. 'I'll bring my gear in after I'm done.'

Rhiannon had come back through to see who it was, and she and Miriam looked at each other, confused.

'So, where's Joanna? I sent her a text earlier to say I'd be a bit late, but it bounced back.'

Miriam sighed. 'Joanna is away at the moment for a break. I'm renting the house and taking care of things. She's fine.'

'Oh …what's the matter with her?'

'Nothing,' said Miriam firmly as the man came out of the downstairs toilet dressed entirely in black.

'Like the new outfit?'

'Very ... nice?' Rhiannon said slowly.

'Basically the same as the last one, only I've gone for the black leather jacket and shirt rather than roll neck, you know.'

Both women looked at him.

'It's about the voice at the end of the day though, isn't it?'

'Well, we hope you enjoy your meal ... whatever you're wearing,' Miriam said eventually.

'Meal?' He laughed. 'I'm the entertainment. But Joanna normally flings me a few morsels.' He stepped forward and held out his hand. 'I'm Dr Tom Jones. Nice to meet you.'

Miriam shook his hand. 'Oh, that's what TJ stands for on the spreadsheet. You're providing entertainment? So, where is your practice, Dr …?'

'Jones,' he said. 'Dr Tom Jones. That is my real name. My parents were having a laugh, weren't they? So, what with the name and the voice, I sort of drifted into the tribute thing. There's loads of Tom Joneses in Wales. I mean … it's not unusual.' He burst out laughing then walked back out to the car. 'I love saying that.' He pulled a PA system out of the boot and dragged it in. 'My patients do too, to be honest.' He laughed again. 'Ladies. You haven't told me your names.'

'Rhiannon. I love Tom Jones, I do. This is going to be fabulous.'

'Well, get involved, lovely girl. We love a sing-along.' He smiled at Miriam expectantly.

'I'm Miriam. I'm ... in charge isn't the right word ... but I'm keeping things going whilst Joanna's away.'

'Right you are.' He nodded. 'I'll set up in here, then I'll go and sit in the summerhouse out of sight until the guests are ready. Is Alan about?'

'No, he's away for a couple of days,' said Miriam.

'Pity. Never mind. I'll catch him at the Look-Alike Festival, no doubt. I'll go down to the orchard and do my warm-ups there, then.'

As Tom took his equipment into the living room, Miriam and Rhiannon began to laugh. 'I've always wanted to see Tom Jones,' giggled Miriam. 'But not like this ... very unexpected.' She took two bottles of red wine and carried them to the dining room.

'I'm all done.' Tom headed out to the garden. 'I'll help myself to some water from the tap if that's all right? I usually appear when they've had a couple of glasses of whatever it is they're imbibing. Come and get me just after the first refill.'

'Thank goodness he knows what he's doing,' said Rhiannon. 'I can hear people outside. Shall I?'

Miriam nodded, butterflies suddenly fluttering uncomfortably around her stomach, combined with an unpleasant surge of nausea. She glanced at the table and fought the urge to climb under it, pouring a glass of water to calm herself down instead. 'Where did you come from?' she muttered.

'Hiya!' she heard Rhiannon shout. 'Welcome! Everyone come in. Who's in charge?'

'Me!' a young woman said excitedly. 'We're from Swansea University International Students' Association. We've come to experience an interesting Welsh night out and we're looking forward to the Tom Jones tribute act ...'

'And the seafood too,' shouted someone at the back of the group.

'Well, Tom is just warming up, so why don't we take your coats and get you settled in? Miriam ... Miriam!'

Miriam smoothed down her dress for the umpteenth time, put on a calm smile and joined the guests. 'Hello. If you all go through here ...' She waved her hand at the dining room, then hurried back into the kitchen, opening the back door and taking a few deep breaths.

'Coats done. What's up?' Rhiannon touched her arm, concerned.

'Nothing. Just the usual unexpected and unexplained nerves. Which is also very irritating.' Miriam switched her smile on. 'Shall we get this delicious looking food in front of our guests?'

An hour later, Dr Tom Jones took his place noisily in the dining room as Miriam and Rhiannon cleared the table and brought in the main course. 'Hello, Swansea University International Students' Association! My name is Tom Jones. No, really, it is! I'm going to start with "It's Not Unusual". And probably end with it too ...'

Miriam felt herself lifted by the whoops and cheers of the audience, and caught herself swaying to the beat as she worked, laughing when Rhiannon grabbed her and said, 'Let's dance. It's not often you get to be in such close proximity to *the* Dr Tom Jones!'

By the time he'd got to 'Sex Bomb', she felt like she'd reluctantly just been to a party, and rather liked it.

'You've been enjoying yourself.' Rhiannon handed her a full glass of wine. 'I've not known you long but I haven't really seen you smile, let alone laugh properly. And tonight you've done both.'

'Really?' Miriam stared at the glass for a moment. 'I used to be fun, you know?'

'One day you'll tell me everything, won't you? Now, come on, drink up. He's gone into "It's Not Unusual" *again*, and it's going to be a bit of a job getting our guests out.'

They took their glasses into the dining room and began dancing as the group sang and swayed to the song. For a few moments, Miriam felt different. As Dr Tom posed for photographs with the revellers, she realised why. *I feel like me*, she thought. *I feel like me again.*

Chapter Nine

Miriam opened up her journal to check what she'd written the previous evening.

This evening was ... stressful.

But a tiny, tiny, tiny bit of me almost enjoyed some of it.

I don't want to do it again though.

The alarm on her phone buzzed. It was ten o'clock, so she picked it up and called Fiona.

'How was your break?'

'It was very nice, thanks. How have things been with you?'

'Mixed.'

'In what way?'

'Well, I'm getting drawn into this more and more ... and I'm getting confused.'

'Confused?'

'Well, yesterday evening I realised I was enjoying myself. But I also had to open the door and take some deep breaths because of stress.'

'It *is* a bit of a strange situation.'

Miriam laughed. 'Very!'

'Are you doing anything to distract yourself? Taken up any hobbies?'

'Well.' Miriam looked at the sky, dotted with fluffy cotton wool-like clouds. 'I'm interested in astronomy. There are two telescopes here ... and my father loved it. He never had a telescope though – and there's an expert on site.'

'That sounds convenient. Who's that?'

'Alan. He's the nephew of Joanna and he writes books about astronomy. He said he'd give me a lesson.'

'That sounds fun.'

'Yes ... not sure. Don't want anyone too close, you know.'

'Having an astronomy lesson isn't letting someone too close.'

The image of Alan striding out of the sea as she sat on the beach popped into her mind.

'Mmmm,' she said. 'I don't trust my judgement on anything any more.'

'How is trying to be more kind to yourself going?'

Miriam thought for a moment. 'Letting my guard down with anyone over anything doesn't feel like something I want to do.' She picked up the guidebook she'd read in Tenby. 'I'm going to visit a place called Bosherston today. It's another one of the places my mum talked about ...' She trailed off.

'Are you okay?'

Miriam cleared her throat. 'Yes ... um ... it's famous for its water lilies.'

'Have a lovely time then. I'll speak to you next week.'

'Thanks, Fiona. Bye.'

Miriam put the phone down, silent tears streaming unexpectedly down her face.

'Oh bugger ...' she said, grabbing a tissue and blowing her nose. 'Nope. This won't do,' she muttered, rifling through her wardrobe to find something suitable to wear and settling on a pair of cropped jeans, a designer T-shirt and a pair of sandals. Then she put on her mother's necklace and went downstairs.

As she climbed into her car, Jim walked past with his dog. 'Hiya!' he shouted. 'See you Wednesday.'

'Just for one minute, can I forget about any kind of work or responsibilities?' she muttered irritably, turning the engine on and switching on her "Travelling" playlist to accompany her on the drive.

The verges were bursting with wildflowers, a cacophony of yellows, pinks, purples and whites. The lush green leaves on the trees contrasted with the clear, bright blue of the sky, and as she pulled into the car park, Miriam realised she felt a little lighter somehow. As if the brightness of the day had rubbed off on her and lifted her up with it.

She walked down towards the water, watching the dragonflies hover over the lily pads dotting the lake, hearing only her own footsteps on the path as she got closer to the beach. Sitting for a while, she watched seagulls surf the breeze, and listened to the distant barking of dogs and the gentle rhythm of the waves. Closing her eyes, Miriam tried to remember what her mother had said about this place whilst she'd sat next to her in the care home, hungry for the snatches of lucidity that slipped gradually away as the dementia took her over.

But she couldn't grasp the words her mother had said. All she knew was that she'd loved it. She knew it, but she couldn't hear her say it.

She opened her eyes and scratched a pattern in the sand, frustrated. If only she could get a part of her back … a real memory, the sound of her voice, her laugh, a picture in her mind that she could actually see, not just a flat, immobile photograph. Something. *Anything.* She touched the necklace. *It's just a necklace*. She smiled. A necklace she realised she was wearing almost every day.

A yacht sailed gracefully past, gliding slowly across the bay. Miriam watched it disappear around the headland and stood up, wiping the sand from her legs, then made her way back to the car. She paused on a wooden bridge and took a photograph. *Maybe that will help*, she thought. *It's worth a try.*

When she got back to the house, she decided to heat up a tin of soup rather than simply assemble cold ham and tomatoes on a plate.

Putting a saucepan on the hob, she realised it was probably only around the second time she had come close to cooking anything for quite a while. *Maybe I should do a fanfare or something to mark the occasion.* 'Ta da,' she sang, opening the cupboard to take out one of her emergency stash of cream of tomato soups, but all she saw was a small tin of spaghetti hoops shoved right at the back. Reaching up to the shelf above it, she ran her hand along that, trying to find the missing tins.

'Um …' she said to the saucepan. 'Am I going mad?' Picking it up, she began to hang it on its hook next to the oven when she heard the tell-tale sounds of Alan's camper van rumbling into its parking space.

Still holding the pan, she opened the fridge. There was a solitary piece of cheese next to a tub of butter. 'There's been a raid,' she muttered. 'A raid.' Then she walked out into the garden. 'You've taken all my food again,' she said loudly.

Alan looked up and smiled. 'No I haven't … well, technically not. I've paid for it.'

'I'm not your aunt, and I'm not your mum.' Miriam could feel her voice rise, hunger pangs increasing her irritability.

He walked towards her, holding his hands up in front of him. 'But this has always been the arrangement.'

'What are you doing, holding your hands up in front of you?' Miriam looked up at him.

'You're waving a saucepan at me, so I'm attempting to be conciliatory.'

His warm green eyes held her gaze for a moment, then she stood back. 'I know what you're doing.'

'What do you mean?' He smiled again

'You're trying to be nice and … and … flirtatious … to hide the fact you've taken all my food.'

'Well, technically …'

'Technically … rubbish! You're just a scavenger.' Miriam felt pleased with the description and smiled despite herself.

'Are you hangry, Miriam?' he said softly. 'Because I've got just the thing.' He opened the back of the camper van and climbed in. She heard him rummaging around in a bag, then he jumped back down. 'Here you are.' He handed her a tin of tomato soup.

Miriam bit her lip. She didn't want him to see her laugh. It wasn't funny. She *was* hungry.

'That's my soup. Well, *one* of the tins of *my* soup.'

'Yes, I'm giving this one to you. It's your soup,' he said, deadpan.

'It's the soup I bought, so it was already my soup.'

'Well, you know … this is how we roll, me and my aunt, normally, so I'm having to get used to a different way of doing things. I would be grateful if you showed a little patience.'

Miriam had to stop herself stamping her foot with frustration. 'What am I supposed to do now? Do *another* shop?'

'Well, I haven't got time, so, yes ... I suppose. I just popped back to pick up something,' he said, going into the summerhouse. 'I'm off on another site visit for a few days. Taking a few photographs of the stars …'

'You can't just take all my food. What if I had something on?'

He carried his rucksack out and closed the door, locking it behind him. 'You're on a break though. I didn't think you had anything on. It will be nice for you to go into town.'

'I don't want to go to the supermarket.'

'You could go to the farmers' market, or one of the independent shops, you know. It's your choice to go to the supermarket.'

'That's because I don't want to go and buy food …again!' She watched as he got into the driver's seat of the camper van.

'You can use my telescope if you like,' he said. 'While I'm away.'

'The one in the attic in the house is superior.' Miriam didn't want him to get the better of her, so she decided to carry on arguing.

'It's harder to use. For someone of your level anyway.' He turned on the engine and smiled at her. 'I promise I'll give you a lesson when I get back.'

'I'm not sure I …' Miriam trailed off.

'Bye then.' He waved and reversed the van out into the road, still smiling.

'I really don't know what to think of you,' she said quietly, throwing the tin into the saucepan and walking back towards the house.

'You've got to open it first,' he shouted, then drove off, waving.

And Miriam tried not to smile.

Chapter Ten

On the morning of her meeting with Jim, Miriam checked her bank account. The money for the catering had been transferred from Joanna's solicitors to her overnight. She sat back and sighed, wondering how transactions like these seemed to follow her about. Unwanted.

Clicking onto her business account, she examined the figures for a while, making sure that everything was in order before moving the new money from her current account. Then she stopped.

Keep it separate, she thought. *Then when I go, I just pay it all back and cancel everything that reminds me of it*. So, she reluctantly set up a new online bank account, transferred the cash and switched off the computer, knowing she would also have to do some bookkeeping too. Which was also work, and something she used to pay her accountant to do.

'I could get them to do this,' she said to herself, turning the laptop off. 'But that's more money down the drain … and now, on my long holiday, I have a meeting about some work.' Grabbing her jacket, she opened the door. Oh, bloody flippin' … flip!' she said to the computer as she went. '*Flip!*'

'Latte, cappuccino, hot chocolate, tea – herbal or common garden variety – chai latte?' Jim waved in the general direction of the bar as Miriam sat down.

She looked outside as the grey waves crashed dramatically on the rocks, the clouds so low they merged into the sea. 'Hot chocolate would be very nice.' She put her jacket on the back of the chair whilst Jim ducked back behind the counter and made her drink

'Pity about the weather,' he shouted above the hissing of the coffee maker. 'Should be all right tomorrow though.'

His dog ambled in from upstairs and lay at Miriam's feet, sighing forlornly.

'He doesn't like the rain.' Jim carried the mugs over to the table and sat down. 'Bit of a problem if you live round here. I think he's got a dog version of – what is it? – seasonal affective disorder, although it runs all through the year.' The dog grunted as he rubbed his ear. 'Never mind though, boy. The sun will come out tomorrow as the song goes.'

Miriam took a sip of the hot chocolate, enjoying the steam brushing her face. She put on a smile for Jim's sake, but the knot in her stomach she had woken up with was now churning around slowly.

'Well, this is going to be fun.' Jim moved his laptop screen to face her. 'Here's the marketing and publicity materials and such,' he said. 'But you don't have to worry about that. It's helping with food and logistics and everything.'

'Okay!' Miriam tried to sound bright to match his enthusiasm.

'To be honest, I'm hoping this year goes a bit more smoothly than last year.'

Miriam took another sip of her drink. 'Why? What happened?'

'Well …' Jim clicked on a link to some photographs. 'There was a bit of a to-do. A bit of rivalry between the Elvises. Or Elvi as I like to call them. You know, like a flock of sheep or a shoal of fish?' He smiled.

Miriam laughed and peered at the photograph.

'Young Elvis got into a ruck with the Las Vegas Elvis. Pulled off his sequins, he did. Quite late in the evening. And look, there's an Oasis look-alike and a Dylan Thomas look-alike … I told him it was a singing look-alike competition, but he didn't listen. Then they all piled in.'

Miriam tried not to laugh again as Jim's face was deadly serious.

'Doesn't do our image any good.'

'No ... are you doing anything to make this less likely to happen?' Miriam could feel herself click into management mode and tried to fight it. 'I mean, did you get lots of publicity out of it?'

'No. Thankfully. Didn't go much further than a splash on social media.' He leaned forward. 'There's going to be no free drinks this year. Joanna said I needed to put my foot down. So, it's on all of the entry forms.' He clicked on another link and showed her the page. 'See – all drinks must be paid for. It says there. I had an over-enthusiastic barman called Reg. He used to help out occasionally. Eighty years old, didn't care ... he's off in Hawaii with his girlfriend at the moment. He does Joanna's garden, come to think of it ...'

I'd forgotten about the garden. Another thing to sort, thought Miriam, reluctantly putting it on the list of to-do's in her head. 'Well, it sounds like you'll have more control of things if people aren't getting unlimited free booze.'

'Yes. So, I have a couple of marquees and we have a sort of Glastonbury Pyramid Stage and Acoustic Stage vibe ... and Joanna organises the catering – does some stuff herself, gets a couple of stalls in. I provide the staff.'

'Oh, that sounds—'

'Basically they're the same kind of acts – look-alikes but we like to put them in different locations so it sounds grander, you know. But mainly it's the pub garden and by the harbour.'

'Ahh ...' Miriam hoped she'd be gone by the time the festival came. But as soon as that thought arrived, she felt a bit sick. *Gone*

... she thought, a pinprick of doubt surprising her. She leaned forward, focusing on the computer, pushing her confusion away.

'How many years has this been going for?'

'Four years. I went to the Elvis Festival in Porthcawl a couple of times and thought it would be a good idea to have something similar here.'

'But it's not an Elvis Festival?' Miriam picked up the mug again and took another long sip of her hot chocolate. 'This really is delicious.'

Jim beamed. 'Special recipe.'

'Is it a general look-alike festival then?'

'Well, first of all, it was a tribute act festival … then it was a Welsh tribute act festival, but there were a lot of Tom Joneses and Shirley Basseys, a few Manics, quite a lot of Stereophonics, some Super Furry Animals … Dylan Thomas turned up … he always turns up … even though it was *singing* … I keep telling him.'

'It sounds fun.'

'Too many acts and a bit too niche, so we changed it last year to the Look-Alike Festival. Now it's a mixture of performers and people who like to dress up.'

Miriam looked back out at the sea again. Spots of rain were now dappling noisily on the windows, and she rifled through the list of events she and her previous company had catered for. She couldn't find a Look-Alike Festival. *Add it to the list*, she thought, *of things that aren't on the list.*

'So, we need to double confirm the marquees in the next week, and all the lights and such.'

'We?' Miriam felt her heart began to thump uncomfortably. 'I—'

'It's all right, I'll do it. It's just that Joanna pays towards it.'

'Oh, right. That's fine. Just let me know how much.'

114

'And there's all the health and safety forms and risk assessments to do.'

A wave of nausea swept over Miriam. Too much like work – like the past was just there, looking over her shoulder.

'Are you all right?'

'Me?' Miriam took a deep breath. 'Some of the hot chocolate went down the wrong way. Do I need to do those?'

'You look a bit pale all of a sudden. Don't worry, I'll do them. And I'll order the food too. I've got the list from last year. You've been dropped in it a bit, to be honest. Any clues come to light?' he asked. 'About Joanna's whereabouts?'

'No. I'm sure she's fine. But if anything does come up, I'll definitely let you know.'

Some customers came into the pub, dripping the rain from their umbrellas on the floor. 'Hello there.' Jim stood up, smiling. 'Welcome. It's a bit inclement outside, isn't it? But we'll get you warm and dry. Would you mind putting your umbrellas in the receptacle in the foyer?' He began to herd the group towards the coat stand.

Miriam finished her drink and stretched. A refreshing walk in the rain seemed like a good idea. *Because I can. Just like that*, she thought. *That, after all, is what I'm here for. Not work.*

Putting on her jacket, she stood up and waved at Jim. 'Thanks for the drink. I'll be off then.'

He waved. 'Enjoy your day. And, for someone who doesn't want to cook for anyone, I've been hearing rave reviews about your culinary expertise.'

Miriam nodded, feeling her face redden. *Shame on you*, she thought, remembering that she'd booked the outside caterers again for the following night.

Miriam opened the curtains the next morning to watery sunlight, the cliffs and the sea glowing softly in the distance.

Taking out her journal, she wrote:

Today is a beautiful day. And I'm going to stroll along the beach, indulge in a bag of chips before tonight's event.

Think I accidentally made a to-do list.

Putting the book back on her bedside table, she switched on the radio and danced around for a few minutes to 'Hip To Be Square' by Huey Lewis and the News. Then she had a very hot, refreshing shower and headed for the beach, enjoyed her chips on the harbour wall and returned to the house, feeling slightly anxious about the evening's event – only this time it was mainly because she didn't want to be caught outsourcing the curries.

'Helloooo. It's only me.' Rhiannon rapped on the front door. 'Ready and rarin' to go for the curry night.'

Miriam turned off the radio and let her in. 'I really do appreciate this, you know,' she said. 'I've got most of the crockery out already, so it's mainly just getting the food from the caterers and meeting and greeting.'

'Any entertainers booked then?'

Miriam opened the folder and ran her hand down the spreadsheet. 'No, not tonight – I don't think so anyway. No mysterious initials!'

Rhiannon grabbed the kettle and filled it with water. 'Don't mind, do you?'

'Go ahead.'

'Bumped into Jim earlier on. Told me all about the Look-Alike Festival.' Rhiannon got a mug out of the cupboard. 'Fancy a cuppa?' she asked.

'No thanks.' Miriam picked up a glass of water. 'Too much caffeine earlier on.'

Rhiannon leaned against the table. 'He's lovely, isn't he?'

'He is very nice, yes.' Miriam took a swig of water. 'You rather like him, don't you?'

'Well, I think his beard is great. Makes him look a bit like … someone … hang on … tip of my tongue … Justin Timberlake! That's it. But a bit bigger … wider … you know? And only when he's got a beard.' She poured the boiling water into the mug and took some milk from the fridge. 'He may look like him when he's not got a beard too. I'll have to take a closer look.' Throwing the used tea bag in the bin, she looked up at Miriam. 'What are you smiling at?'

'The thought that there's a Justin Timberlake look-alike in the pub. You should persuade him to take part in the festival.'

Rhiannon laughed. 'Oh, yes. I said I'd help out. You know, get to know the people in the area bit more, be part of the community.'

'I was hoping you'd help me if I'm still here?' Miriam looked at her hopefully. 'There's a bit of cooking to be done.'

'Course I will. As long as we get to dress up as something … leave it with me.'

The doorbell rang and Miriam glanced at the clock. 'Must be the caterers. I hope they've not parked on the drive. Don't want to give the game away!'

She opened the door to find a van emblazoned with the catering company's name directly in front of her. The back doors were open and a man was already unloading the food.

'No …' Miriam began to panic. 'I'm sorry. Can you drive round the back? That's what we did last time. I did speak to Pedro about it.'

He looked up. 'The gate's locked at the end of the lane. Already tried.'

'Is it? I didn't see Alan lock it … you can't be seen here!'

'Um.' he looked confused. 'I just need to deliver this lot. We've got an event later I have to prepare for.'

Miriam grabbed her jacket. 'We'll have to do this somewhere else ... Rhiannon!'

Rhiannon came out of the kitchen. 'Everything all right?'

'Is there a quiet country lane nearby where there aren't any cars so that we can transfer the food between us?' asked Miriam, picking up her car keys.

Rhiannon thought for a moment. 'I don't know the area very well yet, to be honest ... but ... oh yes, there's a road called Nathans Lane. I remember it because of you know ... Nathan Lane ... the actor ... makes me laugh. It's about five minutes away, and there's a lay-by.'

'Excellent.' Miriam hurried to the car. 'Can you help, Rhiannon? We need to transfer the food quickly, so we can get away and hopefully no one will notice.'

'This is odd,' the driver said, closing the doors and climbing into the van. 'Very odd, but I'll follow you there if you insist.'

'No!' shouted Rhiannon. 'Somebody might see you with us.'

'Good point.' Miriam got into her car. 'Can you put Nathans Lane in the sat nav and we'll follow you there in five minutes?'

He looked at them both, muttered something, set the sat nav and turned the engine on. As he drove off, Miriam thought she heard him say, 'Not paid enough for this.'

Moving the car to the end of the driveway, they sat for a few moments in silence. Then Rhiannon burst out laughing.

'Oh, this is funny. Curry smuggling, we are.'

Miriam looked at her and joined in. 'Is that a crime? Curry smuggling ...'

'Not in these parts.'

'But don't want to be caught, just in case.'

A motorbike sped past and Miriam followed it. 'We can hide behind this,' she said, and Rhiannon snorted.

'Oh, no. Lost control. Snorting laughing ...'

A few minutes later, they pulled into a lane at the far end of the beach. 'Is this the right one?' Miriam slowed down to a crawl.

'Yes. There's a house just been put up for let right up the top of the hill over there, which is how I know it. The lay-by is down here.'

The catering van was hidden just out of sight, and as Miriam parked behind it, Rhiannon opened the car door. 'Got to be quick,' she said. 'It's quiet, but cars do go past.'

Miriam jumped out and opened the boot as the van driver began to pass her the steel dish sets. 'I'll certainly have something to tell the guys when I get back to base,' he said. 'How am I going to get them back by the way?'

'Shall we meet here tomorrow at midday?' Miriam began to load some of the sets into the back seat. 'Just in case I can't find the keys to open the gate at the house?'

'Okay, but why are you being so furtive?' He climbed back into the van and closed the door.

Miriam felt her face redden again. *Shame, shame, shame*, she thought. 'To protect my reputation and that of others,' she said.

She saw him laugh as he put the engine on and drove off.

'Can you sit in the back and make sure those don't spill?' she said to Rhiannon.

'Okey-dokes.' Rhiannon got in, and Miriam turned on the engine. 'You're quite firm, aren't you? Quite business-like and *very* efficient.'

'Mm, well ...' Miriam pulled out into the lane, trying to push the company director in her as far away as possible.

Miriam forced herself to click into event host that evening, somehow filing her feelings of resentment and panic into the "to-do ... or to-feel later" part of her brain. The guests enjoyed the curry, and Rhiannon seemed to like helping out. By the time Miriam loaded the empty dish sets into the car to return to the catering company in a secret liaison arranged for the "usual" lay-by the following day, she had decided that quietly outsourcing the bigger events was the way to get through it. Even though she was having to spend her own money.

Ah, well, it's not for long, she thought to herself, turning off into the side road then parking up next to the catering van.

'Hi,' she said, climbing out of the car and opening the boot.

Pedro was already waiting there and smiled at her. 'My driver yesterday was very bewildered by all of this,' he said. 'I told him it would be something to write down in his autobiography.'

Miriam laughed. 'Do you think anyone would believe it?' She handed him the first tray.

'True enough,' he said, beginning to load the van.

Miriam heard the distant sound of an engine moving closer. 'Can you hear that?' she said.

'Yes, it's a car. We are on a road so ... not surprising!'

Panicked, she noticed a stile hidden between some bushes and hurriedly clambered over it. 'Just in case,' she said, 'Don't want anyone I know to see me here.'

Pedro shook his head, laughing. 'I'll just stand here all nonchalant, then.'

Miriam crept along the field and hid behind a bush, waiting for the car to pass, her stomach churning anxiously. But it didn't. It slowed down and sounded like it was parking in the lay-by too.

'Oh ... no,' she sighed, edging further along. 'Please don't be anyone I know.'

She held her breath as she heard the slam of a car door, then a familiar voice. 'Everything all right?' said Alan to Pedro.

'Oh, for God's sake,' Miriam muttered, darting behind a tree.

'Fine, fine. Just stopped for a break. Bit of fresh air.'

'Is Miriam around?'

There was a pause.

'Who?'

'Miriam. I only ask as that's her car.'

'No idea who Miriam is.'

There was another pause. 'What's she doing with all those food trays in her back seat?'

'Food trays? No idea.'

'Look – the same as yours.'

Miriam moved even further away, almost pushing herself into a bush, getting her shirt caught on a branch in the process. She wanted to shoo him away. How dare he drive past exactly when she didn't want him to? She tried to free herself in order to look like she was having a relaxing morning stroll along a public footpath.

'Ah, there you are. I was worried.' Alan had jumped over the stile into the field. 'Have you been hiding in some bushes or something?'

Miriam sighed inside but smiled outwardly, feeling like a naughty child. 'Why are you worried?'

'Well, I was driving past and saw your car in a strange lay-by and—'

'I was having a walk.' Miriam pulled herself free of the twig that was trapping her and turned to face Alan. 'I am allowed. Nothing to see here.'

He walked towards her. 'Nothing to do with the catering van then?'

Miriam hesitated. 'Catering van?'

121

'The one parked next to you.'

'Well, I've been walking for hours so didn't notice.' Miriam stepped back, her mind screaming, *Why are you lying about a catering van? It's up to you whether you get outside caterers in. You're going mad!*

Pedro jumped over the stile into the field. 'I'm sorry, Miriam. I've got to get going. There's an event at two, and I have to drive back to the depot to pick up the food.'

Alan looked at her. 'I know what you've been doing.'

'I'll be off then,' shouted Pedro. 'Yes?

Miriam looked at him unsure what to say, so waved. 'Of course. Lovely to bump into you again … by accident …' Her voice trailed off as he climbed out of the field, and she heard the clattering of trays followed by a door being slammed shut and the engine rumbling into life.

'You are a very bad liar,' muttered Alan eventually, to the sound of the catering van driving off into the distance.

Miriam could feel her heart racing. 'What are *you* doing driving round country lanes?' she said.

'I'm popping in to see a friend on the way back to the house. It is allowed.'

'Why are you spying on me?' She could feel her voice rise.

'I'm not. But … if word got around that my aunt was using outside caterers and ready meals, her strange, odd and frankly loss-making business would lose *all* credibility.'

Miriam searched her mind for a justification. She knew how important reputation and credibility were to a business. *But … but …*

And then it came. It swept over her like a tidal wave. Sudden and overwhelming and unstoppable. She was standing in the middle of a field with people milling around, music drifting from the stage, queues snaking around the food stalls. Then someone asked her a question. '*There's a problem at the ticket office, who do I get to help?*' That was it. The straw that broke the camel's back. At that moment, all she had wanted to do was sink to the ground and not deal with anyone or anything. Be invisible. But of course, Miriam Ryan couldn't do that. She had to power through, so she just took a deep breath, smiled, answered, and then ran to the portacabin to hide under the desk.

'Miriam?' Alan's voice brought her back to the present.

'But I'm supposed to be having a break from all this.' Her voice shook. 'If you only knew.'

He stopped smiling and walked towards her, his expression suddenly concerned and kind. 'Knew what?' he said softly.

Miriam looked at the ground and tried to control herself. *No, no, no,* she thought. *Not ready to tell.* She breathed and smiled.

'Nothing, nothing,' she said. 'However, your aunt did disappear suddenly, and I signed the lease without realising what I was committing to. I could have just said no. Or have run off. But I haven't.'

Alan sighed. 'Fair point,' he said. 'Strange old thing all round, truth be told.'

'Yes.' Miriam walked towards the stile and climbed over it, trying to regain some dignity and control, having been caught in the act of passing someone else's food off as her own. As well as almost having a panic attack in a field in south west Wales.

Alan followed her over. 'Best double check your friend has taken all the trays with him. He did leave in a bit of a hurry.'

'Why did you lock the gate at the end of the lane?' Miriam opened her car boot.

'Because I was going away for a few days, and it's sensible.'

'You didn't before.'

'That was a mistake. Don't tell on me.' His eyes crinkled as he smiled, and something in Miriam melted a little. She didn't like it, so she stood a little taller to stop herself giving into it.

'I thought you had a Jeep, or a camper van?'

He opened the door of an old yellow Citroen. 'Oh, I did. My mate keeps lending me cars because mine's shot really. I need to get a new one. But none of them are any good, so I keep complaining and he keeps giving.'

'Oh, I did wonder.'

'Right, Pedro,' he said. 'Sorry, I mean Miriam. Looks like all evidence has been removed. Let's get out of here before anyone finds out we've been dealing in contraband industrial-sized catering trays.'

Chapter Eleven

Miriam sat at the kitchen table nursing a mug of tea, the clock ticking comfortingly in the background. The previous evening she had lain a suitcase on the bed and opened it, wanting to run away somewhere. Anywhere. Where there were no people and no responsibilities.

But it had remained empty. She had just looked at it for a while, feeling trapped by her own indecision. And by the thought of Artie Morgan twisting his story to make her look bad if she didn't fulfil her obligations. Then she put it back on top of the wardrobe and climbed the stairs to the attic room, where she watched the stars glitter through the telescope for a while before going to bed.

Her phone alarm went off at 10 a.m. and she called Fiona.

'Hi,' she said. 'Thank goodness you're free at such short notice.'

'That's fine.' Fiona's voice sounded calm and measured as usual. 'The voicemail you left last night sounded a bit frantic, so I wanted to make sure I spoke to you today.'

'I do appreciate it.'

'Has anything in particular happened to make you feel like this?'

'Well …' Miriam didn't know how to explain everything without sounding like a child. 'This is going to sound childish,' she said eventually.

'I'm sure it won't.'

'I booked some outside caterers to look after a couple of events. I did it on the quiet. And I got caught out by Alan, Joanna's nephew.'

'Caught out?'

'He found me in a lay-by moving empty dishes into the catering company van.'

'Ahhh … is that what's made you feel so anxious?'

'Not that in particular. It's the feeling of being sucked into all the responsibility. And the fact that, because of what happened, and the way I am, I can't seem to just leave it and clear off. I got a suitcase out last night and just stared at it.'

'So, that feeling of responsibility. How does it make you feel, apart from anxious?'

Miriam thought for a moment, watching a robin hop around in the garden. 'Trapped. I feel trapped. Like I did before.'

'When your mother was ill?'

'Yes, and then all the business with, well, you know, the business.'

'Why are you unable to just walk away?'

The door of the summerhouse opened, and Alan walked out carrying a surfboard.

'It's complicated … legalities … my brain …'

There was a pause at the end of the line. 'I think there may be more to it than that. Do you think a part of you wants to be involved?'

'If I do, that's out of habit. I mean, I wanted to come to this part of Wales to get something back ... to do with my parents, somehow. But I can't even do that.' She watched Alan attach the board to the roof of the car.

'Apart from the telescopes reminding you of your father?'

'Yes, he loved gazing at the stars.'

'So …?'

'So?'

'If you can't leave because you won't let yourself, perhaps if you just went with it, you may find what you're looking for?'

'Mmmm.'

126

'There's no guarantees that will happen, of course. But something's keeping you there.'

Alan slammed the door of his car and started the engine.

Miriam turned away and looked at the wall. 'Maybe. Can I book a proper session in for next week?'

'Of course you can. A normal length one. We can do it via Skype if you want?'

'Okay. It'll be nice to speak to you and actually see your face. I miss your cosy room.'

'I'll look forward to getting a glimpse of your gorgeous house,' said Fiona. 'Just book yourself in via the app, and I'll speak to you next week.'

'Will do. Bye.'

'Bye,' said Fiona.

Miriam put the phone on the table and took her tea out to the decking. 'As counsellors go,' she muttered to the robin who had now jumped onto the table, 'she's very, very good.'

The sound of birdsong and the light rustling of the breeze through the trees slowly stilled her, the warmth of the sun calming her busy mind. She closed her eyes and breathed in the delicate scent of the roses blooming around the garden.

'You fall asleep out here a lot, don't you?'

Miriam opened her eyes, startled. 'What? Oh, I ...'

Alan was standing next to her with a tray. 'Thought I'd make you a refreshing cuppa.'

'Thank you,' she said, rubbing her eyes. 'What time is it?'

'Around midday.' He sat down on the chair next to her and picked up the teapot. 'Milk and sugar?'

'Just milk, please. I must have slept for nearly two hours.' She glanced over at him as he poured the tea. 'I didn't snore, did I?'

'Quiet as a mouse,' he said, passing her a cup.

127

'Did you enjoy your surfing? I saw you go out earlier.'

He took a sip of his drink and leaned back in his chair, his hair still slightly wet. 'Only did an hour. I've got to get down to some writing this afternoon.'

'Another book about the stars?'

'Indeed.' He smiled over at her, and Miriam felt an unwanted flutter. 'But before that, I have to go into town. I wondered if you'd like to come with me?'

'Oh … to do what?' Miriam wished she could be nicer to him, but for some reason the words that came out of her mouth when she was near him just weren't.

He leaned forward and smiled. 'You could sound more enthusiastic!'

'Sorry.'

'I just thought that it would be nice for you to have a tour of some of the independent food shops and the farmers' market. And if you came with me, whatever pressure you are feeling about whatever it is … well, it might not be so big.' He took another sip and looked away towards a distant tree.

'Oh.' Miriam felt the flutter again. 'That's very thoughtful of you.'

'And it's going to be clear tonight, so I could give you a half-hour tutorial on the stars.'

'Thank you. That sounds lovely.'

'Right.' He stood up. 'Drink up then. Busy day. I'll meet you by the car in five minutes.'

Miriam watched him stride back towards the summerhouse and wondered what had happened. Then she hurried into the house to change into something suitable for going into town.

'When did you start with the cooking then?' Alan asked, rolling his window down as he drove along the cliff-top road.

128

'I went to catering college when I was eighteen. Then went travelling with Felix – my ex-husband – then we started up a food truck and everything grew from there.' Miriam felt like she was talking about another person somehow. Someone with a spirit of adventure, not someone afraid to buy a tomato.

'I meant the cooking though. When did you decide you loved to cook?' Alan scratched his unshaven face absentmindedly. Miriam forced herself to look at the scenery outside, realising she had been staring at him.

'Oh, I see what you mean. I suppose with my mum. She loved feeding us. Was always coming up with new recipes, and I'd be in the kitchen helping her out as much as I could.' Miriam tried to summon up a picture in her mind. But all she got was a wall – a static image of her mother smiling, like she did when she looked at the photographs or put on the necklace. The essence of her seemed to have got lost somewhere – the only real memories Miriam was able to conjure up were of her illness and what had happened after she'd died.

'My aunt's the same. Learned to cook from my gran. My mum wasn't so keen.' He laughed. 'Anything out of a tin! That was her mantra. Made lovely tea though, has to be said.'

Miriam watched the waves surge over the rocks below, as Alan switched on some music. 'Bon Jovi all right for you?'

'Fine, yes.' Miriam smiled as 'Living on a Prayer' blasted out from the speakers whilst they sped on, turning inland through quiet lanes, the hedgerows bursting with yellow, purple, white and red wildflowers.

'Beautiful, isn't it?' Alan said, as Bryan Adams began to sing 'Summer of '69'. 'I love a soundtrack to my drives. I plan them according to the route.' He glanced at Miriam. 'This is "Home to St David's across country". Don't like to be too specific in case there's a road closure.'

Miriam leaned back in her seat and began to laugh. 'Do you have one for the M4 or the A48?'

'Road to Nowhere!' he shouted, then began to laugh too. They sat in companionable silence until they reached St David's.

'Ever visited the cathedral?' Alan asked as they walked from the van towards the market.

'Don't think so,' said Miriam, searching for any connection to the bustling little city. 'Honestly, I was so young when we used to come down here, I've very few actual memories.'

'It's worth a visit.' He checked his watch. 'Not today though. Got to get an article finished by six.'

'I can just pop in anytime.' Miriam hurried behind him as he strode along the street. 'It's not too far from the house, is it?'

He disappeared into a crowd of tourists next to a coach, and Miriam stopped, confused, then spotted the back of his head. He was taller than everyone else around him, his wavy hair touching the top of his jacket collar as he stood at the entrance to the farmers' market.

'Where'd you go?' His eyes crinkled as he smiled.

'You've got long legs,' said Miriam. 'I think one of your steps is the same as three of mine.'

'So. This is it.' He pointed towards the stalls, piled with all sorts of fresh fruit and vegetables, cheeses, bread, meats, chutneys, cakes, herbs and everything that had once made Miriam's heart sing with excitement.

She looked at it, wanting to run in and buy everything, and sprint off away from it at the same time

Alan touched her arm. 'Your mission, Miriam, should you choose to accept it, is to buy something to make for your own meal tonight. It could be anything from a full-blown casserole to a watercress salad, or even a ham sandwich. But it must all – I repeat all – come from here.'

Miriam smiled. 'You must think I'm really odd, getting anxious about cooking food.'

'I think it makes you interesting,' he said, looking into the distance over the top of her head. 'But you've got to be quick. I've only got half an hour. Now, go!'

Miriam laughed and started to move swiftly through the stalls, buying some fresh tomatoes, onions, mozzarella, lemons, garlic, olive oil, a loaf of sourdough bread and some cockles. As she rushed to meet Alan by the entrance, she paused by a stall selling yoghurt and honey, and bought some of that too.

Alan smiled as she walked towards him. 'I haven't seen you that relaxed since … well ever … as I haven't known you long, to be honest.' He took one of the bags and began to walk back to the van.

Miriam followed him, feeling more alive than she had done for a long time. *I only bought some food*, she thought. *How odd …*

They climbed back into the car and set off for the house. 'I watched you,' Alan said, looking steadily ahead at the road. 'You whizzed around there like you were in a race. Didn't pause at all. Just buy that, buy that …'

'I didn't stop to think. It just clicked.' She laughed. 'We're talking about me buying things from a market as if I've just climbed Everest or learned to fly a plane.'

'Well, I don't know what's been going on with you, but the way you reacted when I caught you with the outside caterers … I think this *is* your Everest.' He burst out laughing and turned the music on again, so their drive was accompanied by the Red Hot Chili Peppers singing 'Under the Bridge'.

Miriam looked over at him, the unwelcome flutter returning. 'I suppose you're right. Don't know what I'll be like when I have to cook for other people.'

'If there's any left of what you make for yourself this evening, I'll take it. Then you'll have cooked for me.'

Miriam wanted to fling her arms around him as much as she wanted to jump out of the car and run away. She dug her nails into the seat and tried to work out why. 'No idea,' she said eventually.

'What?' Alan looked at her, confused.

'Did I say that out loud? I mean, *good* idea. I'll leave it in the fridge for you to forage, like you normally do.'

'Very funny,' he said. The song changed to 'Best of You' by Foo Fighters, and Alan began to sing loudly and out of tune. Miriam smiled, took out a lemon from the bag, scratched its skin and breathed in its refreshing citrus scent that always made her feel like it was summer. Then she leaned back into her seat and closed her eyes.

Miriam studied the plate as she sat outside, enjoying the contrasting colours of the food. The mozzarella and tomato salad looked bright and inviting, and the bowl of cockles in vinegar next to it made her mouth water in anticipation.

She'd forgotten how to enjoy the simple things she had always taken for granted. The joy she had always had from creating a meal had disappeared with so much over the past couple of years. And now, fleetingly, she remembered what it felt like.

The early evening sun shone a soft glow over the garden; the grass looked a lush, thick green and purple fuchsias cascaded from their plant pots along the path. Miriam stretched her arms then took a bite of her salad. The tartness of the onion mingled with the sweetness of the tomato, and the sharpness of the lemon and olive oil she'd drizzled on almost made her laugh with happiness. She took a mouthful of the cockles and stood up, wanting to give herself a high five, but waved her arms in the air with delight instead.

'That's a rare sight.' Alan was dragging a lawnmower across the grass. 'Someone about to give themselves a round of applause for a salad.'

Miriam paused and put her arms down, embarrassed. 'It's the first one I've made for a while, so …'

'Well, I hope there's some left. I'm going to be ravenous after this.'

'I wondered who normally did it.' He was wearing shorts. Miriam tried not to stare.

'Reg used to do it. But he's off in Hawaii with his girlfriend. I said I'd look after it while I was here until Aunt Joanna found a replacement. So here I am.'

'Finished your article?' Miriam picked up her plates and turned towards the house.

'Yes. Then this. Then our introductory stargazing session. Then down the pub. What a day it's turning out to be.' He laughed and switched on the mower. 'See you on the other side,' he shouted, as Miriam walked into the kitchen.

After she'd finished her meal, she checked the diary for the next appointment, hoping it would be for two people rather than a crowd. She surprised herself as she smiled when she saw Julie and Henry's names written down for the evening after next. The sound of the mower drove her up to her bedroom, where she took out the jiffy bag of photos and spread them out on the bedspread. They still all just looked like pictures of someone else's family. Someone else's two-dimensional life.

The sun hung low over the sea, glowing orange as it set, the sky oozing blues and pinks around it. She watched the stars begin to appear, dotting the horizon like fairy lights, and she managed to empty her mind of all those thoughts until Alan shouted from the kitchen below.

'Astronomy lesson to start in half an hour. I'll bring the beer.'

Miriam pushed the door open and turned the light on in the attic room. The tiny crescent moon hovered in the distance, the horizon full of sparkling stars. Alan walked in, turned the light off and handed her a bottle of beer. 'The only light we want is whatever is in the sky,' he said, pulling out a couple of folded garden chairs from behind a chest of drawers. 'There you go.' He opened them up with a flourish. 'You sit by there, and I'll sit by here.'

Miriam took a seat and watched as he adjusted the telescope, his forehead creased into a frown of concentration. He smelt of fresh grass and aftershave, and she pushed her chair back slightly to stop herself from leaning closer to him.

'All right?' he said.

'Yes, just wanted to stretch my legs a bit.'

'Well, you'll have to *cwtch* up a bit closer I'm afraid.'

'*Cwtch*?'

'It means cuddle, but I don't mean cuddle … I mean … I *don't* mean cuddle. You know what I mean.' He moved the telescope slightly. 'Come on. Not going to bite.'

Miriam moved the chair again but leaned backwards.

He looked at her and smiled. 'I'm not going to take advantage of you,' he said. 'Even though we are sitting in the dark ... alone.'

Miriam laughed. 'I know that!' she said. 'I'm a fully grown adult, and I know this is an astronomy lesson.'

He caught her eyes for a moment, then picked up his bottle. 'Cheers,' he said.

134

'Cheers,' said Miriam. 'So ... I've been listening to some podcasts. I know a little bit. A teeny, tiny bit.'

'Let's pretend you haven't, shall we? Makes it easier. Right ...'

'Right.'

'On a night without clouds – which this is ... unusual for Wales, to be honest, even in the summer ... but there you are – the dark sky is full of pinpoints of light, and we can see more than two thousand with the naked eye. '

'Two thousand?' Miriam leaned forward. 'Really?'

'Really.' He smiled at her. 'With binoculars, it can be more than forty thousand. When you look closer, you can see that some are not actually points of light – they are galaxies full of stars ... see the fuzzy patches there ... or disc-shaped planets.'

'Is that the celestial sphere?' Miriam decided to show she had some knowledge.

Alan nodded. 'The celestial sphere is a very important way to help us understand what is up there. Very good,' he said. 'But that's for another time. On this occasion, we need to just get a feel for what you can see.'

Miriam took another sip of beer and looked out of the window.

'Right, standing up is better, I think. Look ... there's Ursa Minor – The Little Bear.' He moved out of the way, and Miriam put her hands around the telescope.

The sky was scattered with thousands of glimmering lights, stretching to infinity.

'There's a large bright star high on the left of where you're looking ... and then three smaller ones lower down in a sloping line ... and that's attached to a kind of box with another bright star on the corner ...'

135

'Oh, I see it!' Miriam squealed, excited. 'I've been wondering what all this meant …'

'The Little Bear is normally easy to spot in the northern hemisphere. The sky changes depending on the time of year, to be honest.'

'What's that?'

She moved the telescope to track what she was seeing. 'It's white and it's moving. Is it part of a meteor shower?'

'Shouldn't be. Next one's not till next month.' He took it from her, his fingertips accidentally brushing her hand. Miriam felt something like an electric shock and stepped back, once again fighting the urge to move closer. 'It's a plane.' He laughed and looked at her, the tiny sliver of moonlight illuminating his face for a moment.

Miriam edged away again and bumped into the pile of boxes Joanna had left in the middle of the floor.

'Careful there,' said Alan holding out his hand as they crashed to the ground, along with Miriam.

'Oh, bugger,' she muttered sitting amongst photographs and files of paperwork spilling out onto the floor. 'I keep doing that.'

Alan kneeled down next to her. 'Are you okay?'

'Just embarrassed,' sighed Miriam. 'Can you pass me my bottle of beer. I'll drink it whilst clearing this up.'

He handed her the drink and sat down next to her. 'I hope that whet your appetite for stargazing,' he said. 'A short but informative lesson, I feel.'

Miriam swigged her drink. 'I definitely know the difference between a plane and a meteor shower now.'

'Right.' Alan stood up and switched on the light. 'Might be easier to file everything away if we had more than the light of the silvery moon to guide us.'

'That sounds very poetic.'

'My mum was a Doris Day fan. I know all the words.'

Miriam began to tidy and gathered up some papers that had fallen out of a green file. 'I found a recipe in this box not long ago. Exactly something my mother made,' she said, studying the heading on a lined page. 'And this looks familiar too. How strange. This is for a lamb casserole. It says cawl on the top of this, but it's exactly what my mother had written down. Word for word.' She looked up at Alan. 'Do you think your aunt would mind if I borrowed this?'

He smiled. 'She wanted you to cook for her customers. So, no. She'd want you to use it, I expect.' He held his hand out. 'Come on. I'll help you up. I've got to meet Jim at the pub in ten minutes, and I don't want to leave you here on the floor.'

Miriam tried to stand up and he grabbed her, pulling her towards him as he did so. They stared at each other in silence for a moment, as a cloud passed across the moon.

'I ...' said Alan as his phone buzzed in his pocket. 'Oh.' He sighed. 'No rest for the wicked.' He read the message and a scowl passed briefly over his face. He put the phone back in his pocket. 'Right. Well, I'd better be off. See you in the kitchen sometime.'

Miriam watched him go, confused by the speed at which he'd left. She closed the door of the attic room behind her and took the recipe to the kitchen, checking the diary to make sure there were no special requirements for Julie and Henry's meal.

'Right,' she said out loud. 'I'm going to cook you two a proper dinner. I've got to start tomorrow evening and finish it the day after, so, if I get stressed, there'll be no one to see me.'

Then she made herself a cup of chamomile tea and went to the living room to watch *You've Got Mail*.

Chapter Twelve

Miriam noticed Alan's car wasn't in its parking space when she went down to the kitchen to make a cup of tea at just after seven the following day. The early morning sun had peeped through the curtains, rousing her from a deep, relaxing sleep, and she had climbed out of bed, almost chanting the list of ingredients for Julie and Henry's meal.

Switching on the kettle, she sliced herself some bread and put it in the toaster, wondering if it was warm enough yet to eat her breakfast at the table outside, then she checked Joanna's recipe, which she had left on the worktop the night before.

Buttering her toast, she put on her fleece and went out to the decking, taking the folder of local suppliers with her and, sipping her tea as she read, she planned the shopping visit to the local town in her head.

'This is just one meal,' she said to herself. 'It's not an event.' She grabbed her phone and sent a text to Rhiannon.

If you're free tomorrow night, I'm actually going to cook a meal. It's at 7.30. Let me know if you can come. M.

Now I'm just cooking for friends, she thought – *I'll call Julie and Henry friends for this evening, not customers – so no pressure.*

Then she took a shower, got dressed and drove into town for a stress-free food shopping trip.

Miriam placed the recipe on the worktop and read through it carefully, arranging all the ingredients in the order she was going to use them in a row next to the chopping board.

She put on her "Hearty Meal Playlist", and as 'Life Is a Minestrone' filled the room, she began to prepare the food, her mind clearing of everything except for the task at hand. She forced herself to work, slicing the onions aggressively every time a negative thought popped into her head, and slowly she forgot where she was for a while and why she had run away.

As she put the casserole dish in the oven, the door slamming behind her made her jump.

'Sorry.' Alan put his laptop down on the kitchen table. 'Don't mind me. I just need a change of scenery from the summerhouse.'

Miriam glanced at him, her eyes momentarily resting on the hair peeping over the top of his T-shirt, the sudden now familiar flutter unbalancing her. She felt the intensity of the night before again. And remembered how abruptly he'd left, leaving her standing in the moonlight, confused and alone.

Alone ... where the hell did that idea come from? she wondered, and felt a mild panic on top of everything else. She took the oven gloves off. 'I wanted to go out for a walk anyway. You can keep an eye on the oven when I'm gone.'

'Oh. Okay ... I was hoping for a bit of company,' he said, opening the computer and switching it on.

'I thought you were writing?' Miriam began to load the dishwasher.

'I don't want to talk. I just want to sit in silence with another human being who is doing something else in silence.' He looked up and smiled. 'Couldn't put the kettle on while you're there, could you?'

'And your last maid died of what exactly?' Miriam filled the kettle anyway.

'It's the least you could do,' he said, standing up. 'After I took you into town yesterday and helped you buy actual food.' He began opening the cupboard doors irritably. 'Where are the biscuits?'

'I ate them all.'

'Place is going to pot,' he muttered. 'I'll do without.' Then he sat down again.

Miriam silently made a mug of tea and put it in front of him.

'You not having one?' he said, not looking up.

'No. Like I said I'm going out for half an hour for some fresh air.'

'Couldn't get some biscuits from the corner shop while you're there, could you?'

Miriam took her sunglasses out of her bag and put them on, grabbed her keys and walked towards the front door. 'Maybe yes. Maybe no,' she said, then stepped out into the warmth of another perfect summer's day, pondering on why part of her wanted to stay in the kitchen with Alan and just be. And why the other part wanted to run away very, very quickly.

When she got back Alan had gone, but there was a packet of custard creams on the kitchen table with a note.

Here's some of my stash from the summerhouse. Couldn't leave you without sustenance. Casserole smells nice. Had to dash to Cardiff at the last minute. Work. Back tomorrow. In case you're wondering. A.

The house felt suddenly very empty. Even though he was hardly in it. And she barely knew him. And he was both very kind and easy-going, but confusing and difficult as well. Which she really didn't need. *Except* … but this is what she wanted. Solitude. Alone time. No one to care about. Apart from herself. And she was leaving. As soon as she'd stayed long enough to complete at least some of her contracted obligations. Then she would give Jeffrey Goldstock the nod, and he'd set the escape route in motion. So, none of this really mattered. *Did it?*

Her phone buzzed. It was a message for Rhiannon.

Yes please to the free food! See you tomorrow.

Miriam turned the oven off, took the cawl out to cool overnight, booked herself a ticket to see yet another *Mission Impossible* film, then drove to Haverfordwest where she could sit in the cinema on her own but be with other people.

'Ooh, now that smells lovely.' Rhiannon opened the oven door and took a deep breath. 'I haven't had cawl in years. Reminds me of my gran on my father's side, it does. We'd go round on a Sunday and the house would be full of this amazing smell. And this is the same.'

Miriam smiled. 'Glass of wine? Or beer?' She opened the fridge door. 'I'm on my second. *Glass* of white wine, not bottle.'

'Beer for me, please. I popped in the pub earlier for a latte. Mentioned to Jim I was coming over tonight.' Rhiannon took a glass out of the cupboard. 'I suppose as you have real guests, drinking from the bottle is out of the question.'

'Must keep the standards up,' said Miriam passing her the beer. 'I hope you all like the food.'

'You're an expert, aren't you?' said Rhiannon, pulling out a chair. 'Just because you've taken a sabbatical doesn't mean you've forgotten how to cook.'

'I haven't done much cooking for a few years, to be honest. Just the occasional event to keep my hand in.' Miriam felt her stomach churn as she remembered the last time she'd got involved and stood up, pushing the thought away. 'But this isn't an event. This is a meal. That's all. A meal.'

'Cheers to that,' said Rhiannon. 'Lovely necklace that. Gorgeous blue stone.'

Miriam touched her neck. 'It's a family heirloom,' she said quietly as the doorbell rang.

She took a deep breath, smoothed down her dress and walked into the hall. 'Right. We're on,' she said, making herself smile welcomingly as she opened the door.

'What a lovely evening.' Henry handed Miriam a pot of honey. 'We were at that craft place earlier – we always visit on a Thursday – and thought you should sample some local produce. Didn't we, Julie?'

'Good for your health too,' Julie said, hanging up her jacket. 'You aren't getting any younger.' Then she put her hand over her mouth, embarrassed. 'That came out wrong. I've no idea how old you are. But none of us are getting any younger.'

Henry laughed. 'I think you should stop talking, dear.'

'Oh, yes. You're right. Maybe a drink would do the trick.'

'They're in good spirits,' said Rhiannon under her breath.

'Thank God for that,' muttered Miriam as they went into the dining room.

'That smells delicious.' Henry pulled out a chair and sat down.

'It's a traditional cawl with a bit of a twist. What would you like to drink?'

'A bit of a twist. Interesting.' Julie sat down. 'I think Joanna made us one a few years ago. That had a bit of something extra. I'll have a glass of red wine, please.'

'Same for me,' said Henry. 'Are you using her recipe?'

'Yes. It's remarkably similar to one my mother used to make too. Only she just called it lamb stew.' Miriam went to the kitchen and poured the drinks. 'Rhiannon is joining us today as a special guest,' she shouted.

'Special guest?' Rhiannon looked confused.

'You can tell them about your adventures working in the property market in Cardiff …' Miriam's voice trailed off.

'Doesn't sound very exciting, to be honest. And I'm saying that about myself.' Rhiannon glugged down her drink and took another beer out of the fridge.

'I've only just thought of it,' said Miriam. 'I just thought I'd cover us – they are paying after all.'

'Ok. Fair dos.'

Miriam touched her arm. 'I'm really grateful you came. This is quite a big thing for me. You'd be surprised.'

'Oh, no worries.' Rhiannon's face lit up. 'I'm always up for food, I am.'

'Shall we?' Miriam smiled, carrying the bottles into the dining room.

'Yes, sir, boss, sir!' Rhiannon laughed, following her.

'Rhiannon here,' said Miriam pouring the drinks, 'is going to give us an insight into the world of property in Cardiff.'

'Oh, we dabbled in property a few years ago, didn't we Julie?' Henry took a sip of his drink. 'It was in London – we made quite a bit of money when we sold on.'

'It was a bit of an adventure.' Julie looked at Miriam. 'Are you going to join us too? Wouldn't want you to be sitting out in the kitchen all on your own.'

'I was hoping you'd say that.' The door to the garden banged shut, and they heard the fridge door open in the kitchen.

'Got any leftovers?' shouted Alan.

'We haven't even started it yet.' Henry laughed. 'Why don't you join us? It's going to be a lovely little dinner party.'

He appeared in the doorway, his wavy hair ruffled, his face unshaven. Miriam felt the flutter again and took a glug of wine.

'Well, thank you, Henry. I've had a bit of a strange couple of days, so that would be very nice.' He looked at Miriam. 'As long as there's enough?'

'I did make a big batch. Not sure I can stretch the starter though.'

'Oh, what is it?' Julie said.

'Avocado with prawns. Thought I'd go a bit retro and classic. There's more than enough homemade cheesecake though.'

'Tell you what, I'll go and get showered and be back for the mains.'

'What a lovely man,' Julie sighed as he left.

Henry rolled his eyes. 'She's had a crush on him for years. Even though he is so very much younger than her.'

'Oh meow, Henry.' Julie laughed. 'Now, Rhiannon. Sit down and tell us all about working in the big city.'

Miriam carried the casserole dish into the dining room, and placed it next to some crusty bread and Caerphilly cheese.
'That smells delicious,' said Julie. 'In fact, the whole house smells delicious!'

'It's a very comforting feeling,' sighed Henry. 'That warm, meaty aroma spreading everywhere.'

Miriam cleared her throat as she picked up the ladle. She waited for the anxiety to come, the nerves to flood back, the feeling of panic she'd felt before as caring for other people became too overwhelming. But there was nothing. Just hunger.

'What are you smiling about?' asked Alan.

'Am I smiling?' Miriam said. 'I didn't realise.'

'I think she's smiling because she knows how ravenous we all are.' Henry laughed. 'Come on! Open it.'

144

Miriam took off the lid, watching the faces of her guests light up with pleasure as she did, and felt relieved. This, after all, was her comfort zone. She'd just not been here for a while.

The doorbell rang just as Julie started to pile the food onto her plate. Rhiannon stood up quickly. 'I'll get it,' she said brightly. 'There's plenty, isn't there?' she muttered to Miriam as she walked to the door. 'Hiya! What a surprise!' Rhiannon could be heard giggling in the hallway. 'Come on in, Jim.'

'Hope you don't mind … I was just passing.' Jim stood in the doorway, eyeing up the food.

'I said Jim should pop by at some point,' said Rhiannon. 'He's got a few ideas about Joanna's whereabouts.'

'Lovely to see you, Jim,' shouted Henry. 'Please, sit down. There's a lot of tasty stew to be had here. Up to Miriam's strong standards, I'd say.'

Miriam flushed, remembering the ready meals she'd served up before. She moved her plate around to cover up her discomfort.

'Oh, thank you.' He sat down and poured himself a glass of water. 'Smells lovely, Miriam,' he said.

'But. Before we talk about Joanna,' said Henry, 'I think we should find out a bit more about our current hostess.'

They all looked up at Miriam and murmured in agreement. 'No, we don't know very much about you. You're clearly a talented cook,' said Julie. 'Henry and I were talking about it earlier. But you are a little bit mysterious.'

'Mysterious?' Miriam thought she was anything but.

'I think what they mean is that you arrived very suddenly, got caught up in all this catering business, and we've not had time to talk about you.' Alan took a glug of his beer.

'So …?' Julie looked at her expectantly.

'Well, not much to tell,' said Miriam uncertainly. 'I sold my business. I'd started it years ago, and it was like my family.'

'Mine was like that, wasn't it?' Henry nodded at Julie.

'Why did you sell it?' Rhiannon grabbed some bread and dipped it in the stew.

Miriam was silent for a moment, not wanting to say too much. Revisiting that part of her past was still difficult. 'My mum got ill. Alzheimer's. I'm an only child. And what with looking after her and the demands of the job, I came to the conclusion I needed a life outside of it. So, a few months before she died, I decided to sell it.'

'And how do you feel now?' Henry leaned forward. 'I ask because I remember how strange it was when we sold our business.'

'It all got a bit complicated, to be honest ...' Miriam trailed off and began to eat.

'So, why here?' Jim was looking at her intently.

'I used to come here as a child with my parents. I was so young. Really don't remember it. But my mother talked about it all the time. Especially when she was ill. And so, when the business was finally sorted out, my plan was to come to somewhere in the area and hide out.'

'And you ended up here. With us.' Rhiannon smiled.

'And what about Father?' said Julie gently.

Miriam took a long drink of wine. 'Well, he died about fifteen years ago. Suddenly. Heart attack.'

'He couldn't have been very old.' Julie's voice was kind and encouraging.

Miriam felt her words running off, out of control. 'It's funny, isn't it? Having the telescopes here. My father loved astronomy, and when I found them it was like I found him again. I've got a clear picture of him in my mind ... I can conjure up his voice and hear his laugh.' She looked up. 'Is that because he went so suddenly? Because ...' They were all looking at her intently.

'Because … I can't do that with my mother. I have so many photographs, but when I look at them, all I can see is her illness. And all the difficult times. I can't find her …' Miriam stopped, suddenly embarrassed.

Henry sighed. 'I think sometimes it's because if you think about the bad times, it dilutes how much you miss them. It blocks it.'

'That's the conclusion we've come to,' Julie said. 'We've thought about that kind of thing a lot.'

'Did you say this recipe was the same as your mother's?' Henry took another mouthful.

'Exactly,' sighed Miriam, not wanting to talk about it any more.

'Well, you've found a bit of her, haven't you?' Julie smiled. 'By accident.'

Alan picked up his beer. 'What were your parent's names, Miriam?'

'Frederick and Lillian.'

'A toast,' he said. 'To Frederick and Lillian.'

Then everyone raised their glasses. 'Hear, hear,' they all shouted. And the names Frederick and Lillian echoed around the room.

'Are you all right, Henry?' asked Julie quietly. 'You seem distracted suddenly.'

Henry frowned slightly, then smiled. 'Did I? Sorry. I was just rifling through the Filofax in my brain … you know how I get. Thoughts fly in and out …'

'Very eighties, dear,' said Julie, squeezing his arm.

'Oh dear.' Rhiannon stood up and hugged Miriam. 'Crying, I am. Poor dab.'

'Thank you,' she whispered, then she stood up and took a deep breath. 'Right ... um … enough of me.' She looked at Alan.

'Alan has an interesting selection of music, don't you? Could you connect it to the speakers?'

His eyes crinkled around the edges as he smiled. 'Of course,' he said. 'What about the, "Travelling To See the Stars" set – a relaxing night with Aerosmith and Bon Jovi.'

As everyone got up to leave after the meal, Jim picked up his jacket. 'Oh, I forgot to say earlier. Joanna. I've been thinking. You know those initials … well, I messaged Reg in Hawaii. I mean, he's known Joanna for years. He said there was a romance with someone years ago that ended badly. Despite all the men she had in her life – and there were a few – she never got over it, he reckons.'

'Ohhhh,' Julie, Henry and Rhiannon said at the same time.

'But that's all he could remember. Didn't have time to linger as he was off surfing.'

'There must be some clues in the house,' Rhiannon said excitedly.

Miriam looked at Alan, who shrugged. 'Don't look at me. She never told me about her love life.'

'If I come across anything, I'll let you know.' Miriam felt suddenly tired and yawned. 'Sorry. Nothing personal.'

Henry laughed. 'No offence taken. See you next time, Miriam. That's a lovely necklace by the way. Antique?'

'I forgot I had it on.' She smiled, touching her neck.

Jim turned to Alan. 'Fancy a pint? Last orders in half an hour.'

'Why not?' Alan followed him out of the door. 'I could do with some fresh air.'

Rhiannon hovered by the coat rack. 'Can I help you tidy up?' She watched Jim walk down the path.

Miriam smiled. 'No thanks. That's fine. You've earned a pint at the pub for being the special guest.'

'Didn't really do anything though,' she said. Then she hugged Miriam again. 'I've had a lovely time. And you cook fabulous food. See you.'

As she closed the door behind her, the house fell silent. Miriam looked at the piles of glasses and plates in the dining room, switched on *Songs for Swingin' Lovers* by Frank Sinatra and quietly tidied everything away.

Chapter Thirteen

The buzzing of the phone ringing woke Miriam up from her deep, comfortable sleep. The rain pattered on the windows outside, accompanied by blasts of wind rattling the plant pots below.

She checked her watch and jumped out of bed. 'Eleven o'clock. Bloody hell!'

The phone stopped buzzing, but a ping indicated a voicemail had been left. Woozily, she listened to it.

'Miriam. Hello. It's Jeffrey Goldstock. I need to talk to you about a couple of things. One is connected to the house you are staying in. And other one is connected to your business … or should I say, your previous business. Can you call me back on this number?'

Miriam felt a surge of anxiety wash over her and tried to slow her breathing down. 'The business. I haven't got a business any more. Please don't let it be …'

She got up and opened the curtains, watching the wild surf crash onto the distant cliffs. 'Right, right … let's just do this.'

She picked up her phone and called him back.

'Hello, Miriam. How are you?' He sounded upbeat and not too solemn, so Miriam began to relax.

'I'm fine, thanks. Is everything all right?'

'Yes, yes, of course. Good news is we've found some small print and a loophole, which means that you can employ someone to do what you're doing in the house you're currently renting. Of course, we also have the option of contacting the solicitors and asking them to release you from the contract entirely. So, you do have a choice.'

'Ahh, good news indeed.' Miriam glanced out of the window as Alan set off for a jog along the road and felt oddly flat.

'Secondly, we've had a communication from the solicitors acting for Mr Morgan.'

'What?' Miriam felt sick. *Surely he'd long gone?*

'Some dispute about the ownership of a food truck. He says his company hasn't been paid for it.'

'Yes, they have.' Miriam felt her heart begin to race. 'Everything to do with his company was dealt with. I'm really confused.'

'It's probably just an oversight somewhere along the way. We were very rigorous with everything …'

'When it all fell apart … I'm sorry. I didn't mean to say that out loud.'

'It's fine, Miriam. I just needed to check with you. There is also a bit of paperwork to do with your mother's estate I need you to sign. I can e-mail it to you.'

Miriam remembered the crucial page of the paperwork somehow missed by both her and Justin when signing the lease for Joanna's house, because it was all done online and in a hurry.

'Can I do it in person? Do you have any offices in Wales?'

'Let me see … yes, there's one in Swansea. If you let my secretary know when you can do it, I'll book you in with one of my associates.'

'Okay. I'll do that.' Miriam was desperate to end the call as if that would keep Artie Morgan and his food truck away from her.

'Miriam. Please don't worry about the food truck. I'm confident it's an oversight on his part.'

Miriam sighed. 'I won't. Thank you. I'll be in touch soon about the appointment.'

She put the phone down and began to pace the room, wondering why, when she was beginning to feel better, the past had come to rear its unpleasant head again. She messaged Fiona to see if she could get an emergency appointment, got dressed without showering and went outside, hoping the wind and rain would blow her worries away.

The beach was empty apart from a young couple and a small child flying a kite. Miriam settled at the edge of the dunes and watched the sea churn and crash on the sand, grey and angry.

She closed her eyes, but it was as if she'd switched on a film. Artie was sitting opposite her at a café. One of their snatched moments together. '*I think once I've sold the business, I'll feel a lot better,*' she was saying. '*I'm worried about the staff though. I'm worried about my mum. She's getting worse.*'

He put his hand out and squeezed hers.

'*It's okay. I'm here. You're not alone.*'

'*I don't know what I'd do without you,*' she whispered. '*I used to talk to my mother about all the business stuff, you know. Bend her ear ... but now that part of her is gone.*'

'*I'll make sure everyone who works for you is fine. You know me. And you can take the keys of that food truck and drive off into the distance, knowing you've done the right thing.*'

She forced herself to push the image away, making her breathing match the rhythm of the waves, the chatter in her head slowly calming as she did.

How could I have been so stupid? Snatched moments? I saw what I wanted to. Of course he was married. Of course he was ... I was just so *lonely. And he was my escape.*

She heard the child screech and opened her eyes as a kite floated towards her and landed with a thump on her head, then bobbed away gently. She couldn't help but laugh and waved at him as he caught it, his parents beaming at him as he did. A gust of wind shook the kite string out of his hand and he screamed, then began to cry, as his father ran faster to try to catch it. Miriam clambered onto her feet and grabbed the kite before it could get swept away into the sky, watching as the father slowed to a walk and the mother picked up her son and pointed towards her.

The boy stopped crying, his face lighting up into a beaming smile.

And so did Miriam's.

'Thank you,' said the father breathlessly as Miriam handed him the kite. 'It's his first one, and he would have been heartbroken to lose it.' He smiled. 'Until we'd bought him another one.'

'You're welcome.' Miriam watched as he walked back to his wife and son, then sat down again and closed her eyes, enjoying the little boy's happy laughter and the calls of the gulls swooping on the breeze.

Then her mind started racing again. *It's nothing to do with the affair... you know that ... he's just not letting go because he wants to make you squirm.*

Miriam dug her hands into the sand and let the grains slip through her fingers, her eyes still closed.

It's just his last hurrah, Miriam, my lovely girl. You know that. Just flexing his muscles. Let your solicitor sort it out. Don't let him get the better of you. Hope that bump on the head knocked some sense into you.

Miriam opened her eyes. 'Mum?' she said, confused for a moment. The family had gone; all that was left were their footprints and the memory of her mother's voice in her head.

She stood up and put her headphones on. *This place is making my imagination go haywire*, she thought, clicking on Kylie Minogue's *Greatest Hits*. 'Can't Get You Out of My Head' came on first, and she forced herself to walk home in time to the beat, which meant she got back very quickly.

Alan was in the kitchen making a cup of tea when Miriam arrived back at the house.

'You look stern,' he said as she took her headphones off.

'Do I?' Miriam glanced in the mirror. 'I don't. At all.'

'You did. I can assure you. Everything all right?'

'Yes. Just had something to think through.' She pulled up a chair and sat down. 'As you're making one …?'

Alan rolled his eyes. 'If you insist.'

'You are in my kitchen. You do have a kitchen of your own.'

'Fair point. Although more of a tiny kitchenette.' He took a mug out of the cupboard. 'I was wondering if you'd like to come to a stargazing event with me next week?'

Miriam looked up at him, fighting the now familiar tug between wanting to stand very close to him and running away into the distance.

'Last night, you said …' He glanced at her, falling silent for a moment, then he carried on making the tea. 'I thought it would be a good way of showing you the night sky from another viewpoint.' He handed her the mug and sat down opposite her. 'Jim said he'd like to come when we were at the pub – and then, of course, so did Rhiannon. So it'll be a nice night out.'

Miriam smiled. *No harm in it,* she thought, *with the four of us there.* 'I've never been to anything like that. Thank you. Where is it?'

'Brecon Beacons. And the forecast is good. Last thing you want is to stand on top of a mountain in the rain trying to find the sky.'

'It's not something I've ever heard of.' She took a sip of the tea. 'And because I need to do new things rather than just muse over the past, it's a yes from me.'

Alan grabbed the biscuit tin and put it between them on the table. 'Is that what the stern face was all about?'

154

'Yes.' Miriam sighed.

He opened the tin and waved it in front of her. 'Custard cream or digestive?'

Miriam closed her eyes and put her hand in. 'Pot luck,' she said.

'Wow! That walk on the beach has changed you.'

'Has it? I used to be very much about diving in and getting on with things.'

'Ahhh.' He took a bite of his digestive. 'And are you getting that back one custard cream at a time?'

Miriam crunched the biscuit. She did feel a bit different. As if that walk on the beach had swept some of the past away. Or hearing her mother's voice. *Not her voice. It was my voice. My thought. My voice. It just sounded like my mother. That was all.*

'Now you're looking confused.' Alan leaned back in his chair.

'Confused?'

'You have a very expressive face.'

'I never knew.' They sat in silence for a few moments, listening to the wind blowing through the trees, a door in the distance banging open and shut.

'I'll have to sort that out,' sighed Alan, standing up. 'It's the outbuilding at the end of the garden. Can't ignore it any more.'

'When is the stargazing event?' asked Miriam as he opened the door.

'Next Tuesday.'

'I've got to go to Swansea for an appointment. If I arranged it for that day, could I meet you somewhere and follow you up to the Beacons?'

He thought for a moment. 'I could drop you off, and after your appointment we could all drive up together. Save on petrol. Use one vehicle.'

155

'Okay.'

He flashed her a smile, sending unwanted butterflies careering around her stomach. 'It's a date. I mean ... it's *not* a date. It's a thing on a particular date.'

Miriam laughed. 'I know what you mean,' she said.

'Good. You're a very good cook by the way.' Then he closed the door and strode off across the garden.

I am *a good cook*, thought Miriam. *I know ... I just don't enjoy it any more.* The image of the boxes in the attic room floated into her mind, and she felt an overwhelming urge to go upstairs and search through the recipes.

She got up and checked through the list of bookings and ran her finger down the page. 'One over the weekend.' She sighed. 'And ... oh ... the Look-Alike Festival.' Miriam felt sick again. 'I could just get in the car and drive away,' she said to a chaffinch that had settled on the windowsill. And then she remembered Artie Morgan and what he'd done, and how she would not let him make it look as if it was *she* who let people down. She realised there was now a surge of anger mixed in with her nausea.

'Trapped!' she said to the bird. 'Trapped by my own sense of bloody responsibility.' Leaning against the door, she slid down to the floor slowly as she watched Alan carry a wrench back to the summerhouse, his wavy hair ruffled untidily by the wind. He closed the door behind him, and she pulled herself up to her feet, the call of the recipes upstairs proving too irresistible. 'Maybe I can cook myself something every day so that I get used to it,' she muttered. 'Said the pathetic professional cook who has been known to hyperventilate at the thought of chopping an onion.'

She pushed the door of the attic room open, admiring the view of the coast as she did: the waves and cliffs framed by a dark grey sky, mottled with splashes of white and blue as the sun tried to push through the clouds. Opening the nearest box, she took out a dusty file full of recipes and looked through, trying to feel the same excitement she used to when finding new things to cook. But she couldn't – they were just names and lists of ingredients and instructions.

One piece of paper had a red stain on it. Miriam took it out of the folder and read through it. *Brazilian fish stew*, she thought. *Sounds interesting enough.* So, she took it downstairs and wrote a list of ingredients, then drove into town, bought them and forced herself to cook a meal. A delicious meal. Just for herself.

'Hellooo! Hiya ...' Rhiannon was standing at the kitchen door.

Miriam looked up, confused. She'd been lost in preparing her food for the last hour and had almost forgotten where she was.

'Sorry. I tried the front door but couldn't get an answer.'

'Oh, I was miles away. Come on in.' She turned the hob off and smiled at Rhiannon expectantly.

'Wow! That smells delicious. What is it?'

'A Brazilian fish stew.'

'You should go out and come in again to get the full effect of it.' Rhiannon sat down at the kitchen table.

'It smells nice enough in here!'

'No ... go on. Honest.' Rhiannon laughed. 'It's gorgeous. You could bottle it up and sell it as a smell for a diffuser ... for people who like cookery smells.'

Miriam smiled, buoyed up by her enthusiasm, and stepped out into the garden.

'Now, breathe in some fresh air,' shouted Rhiannon, closing the door behind her.

'Okay.' Miriam did as she was told. 'Done!'

'Now, open the door and come in.'

Miriam laughed, pushing open the door and stepping inside. Then she stood still and gasped. Because for a second, she wasn't in Wales. She was in her family kitchen. Her father was sitting quietly doing a crossword, her mother was chattering as she dished up one of her masterpieces onto the plates, the warm coconut curry aroma filling the room.

'Lovely, isn't it?' Rhiannon said.

Miriam blinked. 'It is.' she walked over to the worktop and checked the recipe. *Could it be the same one her mother used?* she mused. *Like the cawl ...*

'Now, that smells nice.' Alan's voice brought her back to the present, and she turned to smile at him.

'Brazilian fish stew.'

He stood expectantly. 'Don't suppose you've got any spare?'

'Oooh. I haven't eaten, to be honest,' Rhiannon said. 'If you have, I'll join. I'll buy you a takeaway next week as payment.'

Miriam looked at them both, her hope for a solitary meal ebbing away. But they looked so keen. On her food. *Her* food. That *she* had cooked. She thought of her mother and the smile on her face as she dished up the fish stew, the pleasure it gave her to feed Miriam and her father.

'I've got plenty,' she said. 'Just not much rice.'

'I've got some fresh crusty bread in the summerhouse.' Alan set off across the garden.

'Got nothing, me,' Rhiannon sighed. 'Apart from my sparkling personality.'

Miriam laughed. 'It's lovely to see you, but was there anything in particular you popped round for?'

'I keep wanting to go to the pub to catch Jim.' She sighed again. 'But that's a bit weird. Don't want to, you know, be too pushy. So I was driving there, then decided against it and thought I'd see you instead. As we're all going stargazing next week anyway.'

'You look very nice by the way,' said Miriam.

Rhiannon flicked her hair and laughed. 'New dress and just had a manicure.' She waved her hands at Miriam. 'Lovely colour, my nails are, aren't they? I left the beauty salon all dressed up and nowhere to go, so the car sort of brought me to you.'

'Well, you're welcome any time. Even if I'm second best.'

Rhiannon was about to say something when Alan pushed the kitchen door open.

'Here we are,' he said. 'Plus a couple of bottles of Sauvignon Blanc I had stashed away.'

Miriam poured the stew into a serving dish, sliced the bread and sat down. '*Bon appétit,*' she said and watched, smiling, as her unexpected guests began to enthusiastically eat the food.

Chapter Fourteen

Miriam switched the computer on and clicked the Skype icon, waiting for Fiona to call. The past few days had been grey and drizzly, but this morning the sun had returned, making everything sparkle and glow.

'Hello, Miriam.' Fiona looked healthy, tanned and calm, her room still the oasis of tranquillity Miriam had hid in for half an hour once a week for nearly a year.

'Hello. It's lovely to see you rather than just hear you.'

'Yes, it does make it easier, doesn't it? Where are you in that gorgeous house?'

'The living room.' Miriam picked up the computer and pointed it at the window. 'The view is lovely.' She lowered her voice. 'I spend a lot of time in the kitchen but, despite the fact I live on my own, I'm not on my own that often.'

Fiona smiled. 'How is that for you, considering you were so keen to get away from everyone?'

'Mixed.' Miriam thought again. 'Yes. Mixed. I've relaxed into it over the past few days. And … I've even cooked a couple of meals without feeling too traumatised.'

'That is good news.'

'Although I've got some small dinner parties to cater for.' Miriam could feel her heart begin to race anxiously. 'And just as I've said that, I'm starting to fret.'

'You could just walk away and get someone else to do it.'

'Yep. I know … but, as I've said, not that straightforward and … I had a bit of a breakthrough a few nights ago.'

'Ah?'

'I felt I was in my parents' kitchen. It was the smell. Something I'd made ...' Miriam suddenly felt like she wanted to cry and looked down at the table to hide it.

'What prompted that?'

'I cooked something. A recipe I found. My mum and Joanna seemed to have remarkably similar tastes.'

'Interesting.'

'But ... there is also a potential issue with Artie Morgan. And I don't want to go through all of that again.'

'You may not have to.'

'Mmm, you're right.'

'Can I just say, Miriam, that you are looking *so* well. Much less strained than the last time we spoke in person. In fact, you're positively glowing. Perhaps that place is doing you some good after all.'

Miriam beamed. 'Really? That's kind ... but I'm leaving as soon as I can.'

'Of course.' Fiona smiled as the doorbell rang.

'Just a sec.' Miriam opened the front door to the postman.

'Can you sign for this?' He held up a large brown box. 'It's not heavy, just bulky like.'

'Of course.' Miriam took the pen from his hand and scribbled her signature. 'Got to rush ... I'm on a call.'

He handed her the box. 'Bye then,' he said as Miriam closed the door.

She carried it into the living room. 'No idea what this is,' she said to Fiona. 'But do you mind if I open it? I've had a couple of mysterious parcels recently.'

'Go ahead,' said Fiona. 'I'm intrigued.'

Miriam unpacked the box and took out a string of fairy lights in the shape of roses. 'Someone keeps sending me these. I don't know why or who ...'

'Perhaps it's someone who knows you're frightened of the dark?'

Miriam looked at her. 'No one knows that apart from you, to be honest. And my parents when they were alive, so …'

'I meant you *were* frightened of the dark,' Fiona said. 'That was when you were a child.'

'I still have my moments.'

They both looked at the lights. 'Do you know where you'll put them?'

'In my bedroom, I expect.' Miriam placed them back in the box. 'Anyway. Can I book myself in again for next week? I've got that solicitor's appointment and don't know how I'll feel after it.'

'Of course. Just use the app.' Fiona paused for a moment. 'You are doing very well, Miriam.' She said. 'Until next time.' The screen went dark, and Miriam picked up the box.

'Let's get you upstairs,' she said.

The day of the stargazing event was hot and sunny, the sky a clear, bright summer blue. Miriam put on a suitable sundress and sandals, and gathered some warmer clothes for her backpack in case it cooled down a lot in the evening. Checking her hair in the mirror, she hurried downstairs and grabbed some bottles of water from the fridge, then went to meet Alan by the summerhouse.

'Ahoy there,' he said, loading up his car. 'I'll just put the camera and tripod in the boot and we'll be off. Jim can't come – a last minute issue in the pub. And as a result, neither can Rhiannon. So, it's just me and you.'

'Okay, sounds fine,' Miriam concentrated on putting her bag in the back of the car, trying to push away the excited little butterflies coursing around her body. *Oh for goodness sake*, she thought. *Calm down. You're a grown woman. What am I going to say to him for two hours alone on the drive? Shut up, Miriam! Not just a grown woman, but a grown woman who is capable of making small talk with almost anyone because you were an events organiser. For* goodness *sake!*

'Right then.' He got into the driver's seat. 'Now, I have several playlists ready for the journey ahead, so rest assured you won't have to keep thinking of mundane things to say.'

'I wasn't thinking that at all.' Miriam blushed.

'Well, just in case, I've come prepared. I've got, to start off with, "I Love the Stars" – first up, "Death is a Star" by The Clash.' He turned on the engine, switched on the music and pulled out into the road. 'Just sit back, relax and ... don't take this the wrong way, but I've got to get a chapter right in my head and was hoping I could figure it out on the drive.'

'Oh, well, I don't know anything about astronomy. Apart from what you taught me, so I don't think I'll be any help at all.'

'No ... no ... I need to think it over, so is it all right if you listen to the music and I listen to what's going on in my head?'

Miriam smiled. 'Strange way to put it. But, of course. And if the music is as interesting as this all the way, I'll have a lovely time just letting it wash over me.'

'You're not an in-car singer are you?'

'No. I'll be quiet. It'll help you concentrate.'

He smiled. 'Cool.' Then he sped up and headed inland.

A couple of hours later, Alan dropped Miriam off in Mumbles. 'If you cross the road by the mini-roundabout, the office is just up that hill. I'll be parked down towards the pier, so just text me when you've finished and I'll dive back.'

'Okay. Shouldn't be long,' she said, shutting the car door then walking up the hill towards the office.

'Nice to meet you, Miss Ryan. This is very straightforward. Just a probate form to sign regarding your mother's estate.' The solicitor handed Miriam the paperwork, and she began to read through it.

'I just need to make sure I know what I'm signing. I had a bit of an incident with a contract recently, so …'

'Of course. Would you like a cup of tea whilst you read through?'

Miriam looked up and smiled. 'No, that's okay, thank you. Actually ...' She put the pen down. 'I'm a bit concerned about the issue to do with my old business that Jeffrey mentioned on the phone?'

The solicitor checked her computer. 'Oh, that's to do with a food truck that you bought from the company ahead of their potential buy out. Looks like the information got missed when that didn't happen … they claimed that it's not yours … say you only own sixty per cent of it …but you already paid in full in two instalments. That's probably where the confusion arose. Nothing to worry about. It is definitely yours.'

'Oh, that's good news.' Miriam sighed, relieved, then re-started reading the probate form.

'We should get it sorted though. They're asking for interest …'

Miriam looked up. 'What?'

'Very odd,' she said. 'Still … we'll unravel it.'

'Okay.' Miriam could feel her anxiety starting to rise again and turned her attention to the form, breathing slowly but trying to make it not too obvious. 'Right!' She signed it. 'All looks straightforward to me,' she said, handing it over.

'Thank you, and now, yes … there's the issue of the contract you signed for the lease of the property. It ties you into it for six months but …' She scrolled down her screen. 'We have found a tiny loophole. Must say it looks like whoever drew this up was really looking for a strong commitment from the person who took over the house. I know Jeffrey has already spoken to you about it.'

'Yes, that's right.' Miriam felt a strange mixture of relief and sadness.

'We'll cost both options up for you. You'll have to pay someone and also pay to live somewhere else, so that's something to think about if you want to go down that route. It could be easier in one way than trying to do it the other way. That could take a while.'

'Right.' Miriam smiled. 'Thank you.'

They both stood up and shook hands. 'We'll be in touch very shortly. Nice to have met you.'

'You too.' Miriam walked down the stairs, wondering why she wasn't happier about the prospect of moving out of the house and getting rid of her unwanted responsibilities.

Texting Alan that she'd finished, she made her way back to the main road and waited in the car park, watching the scruffy yellow car move slowly towards her through the traffic.

'Everything all right?' he asked as she climbed in and sat down.

'All fine, thanks. Just needed to sort a few things out.'

'Good.' He pulled out and began heading along Oystermouth Road. 'Fancy some fish and chips?'

'I am getting a bit hungry actually.' Miriam smiled. 'How long till we get to the event?'

'Couple of hours. It'll be nearly dark then. So plenty of time for a detour.'

Miriam glanced at the sky, dark grey clouds dotting the horizon to the west. 'Do you think the weather's going to hold?'

'Oh, yes. Forecast is good. We'll go via Neath. Best fish and chip shop there in the entire world. Then maybe go via the Heads of the Valley road, or maybe back on the M4. Not sure yet.'

'Whatever you say. I have no idea where I am.'

Alan turned to her briefly. 'Well, then. It's an adventure. I've got the "Dark Sky Event" playlist ready.' He clicked on his CD player. 'Actually, it's just *Dark Side of the Moon* by Pink Floyd. That all right with you?'

Miriam nodded silently, too polite to tell him what she really thought of Pink Floyd as he was driving her to look at the stars in the mountains, after all. They roared along the motorway to the soundtrack of guitars, then turned towards Neath, the sky a clear, crisp blue in front of them – but behind, it was getting darker and heavier.

The engine rattled and coughed as Alan parked outside the fish and chip shop. 'Oh dear. That doesn't sound very healthy,' said Miriam.

'It's fine. She's an old girl, so I expect has a bit of a wheeze from time to time. Cod and chips?' He jumped out of the car and hurried into the shop without waiting for her reply.

'Yes, please,' she said to his back, and leaned into the seat, thinking about her meeting with the solicitor. Why would that company be trying to get interest on something she already owned? And why had Joanna made sure that the contract she signed was so tight? She sighed, wondering how on earth she had got sucked into the middle of legal issues when she'd been trying so hard to get away from things like that. 'I have to let them sort it out,' she said out loud.

'Who?' said Alan, climbing into the car and handing her the food. 'I put salt and vinegar on. The whole works.' He smiled, turning on the engine. 'I know a nice spot up the hill with a lovely view – we can park up there and eat them.'

The car spluttered and stopped. He started the ignition again, and it did the same thing. 'Just a minute.' Alan climbed out and opened the bonnet, muttering to himself, then got back in and tried again.

'Bugger,' he said. 'For God's sake!' Then he turned to Miriam and smiled, trying to look confident. But she could tell he wasn't. 'I've got a friend who can fix cars. Actually, this is his car. Ten minutes away, he is. I'll get him to sort us out and we can be on our way.'

'Can I do anything? I mean I can't … as I know very little about cars, but, you know, if I can …?'

'No. No, it's fine.' Alan took his phone and walked around the car, and Miriam watched as he paced up and down the pavement in deep discussion with his friend. The smell of the fish and chips got too much for her, so she picked up the wooden fork and began to eat, barely noticing the spots of rain that were beginning to dot the windscreen.

'He'll be here soon.' Alan got back in again and sighed. 'Well, the forecast was a bit off.'

'Maybe it's just a short shower,' Miriam said hopefully, as the heavens opened and the sound of rain pattered rhythmically on the roof.

Alan looked up. 'Of course it is. By the time this is fixed, it will have passed.' He began to eat and they sat in companionable silence for a while, listening to pulsing guitars as the windows steamed up with the heat from the food.

'Oi oi.' Someone tapped on the door. 'Save some for me!'

Alan wound down the window. 'You got here quick.'

'Was just up in Fairyland. Didn't I say? Is she playing up again?'

'Having a bit of a strop. Yes.' He turned to Miriam. 'This is Dewi. Expert mechanic, he is.'

167

'All right!' Dewi waved at Miriam. 'I'll have a quick look under the bonnet, but if it's like last time …'

'Did he say Fairyland?' Miriam looked at Alan as he jumped out, the rain now cascading from the sky, 'And did he say like last time? Were you going to drive me up to the mountains in a less than safe vehicle?' Her voice sounded sterner than she'd meant it to.

'Why would I do that? I'm driving myself up there too. And he did say Fairyland – it's a housing estate. Good name, isn't it? I think the 153 bus via Gnoll Park Road goes there …'

'Wonderful name. Why?'

Alan paused. 'Why the name? Not sure, think there were grottoes built years ago or something, and a house … never thought of it, to be honest with you.' He smiled. 'I like the mystery of it. The otherworldliness.' He laughed. 'If I knew everything it wouldn't be so magical, would it?'

He turned and followed Dewi to the front of the car. She watched them mutter to each other, their faces serious and intense, until Dewi walked over to his pick-up truck and Alan opened her door. 'He's going to tow us up to his workshop and sort it out. Only take half an hour. His van's over there.' He pointed over the road at a battered grey vehicle.

Miriam peered out at the rain. 'I'm going to get wet.'

Alan's voice was quiet but frustrated. 'I am actually getting wet watching you gauge the weather …'

'Okay ... okay!' Miriam grabbed her bag and jumped out, crossing the street, her ankles splashing in grey water as she did, then she clambered into the truck hurriedly.

'You'll have to sit in the middle, lovely,' said Dewi, patting the seat. 'Alan's got to get in yet.'

'Right.' Miriam shuffled over, and as Alan sat next to her, his arm brushed hers. She looked steadily ahead at the windscreen wipers swishing to and fro as Dewi manoeuvred the truck close to the Citroen and hitched it up, whilst she tried not to lean any closer to Alan.

'Not sure you'll get much in the way of stargazing tonight, Al.' Dewi laughed as they drove off.

'Forecast says it will clear,' muttered Alan.

Although the forecast didn't actually forecast any rain at all, thought Miriam. They drove up a hill that took them high above the town, and along a muddy track towards an old farmhouse next to some outbuildings surrounded by old cars.

'It's his workshop,' said Alan.

'I do like to tinker.' Dewi pulled up outside the house. 'Now, you two go inside and I'll get this sorted. Then you can be on your way.' He opened the door to torrential rain and looked back at them both. 'Although maybe on your way back to Pembrokeshire rather than to the Beacons at this rate.' He laughed. 'Door's unlocked, just go in and help yourself to tea and such.'

They both rushed inside and stood in the empty hallway, their hair dripping. Miriam giggled. Alan's face was so serious, his jaw set angrily as he peered outside. 'It's not quite what you promised,' she said.

He looked at her for a moment, then smiled too. 'It is unexpectedly inclement,' he sighed. 'Cup of tea?'

Miriam followed him into the kitchen whilst he turned the kettle on and took some mugs from one of the cupboards.

'So, you and Dewi are old friends?' She leaned against a worktop and watched him move around the room gathering milk and sugar.

'Yep. Friends from five years old. Went to school together. I went off to university. He took over his father's garage. But we have a shared interest in astronomy, so go off to events and stuff together.'

'Ah, so you're from Neath then?'

'Yep.' He flashed her a smile and the butterflies coursed around her stomach again. She folded her arms to try to stop them and cleared her throat.

'Do you divide your time between Neath and your aunt's summerhouse?'

'No. No. I have a place in Cardiff. But I do travel a lot. Because of the job.' He handed her a steaming mug of tea. 'Sugar?' he asked, waving a jar in front of her.

'Not for me, thanks.' Miriam took the mug, the heat warming her clammy, wet hands. 'I know you write … is that your full-time job?'

'I … well … I write, and I work with various planetariums around the world on development programmes and such. I'm also a lecturer but, well, that's becoming a bit untenable, so I'm changing that ... but …' He walked into the hall as the rain continued to patter on the roof. 'Shall I show you where it all began?'

Miriam smiled. 'Yes … here?'

'It did indeed.' He began to walk up the stairs. 'Dewi's father loved the stars. Like yours. And mine.'

Miriam followed him onto the landing, and then up another floor to a large open mezzanine with a telescope in front of some full-length windows spanning the width of the room.

'All you can see here is the clouds at the moment. But when the sky is clear … I mean forget about the Brecon Beacons, or Northumberland, Chile, Portugal, Angola … this, for me, is magic. He pushed a tatty old sofa over to the telescope and sat down. 'This is a prime view.'

Miriam sat at the opposite end and took a sip of the tea as he picked up a remote control. 'Watch this,' he said, pressing a button so the windows slowly slid open. The rain was beginning

170

to subside, slowing to a constant dark drizzle. Alan turned to Miriam. 'I can assure you, the view is spectacular when you can see it.'

'I'll use my imagination.'

'So, Miriam … what's the story?'

She looked at him, confused.

'I mean. You're obviously accomplished, talented and successful. I'm intrigued about the fear of cooking, to be honest.'

Miriam put her mug on the floor. 'I'm confused too.' She sighed. 'And I've tried to get to the bottom of it with my counsellor.' She smiled at him. 'I've had a lot of counselling.'

'And?' His eyes were warm and kind, and something about him and where they were in this dull random room on the top of a mountain, in what felt like a cloud, flicked a switch somewhere in her memory.

'Responsibility … looking after people … I don't want to do it any more. It all got too much. Made me feel very alone.' Miriam looked at him, surprised. 'I didn't mean to tell you that.'

'Did it take it out of you? Looking after your mother?'

'It's not just that. It was looking after my mother and the business too. So I decided I needed to sell the business because that's all I did – work. And I loved it, but there had to be more … but now …' She kicked off her shoes and wiggled her toes, then stood up and walked onto the damp balcony. 'Now, I don't have a mother, I don't have a business and I've lost the love of the only thing that made me happy.'

'Feeding people.'

She turned back and smiled at him. 'Yes, although I stopped being part of the catering side years ago. I began the process of selling when my mother was ill … but … well … not the best timing, is it? Unfortunately, I got involved with the owner of the company who had made an offer … and that's not the best

171

decision I made.' Miriam laughed, but not because it was funny. 'And then my mother died … and then I found out …'

Alan joined her on the balcony. 'Found out what?'

'That he was married, and that he planned to make most of the staff in the company redundant. They were like my family really … so …' She looked up at him. 'I fought. I wouldn't let it happen.'

'This was just after your mother died?'

She nodded. 'Yep. I spent a year trying to sort it out. Worrying about everyone. Not me though.'

The sudden roar of an engine in the yard made them jump. 'Don't get your hopes up!' shouted Dewi from the doorway downstairs. 'Got a bit more to do yet.'

Miriam peered out into the distance. 'What's that?' she said, pointing at a tiny pinprick of light far below.

'That is a sign that the clouds are lifting. It looks like Mumbles lighthouse to me.'

'I didn't realise it had got dark.'

Alan looked at his watch. 'It's later than I thought.'

Miriam smiled at him. 'The stargazing. This is where it started?'

'My father loved astronomy, like Dewi's, and we used to come up here and just study everything around us. I loved it–love it …' He stopped and held his hand out to Miriam. 'Come … look,' he said.

Miriam moved over to him.

'You see. There's more lights … that's Swansea …' He went back into the room and dragged over the scruffy old sofa. 'Sit!' he said excitedly. 'Look …'

The rain clouds were dissipating, the indistinct lights in the distance becoming clearer, one by one, as they did.

He turned to her. 'I'll let you into a secret. It wasn't so much the stars ... it was this. I was about five. I remember—' The sound of an engine backfiring interrupted them, and Alan laughed. 'That happened all the time too.' He sat down on the sofa, closer to Miriam this time. 'It had been raining just like this. It was mid-December, so dark early. The clouds started to clear and these lights began to appear. My dad, he came and stood next to me, and told me what they all were ... Mumbles Head, Swansea docks, Neath ... he pointed out Stockhams, which was his favourite bakery ... down there ... it wasn't obviously – he was good, but couldn't pinpoint individual buildings!' He leaned back and took a breath. 'We did that every time we came here.' He stopped for a moment, his face serious, then turned back to Miriam. 'And over there ... the other side of the valley, he'd name the farms ... and in the distance, there'd be ...' He stood up again and leaned over the balcony. 'Let me show you.'

Miriam stood next to him, captivated. This laidback, difficult, irritating, kind man and his sudden intensity were pulling her closer, and this time her legs didn't want to take her off in another direction.

'There ... oh!' He turned excitedly. 'Look ... the clouds, almost gone ... see right over there – that's Gower, that is. And there used to be BP Llandarcy in the middle there, and it used to spew out this gas and all these flames, and at night it would glow red and orange. It was beautiful ... I mean, horribly polluting and very unhealthy ... but, I used to look at it and try to work out why those colours were there – and over there, see ... Port Talbot and the chemical works with the lights on, and the steelworks far in the distance.'

Miriam watched as, out of the darkness, a carpet of lights tumbled down the mountain along the valley and towards the sea, more and more twinkling to life as the sky cleared, as if everyone had woken up as the rain had slowly ebbed away.

'And look, see ... beyond the lights on the coast and the industry, there's the sea ... all black ... but, if you look closely, you know there are boats out there ...'

Miriam looked at him, fighting the urge to put her arms around him and feel his warmth, the beating of his heart...

He smiled. 'And my dad he'd say – "you can get a man on the moon, and you can even catch a bus to Fairyland from Neath town centre. It's not just the world that's your oyster, Al, it's the whole universe. Infinity".' He paused for a moment, staring into the distance. 'So, I search and I search, and I'll never find all of it ... there'll always be something unknown, mysterious, which is one of the things I love about it. Maybe I'll drive off into the distance just to see the stars from everywhere ...'

Miriam felt herself move towards him, unable to speak. 'Oh,' was all she could say.

He looked up and grabbed her hand. 'See,' he said. 'While we were concentrating on down there, we forgot to see what's up there.'

She followed his gaze and above them was a canopy of stars, stretching off towards the hills beyond, hundreds and hundreds, sparkling in the sky, over the sea and the towns, so that she felt she was swaddled in a cocoon of light.

'It's like being wrapped in the stars, isn't it?' he said quietly. 'You can never be afraid of the dark up here.'

'It's ... it's beautiful. And there's that perfect crescent moon.'

He smiled at her. 'You want the moon? Just say the word, and I'll throw a lasso around it and pull it down.'

Miriam couldn't say anything, and she felt herself being pulled even closer to him.

'It's a wonderful life,' he said quietly.

'Sometimes?' she said slowly, confused.

'The film.' He laughed. 'It's in the film. George Bailey says it ...'

'Oh, of course.'

They edged towards each other, their eyes locked. Then Alan pulled her to him and kissed her, and Miriam fell into it, unable to fight it, not wanting to, losing herself, wanting him so much she almost ached with longing.

The car engine backfired again, and they both jumped back.

'Oh, I'm sorry,' Alan said.

'Don't be.'

'I—'

'Right, you two,' Dewi shouted from the garden. 'The Citroen is currently out of order. So, I'll give you the blue Datsun. My advice, though, is don't take it overnight to the Beacons. I'd just get in it and drive back to Pembrokeshire without stopping.'

'Sounds like a plan,' said Alan steadily, his eyes still locked to Miriam's.

'Sounds fine to me,' she said, pulling him towards her and kissing him again. 'Is there really a place called Fairyland?' she whispered.

'Yes. And there really is a bus ... these old industrial towns. There's more magic in them than meets the eye. Just like those lights in the sky. So much we don't know.'

Miriam stretched, the sound of Alan's soft snoring waking her up. A shaft of light shone through the side of the blinds, illuminating the floor, and she put her feet softly on the ground, enjoying its warmth.

She turned and glanced at him, his unshaven face and untidy wavy hair prompting the butterflies in her stomach to stir. He murmured, rolled over and pulled the duvet over his head, and she leaned over, wanting to run her hand down his back. As she moved closer, a dog barked in the distance and she paused, allowing an unwelcome panicked voice to rise from somewhere in the back of her mind.

Don't get too close ... don't care ... don't trust yourself ... your judgement is off ... remember Artie Morgan ... remember ...

She stood up to try to shake it off.

It was only physical, she thought. *No it wasn't.* She could feel her heart beating anxiously. *This isn't just another one of those things, Miriam. The friendship and sex things. The ones you can manage – sorry,* could *manage – when you were a fully functioning MD of your own company. This man lives in your summerhouse. And you don't want to care for anyone. Do you?*

Miriam pulled her clothes on quietly and padded slowly down the stairs, opening the door and stepping out into the early morning light. The lawn was bright with droplets of dew, shining like sapphires. Taking her shoes off, she walked back to the house, enjoying the feel of damp grass on her feet, and then sat down in the kitchen.

What have I done? she thought. *What have I done?*

Putting the kettle on, she made a cup of tea and went up to her bedroom, picked up her phone and checked Fiona's app to see if there were any appointments available for that morning.

'None, none, none,' she muttered, throwing the phone back onto the bed.

So, Miriam did what she had got used to doing – had a shower, got dressed, packed some breadsticks and went for a long walk, listening to three podcasts about astronomy to drown out the chatter in her head.

Alan was loading the Datsun when she got back to the house and waved at her as she put her bag on the kitchen table.

The butterflies swept around her stomach, so she held onto a chair to stop herself running over to him and pulling him back into the summerhouse. She waved back and smiled, took a deep breath to calm herself back into acting her age, and opened the door.

'Cup of tea?' she shouted, miming lifting a mug up to her mouth and nodding. One leg seemed to want to move whilst the other was rooted to the spot.

'No time, thank you,' shouted Alan, holding up a pair of walking boots. 'Just packing up. Got to head off in five minutes.'

They both stood, looking at each other.

'Okay,' shouted Miriam eventually. 'I'll let you get on.' What she wanted to say was, "Why are you standing over there and where are you going? And why am I standing over here?"

She filled the kettle with water and began to make herself an unwanted cup of tea.

'Miriam!' Alan shouted. She walked to the kitchen door. He was standing in the middle of the garden.

'Yes?'

'Last night ...'

She stepped out onto the decking, still holding the door handle as if it was stopping her floating off into the sky.

He stepped forward. 'Um ... it was ...'

Miriam moved forward slightly, letting go of the door handle but holding onto the side of the table. 'It was ... yes.' She nodded.

'Amazing.' They both moved at the same time. Miriam stopped at the end of the decking.

'I was going to have to go away anyway for a few days. This isn't ... you know ...'

'Oh, good.' She could feel herself leaning forward. 'I just went for a walk. It's a nice day.'

Then their eyes locked, and Alan rushed towards her, throwing his arms around her and kissing her for what felt like forever. Miriam grabbed his hair and pulled him closer.

'I have to go,' said Alan eventually. He looked at his watch. 'Yes … I have to go. Otherwise, I'd ...'

Miriam stood back and nodded breathlessly. 'Yes. Of course. Yes.'

'Although ... ' He grabbed her hand and squeezed it.

'Although?'

'If the traffic's okay, I don't need to go just yet.'

Miriam began to walk back to the summerhouse, pulling her with him. 'No, not just yet,' she whispered.

Chapter Fifteen

Miriam wandered around the house listlessly, looking at the empty space where Alan's car was normally parked every time she found herself in the kitchen. The place seemed full of his absence, even though he had only left three hours ago. She opened the fridge door and pulled out a bottle of white wine, checking the clock as she did it.

'Five-thirty,' she said to the window. 'That's okay.' She poured herself a large glass and took it out onto the decking, as the late afternoon sun flooded the garden with a warm glow, accompanied by a soundtrack of birdsong and the light rustle of the breeze in the trees. Miriam took a sip and tried not to stare at the summerhouse, smiling to herself every time a memory of the last twenty-four hours popped into her mind. A robin perched on the roof. 'I'm going to enjoy this,' she said as it cleaned its feathers, oblivious to her words. 'He's not around till next week, so I can panic about what I've done then.'

The bird flew off, and she gazed into the distance for a while. *I think I need people*, she thought. *I wanted to hide but ...*

She finished her drink, took it into the kitchen, then set off for the pub. The warm evening had brought families out to play on the beach, and Miriam enjoyed listening to the shouts and laughter drifting along the shore, mixed with the gentle lapping of the waves on the sand and the child-like calls of the gulls. She almost floated as she moved, calm and happy. A red beach ball bounced onto the road, and she bent down to pick it up as a car drove past. As she straightened, she heard a familiar joyous giggle that stopped her in her tracks. For a moment, time stood still. For a moment, she forgot where she was, or rather she felt she was standing on the beach, playing cricket with her mum and dad and their friends. It was her mother's laugh. But she couldn't see her face.

The breeze rustled through her hair. She looked over the sea wall to try to find where the giggle had come from, but only saw two little boys.

'Is this your ball?' she asked.

'Yes,' they said in unison.

'There you are.' She gently tossed it to the taller of the two.

'Thank you,' he said, and they both turned and ran towards their parents.

'Mind playing tricks again,' said Miriam to herself, brushing it away, and she carried on walking to the pub.

'Miriam!' Jim shouted across the room. 'Rammed, we are. Not sure there's any space outside at the moment. Fancy propping up the bar?'

She weaved through the people chatting and laughing and grabbed herself a stool. 'Good to see it so busy,' she said, as Jim gave her a glass of wine. 'Ah, thank you. You've read my mind.'

'On the house,' he said. 'Glad you've come. I need your help.'

'Help?'

'I've got a bit backed up with ordering the food for the festival. I know I said I'd do it as Joanna's not here, but with one thing and another …'

'You want me to do it anyway.' Miriam tried to smile, but her stomach began to churn anxiously.

'Not long to it now. Could you? I can e-mail you her usual list of ingredients and such.' He looked at her plaintively.

She picked up her glass. 'Of course I'll do it, Jim.' She took a long gulp of wine. 'Of course.'

'Everything else is coming along nicely. Lots of acts booked. Deadline is tomorrow. Just need the weather to be good, and it'll be a great day.' Someone at the end of the bar waved to get his attention. 'Duty calls,' he said, and went to deal with his customer.

Miriam shifted in her seat uncomfortably, resentment beginning to bubble up from nowhere again. She took out her phone and sent an e-mail to her solicitors, telling them to send her the details of how to employ someone to do her job. *Not her job.* Her *holiday.* Her *break.* She finished her drink quickly and walked back to the house, not wanting to be around people any more, the breeze slowly picking up as she did. Opening the door, a sudden gust of wind knocked over a plant pot. Caught in the whisper of it as it subsided, she thought she heard the laugh again.

Miriam turned around. There was no one there. She shrugged. *It's just my imagination. Again*, she thought, grabbing her headphones and drowning everything out with S Club 7.

After a restless night's sleep, Miriam decided to work off her anxiety with a swim in the sea. Opening the curtains, the sun glowed radiantly over a perfect blue ocean, so she put on her swimming costume and packed her bag, grabbing a book from her "to-read" pile as she did. Her phone buzzed as she poured herself a glass of water, and she shrieked with pleasure when she realised it was a message from Justin

I'm back!! I'm back!! Look out, I'm back!

Miriam laughed and replied. *Does that mean you're back?*

Another message appeared, this time an e-mail.

Thank you for your e-mail regarding employing someone to look after The Grange.

We will send over the paperwork later today or first thing tomorrow. Realistically, it will take about a month or two to find someone and get them to sign your own contract. If you decide to

take the other option and negotiate to leave the contract early,
please let us know at the earliest opportunity.

'A month or two... a month or two!' she said to a chaffinch that was perched on the windowsill. 'Not quick enough to help with this festival. But ... the cavalry have arrived.'

Fancy a visit to beautiful Wales? I need a favour. Rather
urgently. In fact, today if you can make it, she typed and pressed send.

Her phone buzzed immediately.

I'm actually already on my way! Rod has got some family
stuff to deal with so has gone to Edinburgh. And I decided to visit
some friends in Cardiff. Be with you in no time at all! See you
later.

I'll order us in a takeway, and you can tell me all about your
adventures in South America, she replied.

Miriam put the glass back on the table, and her phone buzzed again.

What's the address? That might help!

The beach was quiet with a few surfers floating hopefully in the calm bay, music from a food truck at the far end of the beach trickling out towards the sea. Miriam put her bag down close to some rocks and kicked off her sandals, the sand warm and comforting under her feet. She walked slowly towards the water, enjoying the soundtrack of gulls and waves, and stopped at the shore, waiting as the cool, clear sea drifted towards her, washing over her feet and making her body tingle.

Breathe, she thought, *breathe ... the cavalry's coming.*
Although I must make sure not to tell Justin I just called him that.
She took another step into the waves, and then another. *But ... but*
... I've just had to problem solve! Isn't that like work? She sank into the sea. 'Oh, shut up, me! Miriam, stop tying me in knots!'

182

she shouted, and began to swim and swim and swim, stretching all the stress away, until there was just her and the sea and the splashing of her arms pushing through the water.

Later, she sat on the sand, letting the sun dry her skin, her hair curling in the salty heat. Eventually, she slipped her sundress on and stood up. The food truck sat enticingly in a lay-by in the opposite direction to the house, and she checked the time on her phone. Then she got irritated with herself for feeling she needed to head back at a particular time, when one of the reasons for having the break was not to make lists or keep to schedules, and to actually be a bit spontaneous.

Standing up, she began to walk towards the truck, remembering the plans she'd had for the one she'd bought from Artie Morgan; to just drive off into the distance, casually dipping into one or two events as the mood took her, rediscovering her love of cooking.

As she began to pad along the sand, her mind took her back to the day they'd first met.

He was sitting next to her. 'I'll never forget those days,' he said, his eyes glowing with excitement. 'I'd just go from place to place, getting a licence from the council, seeing how I went and then moving on.'

'Oh, to be free to do that again.' She smiled, clutching at the idea of doing something to please herself, her day having comprised of sorting out a contract with a performing arts company whilst sitting at the care home as her mother slipped in and out of consciousness.

'The company's just bought one, but it was a mistake. No time to use it. Have to unload it.'

'Really?'

'Really.' He leaned closer and touched her arm. 'Why? Are you interested?'

'Yes,' she said.

A car horn beeped loudly in the distance, and she was on the beach again. She shivered. 'Oh, how I wish I hadn't said that.'

The car horn beeped again. 'Miriam!'

She scanned the road to find the voice.

'Miriam! Boss! Miriam?' Justin was waving from a vintage MG sports car.

'Justin!' she shouted, waving. 'You're here!'

He parked the car and climbed out, pulling her into a hug.

'Oh, Justin,' she said. 'It's just *so* lovely to see you.'

'You too, boss. You too.' He stepped backwards and studied her. 'Well, what have they done to you here? Not an inch of make-up or hairspray in sight.' He laughed. 'I meant that as a compliment. You look fantastic!'

Miriam glanced down at her un-ironed dress, pulled her hand through her hair and smiled. 'I've just been swimming, so …'

'Took me two hours to get here, and I decided to grab a bite before we got down to work. This is very famous after all, and here you are anyway!'

'Famous?' Miriam looked at the name on the menu.

'Oh, yes. Been here for years according to my friends in Cardiff. Popular with locals, tourists and the odd celeb. Fab seafood.'

'I didn't realise. I've not really engaged with the food scene here.'

Justin took her hand and led her to a bench. 'You sit there, and I'll surprise you with the order. You know, just like the old days when I was your super-duper uber PA.'

Miriam laughed and sat down, watching him as he chatted to the people serving the food. Justin was more than a PA; he'd become a good friend, making sure that she ate, drank and looked after herself when her mother was ill. And in the aftermath too.

'Here you are.' He handed her a bag of cockles, and put a tray of mixed seafood, salad and chips on the picnic table. 'Fresh, delicious and very, very cheap.'

'Thank you! You look like you had a good time,' said Miriam. 'You're all glowing and tanned.'

'South America did it for me.' He laughed. 'It was a real eye-opener. And the food … well …' He visibly shivered with pleasure. 'We're planning a trip to Thailand in a few weeks – for the food … and ...' He looked at her. 'I have some exciting news.'

'Do tell.' Miriam cut up some fresh mackerel and took a bite.

'Rod and I are going to set up a street food company. Just doing events to start. He'll carry on with his journalism and I'll do some freelance PR.'

Miriam clapped excitedly. 'Wonderful news. When are you going to start that?'

'Next spring. We're just getting the capital together.'

'This fish is delicious,' Miriam took a bite of battered cod.

'Isn't it just?' He leaned forward and touched her hand. 'It was partly you and that food truck that inspired us. Remember?'

'Food truck?' Miriam said. 'Oh no, not that ...'

'It was done with the best of intentions. You were so excited by it.'

'Yes, and look what happened.' She shivered at the memory. 'I don't want to think about it.'

'Well, it was a good idea. Not your fault it got caught up with all that business with … well, the business, and—' he leaned forward and whispered '—you know who.'

Miriam chuckled. 'A lot of stuff got caught up in a lot of stuff. I wasn't making the best decisions at the time, was I?'

'Understandable.' Justin sat back. 'Anyway, you said you needed my help?'

'I need to order food for an event, and as soon as it was mentioned I could feel a minor meltdown coming on.' She stabbed at a chip with a fork and began to eat it. 'I can't believe I've come to this, Justin. I mean, *me*!'

'What's the event?'

'It's a "Look-Alike Festival" at the local pub.'

He sat back and laughed, loudly. 'A *what* festival? How did you, *you* of all people, get involved with that, Ms High Powered?'

Miriam pointed the fork at him. 'I got involved because of a mistake with a piece of paperwork. Remember that?'

'Ahh.' He smiled. 'I think I do owe you. Now eat up, and I'll give you a ride home in my new set of wheels.'

They drove back along the bay. The breeze blew through Miriam's hair, and Justin chattered about his dreams, laughing and shrieking, just like the old days.

Rhiannon was sitting on the garden wall, sullenly studying her phone, and only looked up as they pulled into the driveway.

'Hiya.' She waved, unsmiling.

'Just got to make a quick call,' said Justin as Miriam jumped out of the car.

'What's the matter, Rhiannon?' she asked.

'Why do you think anything's the matter?' She stood up and picked up her bag.

'Well, you're a bit subdued ... for you.'

'Jim's got another woman on the go,' she said, following Miriam to the door.

'Another woman?'

'We're not technically together. Well not together at all really. Last week he suggested we go for a drink … at another pub … but nothing. No time, no date, no contact. I mean, he's got my number … bloody fickle men.'

'You thought things were coming along though?' Miriam put the key in the lock and pushed the door open.

'I did. I was wrong.' Rhiannon flicked her hair despondently. She sat down at the kitchen table and kicked off her shoes. 'Too hot to be wearing these today. Got another viewing in an hour so can't change out of my work clothes.'

'Fancy a cold drink?' Miriam took some glasses out of the cupboard. 'So, what makes you think he's got another woman?'

'He was clinking his glass with this tall, glamorous blonde woman at the bar just now, and they were laughing and joking like they knew each other very well.'

'Could be a friend?'

Rhiannon sighed. 'I think *I'm* just a friend, to be honest.'

'And who's this then?' Justin strode into the room, glowing and tanned, and flashed a flirtatious smile at Rhiannon, whose mood seemed to change instantly.

She flicked her hair, giggled, stood up and held out her hand. 'Rhiannon Jones. Friend of Miriam's. And you are?'

'Justin. Ex PA to the slave driver here. I've come to help out for a day or two.'

'Oh?' Rhiannon's eyes lit up. 'So, I'll be seeing a bit more of you then?'

He winked at her. 'No doubt. I'm going to be topping up my tan on a sunbed in the garden most of the days I'm around.'

She giggled again, then checked her phone as it pinged. 'Damn, don't know where the time went. Got to go. *Ciao* for now.'

'*Ciao*.' Justin blew her a kiss as she passed him, and they heard her giggle again as she shut the front door.

'Your flirting skills have gone up another level,' said Miriam, handing him a glass of water. 'Don't want to get Rod jealous, do you?'

'He'd only get jealous if I flirted with a good-looking man. But I never do. Just lovely women who like to flirt.' He finished his drink and leaned forward. 'So, tell me more about this event. Let's have a brainstorm. Just like old times!'

Miriam ordered a takeaway, and they spent a few hours planning the food for the festival, Justin making notes and checking the list of suppliers that Joanna had left. It was just like the late evenings they'd spent throwing ideas around and making things happen. Miriam became herself again for a while – the in-control, successful, excited self – but every so often, she remembered she wanted to be another Miriam because, when it came down to it, that former Miriam had slowly been unable to cope.

Just before they went to their rooms, she checked the diary. 'Oh, well, there's a small *soiree*, it says here, the day after tomorrow. And the letters AC next to it.'

'AC?' Justin paused by the door.

'Occasionally there's entertainment – random, and usually fun. This is probably one but can't think who. The menu is "Mexican Fiesta".' She sighed. 'Can you help? You can stay, Justin, can't you?'

'Of course. Footloose at the moment. Someone gave me a nice redundancy payment, didn't they? So real life doesn't kick in for a while.'

Miriam wanted to hug him again. *The cavalry? Yes he was.*

Chapter Sixteen

'Who's the lady in your kitchen wearing a dressing-gown?' Justin was quietly knocking on Miriam's bedroom door.

She sat up, stretching her arms above her head for a moment. 'Lady? It's not Rhiannon, is it? She's the letting agent and she's still got a key.'

'Definitely not Rhiannon,' he whispered.

'Oh.' Miriam climbed out of bed. 'Have you asked her?'

'I didn't go in. I saw her walk across from the summerhouse from my window.'

An image of Alan in a pink dressing-gown appeared in her mind, and her heart sank.

'What colour was it?'

'Bright pink. Why?'

'Anyone with her?'

'No. Why?'

'Did you see a yellow Citroen? Or a blue Datsun?'

Justin's voice was getting more agitated now. 'Didn't look! Now, are you coming down to deal with this intruder or what?'

Miriam opened the door, trying to control the pricks of anger that were stabbing at her repeatedly. 'I don't believe this,' she muttered. 'Again. It's happened again ...'

'What?' Justin followed her as she walked down the stairs, and they stopped just outside the kitchen door. 'Aren't you going in?' he whispered.

'What if she's dangerous?'

'In that colour pink? Certainly not.'

Miriam took a breath, tried to compose herself, fixed on a smile and went into the kitchen.

A tall, attractive blonde lady was sitting at the table, drinking tea and eating toast. 'Hello?' she said, clearly confused.

'Hello.' Miriam stood in the doorway with Justin close behind.

'Is Joanna not about?' She put down her toast and stood up.

'No. Joanna went on a trip at the last minute, and I'm looking after the house till she comes back. She's fine, apparently … and this is Justin.'

'Ahhh. Is Alan around?'

'I was going to ask you that as you *are* wearing his dressing-gown.' Miriam bit her lip and tried to be nice. She knew when she saw Alan, she definitely would *not* be.

The woman pulled it around her more tightly. 'Actually, it's mine. I'm Britta. His ex-wife.'

Miriam felt Justin squeeze her arm, then walk past her into the kitchen. 'Well, it's lovely to meet you. I've just got here so have no idea who Alan is, but I do fancy a cup of tea. Do you want a fresh one?'

He clattered mugs and sugar and spoons on the worktop, making enough noise to cover Miriam's breathing. She could hear it herself and held onto the door handle to try to slow it down. There were so many thoughts careering around in her mind that she couldn't focus on anything.

'Sugar?' she heard Justin shout. 'Miriam? Sugar?'

'No, thank you.'

He walked over to her and handed her a mug of tea, then pulled out a chair for her. 'Sit,' he whispered.

She looked up at him, startled, then gathered herself and smiled, sitting down slowly. 'Alan is Joanna's nephew, Justin, and lives in the summerhouse at the moment. Although I don't know where he is as we aren't that close.'

'Doing his disappearing act again, is he?' said Britta, taking a fresh tea from Justin. She laughed. 'That's a rhetorical question by the way.' Then she looked at Miriam. 'That's a bit weird about Joanna though.'

'Yes, people seem to think so. We've tried to get in contact with her – wherever she is – but her solicitors are adamant she doesn't want to be found.'

Britta leaned back and smiled. 'She's gone a bit Alan then. Although it's taken years for his particular kind of—' she put her hands in the air and mimed speech marks '—"free spirited behaviour" to rub off.'

Miriam took a sip of her tea. 'I wouldn't know.'

'You spent the night in the summerhouse?' asked Justin.

'Yes, still got a key. I'm looking for Alan. He's not returning my calls, and I need to get hold of him so I thought I'd track him down in person. Honestly, he never changes.'

Justin leaned forward. 'When you say ex-wife … are you still close? Sorry, can't help it. Just a nosey old so-and-so.'

'I wouldn't call it close. Although ... occasionally we are.' Miriam could sense Britta glance at her as she continued to stare into her tea.

Miriam felt Justin kick her under the table and looked up. 'Will you be staying long? I can take a message if you're not?'

'That's kind, but no thanks. I caught up with Jim last night – you know, the landlord of the local pub – and left a message with him. I've got to get back to Cardiff this morning, but I'll be back for the Look-Alike Festival.' She smiled and stood up. 'Nice to have met you, Miriam. And you, Justin. I'd better get dressed and head off.'

Miriam stood up too. 'Good to meet you too. I'll see you again, then.'

'Absolutely. I'll let myself out. Must run.' She closed the door behind her, and they both watched in silence as she appeared to glide elegantly across the lawn, the pink dressing-gown setting off her sleek blonde hair perfectly.

'What legs she has …' sighed Justin, then he stared at Miriam. 'Come on then. Alan? Spill the beans.'

Miriam sat down and put her head in her hands. *Not again*, she thought. *Not again. This is what happened the last time … married bloody men! But this one lives in my summerhouse.*

'Miriam?' Justin whispered. She looked up and saw him drumming his hands on the table. 'Tell me!'

'*Ahh*!' She jumped up and started pacing around. 'How could I have been so stupid? Let my guard down. How could he? Just because I—it's just sex, Justin, that's all it is … but he lives at the end of my garden, and I can't get away from him!'

'You and your men, Miriam.' He sighed.

She looked at him. 'You say that as if I have an endless stream of them.'

'Well, there was a time, you know, where I thought you were channelling Samantha from *Sex and the City*.'

'No, I wasn't! I just didn't have time to get involved, and then I wasn't involved with anyone in any way for a couple of years, was I?'

'I'm sorry. You're right.' He stood up and put his arms around her. 'I used to enjoy those days though. I never knew who was going to take you to dinner next, and that's not a euphemism. Although sometimes it was.'

Miriam smiled thinly.

'What I'm saying is that you sleeping with someone and not having an emotional relationship is nothing new, so why are you so fraught about this Alan?'

'Because he lives at the bottom of my garden.'

192

'You make him sound like a gnome.'

'Trust me, he is anything but,' muttered Miriam. 'Look. I got involved with he who shall not be named when my mum was ill ...'

'You were entitled to a bit of a distraction, weren't you?'

'Yes, but he turned out to be married, and he turned out to want to buy my business and hollow it out. And—'

'Yes, but Alan isn't him.'

'But he *is* married.'

'Was.'

'Yes, but they are obviously still close – and she looks like the blonde one from Abba.' Miriam sat down and looked up at him. 'It was very recent. Very, very recent, Justin. How could he?'

Justin squeezed her hand. 'Well, I'm gay, and I know you're gorgeous. And since you've gone a bit feral, even more so.'

'I'm very annoyed.'

'Absolutely.'

'Just wait till he gets back.'

'I'm looking forward to seeing that already.' He stood up and turned the kettle on again. 'You've barely drunk that. Have another one, get dressed, brush yourself down and let's get our next *soiree* sorted.'

Miriam leaned back and sighed. 'I rented this house to get away from all of this. And look at me now.' She put her hand to her hair. 'Wait, what do you mean "feral"?'

They spent the morning planning menus, and for a while Miriam sank back into her comfort zone, briefly forgetting why she had run away from it, comforted by Justin's positive presence. She had just finished writing a shopping list when there was a knock at the door.

'You're popular for someone who was planning to be a hermit,' muttered Justin, sauntering along the hallway and opening it with a flourish. 'Oh, hello,' he said.

'Hello.' Miriam heard Jim's voice. 'Is Miriam in?'

'Hi, Jim,' she shouted. 'I'm in the kitchen.'

'Welcome,' said Justin. 'Follow me. I'm Justin by the way.'

'Nice to meet you, Justin.'

'Likewise. Miriam, this is—'

'Jim.' She laughed. 'Yes, I know.'

Jim pulled up a chair and looked at Miriam, confused.

'Justin used to be my PA. He's visiting for a few days and helping out. In fact, he's the brains behind the menus for the festival.'

'Oh, cheers.' Jim studied Justin for a moment.

Miriam smiled, assuming he was trying to work out if anything was going on between them. 'We'll send it to you when it's finalised.'

'Great. That's not why I'm here though.'

'Cup of tea?' Justin filled the kettle.

'No thanks. Just had a macchiato at the pub. Thing is … Britta just messaged me. She said you'd met. You know, Alan's ex?' He chuckled to himself. 'Sometimes.'

'Hmmm?' Miriam bit her lip and tried not to say anything.

'Honestly, those two—'

Justin banged the kettle on the worktop.

Miriam grabbed her phone and tried to open her e-mails. *I haven't replied to the note from the solicitor*, she thought. *I've got to get out of here.*

'Is everything all right?' Jim leaned forward and touched her hand.

'Yes, yes, of course. I just remembered something urgent.'
She tried to log onto the internet. 'But the wi-fi seems to have gone.'

'The thing is, Britta remembered Joanna telling her about some guy she'd met years ago – thought maybe her disappearance was something to do with him. Apparently, he wanted her to go travelling with him, but her dad had just had an accident and she needed to look after her mother. Never got over it, apparently. Could be the same one as the initials on the bench in the garden?'

Miriam put the phone down. 'Right.'

'And there are photos in the attic room she showed her ...'

'Oh, interesting,' said Justin, walking to the doorway. 'Are we going to go and look for them?'

'I just want to know she's okay,' sighed Jim. 'If there's a clue to where she is, it would make me feel better, you know?'

Miriam stood up. 'Come on then, if it'll put your mind at rest.'

Jim and Justin followed her up the stairs. 'There are quite a lot of boxes,' she said. 'I keep tripping over them!' She stopped and ushered them inside the room.

'Oh, nice telescope!' gasped Justin. 'Astronomy is on my list of to-do's next year.' He adjusted it and pointed it towards the sea. 'I know it's not dark, but just checking what's out there.'

'You carry on.' Miriam smiled as she sat on the floor. 'Come on, Jim. There's no point standing up and trying to find what you're looking for. You have to just dive right in.' He moved next to her, and she pushed a box towards him. 'There you go. You take that and I'll take this one, and when Justin's finished his beach-gazing, he can help too.'

Justin sighed and sat down opposite them. 'Don't forget we have to get the ingredients for the event, so we can't take too long here.'

'Yes, boss,' muttered Miriam.

He stretched one of his long legs out and kicked her gently. 'Old habits die hard.'

Jim took some photographs out and put them on the floor. 'I've gone through these with her before,' he said, 'She has a tendency to lose things, so she'll drag me up here when Alan isn't around to help track things down.'

'Just loads of recipes in this one,' said Justin. 'What about you?'

'I don't know what Joanna looks like. So, although this seemed a good idea when we were in the kitchen, actually I'm going to be no help at all.'

'She looks like this.' Jim held up a photograph then passed it to her. 'Well, about forty years ago … but she hasn't changed much, just the colour of her hair.'

Miriam looked at it. In the foreground was a young woman with long dark hair standing on the beach. A handsome blond man had his arm around her waist and was gazing at her, and a few hundred yards behind them was a group of people sitting on towels and eating a picnic. Right at the back, almost out of shot, she noticed something familiar, and looked closer.

She gasped, putting the photo down, her heart racing.

'What's up?' Justin moved closer.

She handed it to him. 'My parents are in that photo.'

He studied it, then grabbed her hand. 'God, Miriam. I recognise your mum from the pictures you showed me.'

'Are you okay?' Jim touched her arm.

'Yes …' Miriam wiped her face with her sleeve. 'Just a surprise out of nowhere, that's all.'

'Do you think she knew Joanna?' he said.

She looked at the photograph again. 'I don't know. I'm not sure if the group she's with was supposed to be in it, or just happened to be there.'

Justin gave it to Jim, who almost jumped to his feet. 'That man … that must have been the one Britta mentioned. What were the initials on that bench we saw a few weeks back?'

Miriam looked at him, unsettled by the photograph. 'I can't remember.'

He turned the photograph over. 'There's a note here,' he muttered. 'Me and H … before he went. I'll go to the garden and have a look if that's all right. Don't know how this helps, but at least if I know who she's with ...'

'Yes, fine,' said Miriam faintly. 'I've just got to go and freshen up, Justin. Shall we go into town for the supplies in about ten minutes?' Then she walked into her bedroom and took the jiffy bag with the family photos in it from the drawer, spreading the pictures along the bed.

Her parents smiled out of each one with Miriam squinting irritably as a child, beaming radiantly, scowling as a teenager, appearing more sporadically as she got older. Then her father wasn't in them any more. And then it was just her and her mother.

But there were no pictures of their Welsh holidays.

Picking up her journal, she wrote,

How strange I'm in this house if my mother knew Joanna. How strange ...

Her pen hovered over the page, but she couldn't write anything else. She wanted to talk to a human being about it. She picked up her phone and clicked on the app for Fiona's practice, but put that down too and stood up. 'I don't want to talk to a counsellor. I want to talk to a friend,' she said out loud. Then she opened the door, walked into the kitchen and threw her arms around Justin.

'Oh, hello,' he said. 'You do know I'm gay, don't you? I mean I've known you for ten years so I assumed you'd worked it out. And my boyfriend is called Rod.'

Miriam laughed. 'Did I scare you? I'm just really glad you're here, because it's all gone a bit weird.'

'Do tell.' He grabbed his car keys. 'But time is getting on, and we need to buy some food for tomorrow's *soiree*.'

'I got hit on the head with a kite and I thought I heard my mother talking to me, and then there was her laugh, or it may have been the wind.' She followed him out towards the car.

Justin frowned and felt her forehead. 'No ... no fever. So, either you're going mad or you're being haunted.'

'Oh, ha ha,' muttered Miriam. But somewhere in the back of her mind, she wondered if he was right. Maybe she *was* going mad. Because she definitely did not believe in ghosts. Just memories.

'Miriam ... Miriam?' Justin was knocking on her bedroom door again. 'Have you finished your yoga yet? It's just—'

She dropped onto the floor mid-plank and lay head-first on the mat. 'I have now,' she muttered.

'It's just that the pink dressing-gown has re-appeared again ... but with someone else wearing it.'

She rolled over and looked at the ceiling. *This is what happened with Artie Morgan*, she thought. I *got involved when I was looking for some comfort ... that's all. Had to deal with the consequences when I was not at my best. And now ... here he is ... and I've gone and done it again. For goodness sake, Miriam.*

'Miriam?' Justin tapped on the door again.

'I'll be there in a minute. I know who it is ... probably.'

'Okay. I'll keep out of the way then. Although I'll be listening at the door.'

She stood up and caught her reflection in the mirror. Her face was red, her hair untidy and there were sweat marks under her arms. She gritted her teeth. 'Perfect,' she growled, and headed downstairs. *I am going to be cool, I am going to be calm, and he will not know how angry and upset I am.*

Alan was buttering some toast as she walked in. 'Hi,' he said and sat down

Miriam paused in the doorway. 'Hi.'

They looked at each other in silence for a few moments.

'Miriam—'

'How could you! How could you! What makes you think you can treat me like that?'

Alan looked confused. 'What do you mean?'

'And you're wearing that dressing-gown,' Miriam shouted.

'Yes, it's my dressing gown, and I was cold. What—?'

'I know it was just sex, Alan, but ...'

He took a bite of toast and chewed it angrily. 'Well, when I woke up, it was *you* who had already gone. So, as far as saying "it's just sex" goes, maybe I could throw the same thing at you.'

'I wasn't talking about that.'

He stood up and pushed the chair away, the legs scraping noisily along the floor.

'Oh, but you did do that. So I could ask how could *you* leave early, then only talk to me from the safety of the decking?'

Miriam folded her arms. 'You only made it halfway across the garden anyway, and I wasn't talking about *that*.'

'What are you talking about?'

'That dressing-gown ...' She trailed off, not wanting to say it, because all the hurt she'd felt when Artie Morgan's wife had told her he was married at a public event when she was standing in front of her new food truck, was waiting in the pit of her stomach to re-emerge, but this time not entangled with all the other stuff.

'I still don't know.' He looked at her, his expression set hard.

Miriam didn't like it; she longed for his kind eyes and smiling face. She glanced at the floor, not wanting to say it because when she did, it would make it real – and that would be the end for them. Although, it was just physical, so it wouldn't be the end of very much. *Would it?*

'Britta,' she said quietly, then looked up.

His face was furrowed. 'Britta?' he said slowly.

'Britta.' The anger began to grow. 'Your ex-wife was here in your dressing-gown. Looking for you …'

'What the hell did she want?'

'Well, she said you were pretty close, even now, so why don't you ask her?'

'Pretty close?' Alan stared at the ceiling in silence for a few moments whilst Miriam bit her lip, struggling to keep quiet.

'And Jim,' she blurted out. 'He said the same thing, or something like it, and goodness knows, I'm no angel, no spring chicken, know what the world is like, *and* I'm leaving here soon … but how could you?' Miriam felt tears prick at the back of her eyes and began to get angry with herself for being so upset.

He looked at her again, shaking his head. 'It's not what you think.'

Miriam stepped back. All she could see was Artie bloody Morgan standing next to the food truck he'd sold her months before. '*It's not that sort of marriage, Miriam … come on, we're all adults here.*'

'Miriam?' *Was it him, or Alan she could hear?* 'Miriam? Are you all right?'

Justin prodded her in the back and the kitchen came into focus again.

'Yes, well, I've heard that before.' Her voice felt thin, like it was about to break, and she turned and rushed up the stairs, as if running away from Alan would help her run away from her past.

'Cup of tea?' she heard Justin say.

'Who are you?'

'Justin ... an old friend.'

'And what are you doing here?'

'Just visiting, you know – so, milk and sugar?'

Miriam closed her bedroom door and climbed into bed, staring at the ceiling. 'I don't want to feel this. I don't want to think about this. I can't ...' She put on her headphones and switched on the meditation app Fiona had advised her to use.

'Take some deep breaths ... count to three, then out to four. '

She repeated the words over and over again until her breathing had calmed down and the image had disappeared. Laying there for a few minutes, the sound of laughter erupted from downstairs, drawing her up and out of her room. She paused for a few moments, listening to the murmur of conversation, then pulled herself to her full height, put on a fake smile and carried on into the kitchen.

'Right. Any tea left in the pot, Justin?' She pulled out a chair and sat down, trying not to make eye contact with either of them.

'Common or garden English breakfast, boss, or a herbal concoction of some kind,' he said, switching on the kettle and staring out of the window rather than at the table where Miriam and Alan were sitting.

'English breakfast, please.'

'So, Justin was telling me about your company.' Alan leaned forward. 'It meant a lot to you, didn't it?'

'Yes, yes,' she said briskly. 'It was like a family to me.'

'Must have been hard letting it go.'

She longed to touch his hand, but somewhere inside she felt rigid, unable to bend – the only way she knew how to protect herself.

'Well.' She looked at him. 'New chapter. Had to be done.'

Justin put the mug of hot tea in front of her. 'She made it an employee-owned trust, so that all her staff became shareholders, and Felix, who always does the right thing, is now in charge. So, she looked after everyone. Didn't you? It took a lot out of her. A long story and one that Miriam will tell you one day, I'm sure. Now—' he took a gulp of water '—I'm going to go for a run and leave you two … to it.' He stood at the door. 'I'm sure you have a lot to catch up on.'

Miriam heard him hurry up the stairs and picked up the tea.

'I'm impressed you managed to look after all your staff before you sold your business, said Alan eventually. 'And I meant it. It's not what you think, me and Britta. She is very definitely my ex-wife.'

Miriam looked at her mug. 'Well, we are all adults here, Alan. It was just rather unexpected to see her in that—' she pointed at his dressing-gown '—unannounced in my kitchen.'

He sighed. 'She's after me to …' He looked up at her. 'I didn't mean she's after me. She wants me to be … more … present – because of the twins, although they're adults now really … the books we wrote together years ago. And Stargazing and Sandcastles. Our event.'

'Are you saying that there is nothing between you? Emotionally or … physically?'

'There is nothing between us—' he paused '—emotionally, apart from our children.'

Miriam picked up a spoon and began to stir the tea. 'And physically?'

Alan scratched his chin. 'Physically …'

'Please don't tell me you're sleeping with her. I mean you literally just—'

'I want to be honest with you, Miriam.'

The pit of her stomach felt suddenly heavy. Part of her didn't want him to be honest with her.

'There was an … occasional … but not recently. That's gone. It's long gone.'

'And when you say recently?' Miriam wanted to stop herself, but it was as if someone else was talking with her voice.

Alan pushed the chair back and stood up. 'I don't keep a diary.'

'Right …'

'I don't believe this.' He opened the kitchen door.

Miriam looked at him. 'Frankly, neither do I,' she said as he slammed it behind him.

'Oh dear,' Justin said from the hallway. 'That didn't go terribly well?'

'I'm going for a drive.' Miriam stood up. 'Don't worry, I'll be back to help with the meal.' She began to stomp up the stairs. 'That I don't want to cook. Because I was here to get away from all of that.' She slammed her bedroom door behind her. 'No responsibility, no caring about anyone. *Anyone!*' She watched Justin from the window as he started his jog, glanced at her journal and picked it up. Then she put it down, changed into her gym gear and ran off in the opposite direction to Justin.

'Go easy with the chopping. It's a bit aggressive.'

Miriam carried on cutting the peppers as quickly and as noisily as she could, taking pleasure in the constant crack of the knife on the chopping board. 'I'm just doing what I always did. Head down and work.'

'Mmmm … well, I hope you're going to be a bit less frightening when your guests arrive.' Justin cut a cherry tomato in half and popped it in his mouth.

'Stop eating the stock,' she muttered.

'I know, I'll put on some music.' He connected his phone to the speaker and held out his hand. 'This should calm you down. Now put down the knife!'

Miriam smiled. 'Am I being that bad?'

'Yes. He's really got to you. Mind you, I can see why. Good taste, by the way.'

'It's not just him …' The soothing tones of 'The Girl from Ipanema' began to fill the room, and Justin pulled her to him, slowly moving her around the room in time to the music.

'Oh, the nights we spent partying in Brazil.' He sighed. 'I've got a whole playlist of this stuff.' He held her face and looked into her eyes. 'So you *will* be calm.'

Miriam burst out laughing and he twirled her around, spinning her and jigging around the table. As she moved, she caught a glimpse of Alan watching from the garden, but when she next looked, he had gone. It was at that point that the doorbell rang.

Miriam adjusted her dress. 'Must be the entertainment. Whoever that may be.'

Justin checked the spreadsheet. 'Oh, yes. AC?'

Mary the Harp was standing on the doorstep without her harp, her face covered in white make-up and black marks. 'Oh, hello.' Miriam stood back to let her in. 'Are you okay? You look a bit— ?'

'I got half ready before I left the house. Takes too long otherwise. Kids keep interrupting.' In one hand was a pull-along suitcase, and in the other was a pull-along sound system. 'Don't do this one very often ... oh, hello.'

Justin was busy making a salad.

'This is Justin. An old friend.'

'Lucky you,' muttered Mary.

'No, he's not ...' Miriam couldn't be bothered to explain. 'He's helping me this evening.'

'Nice to meet you.' He flashed her a smile and she beamed back. 'Nice make-up. Are you AC?'

Miriam poured a glass of wine and handed it to her.

Mary took it and drank it in one gulp. 'Yep. Alice Cooper I am tonight. Just got to put the wig and the clothes on, and I'll be set. Just got to remember to talk with a deep voice throughout and no one will know I'm a girl.'

'A woman of many talents,' said Miriam, pouring herself a glass of wine and taking a long gulp herself.

'Listening to a bit of Latin, are you? My brother does Ricky Martin at some of the holiday parks. He'll be at the Look-Alike Festival next week.' Mary grabbed her suitcase. 'I'll get changed in the bathroom and then get set up.'

Justin grabbed the bottle from Miriam and poured himself a glass. 'Think it's going to be that kind of night, isn't it?' He held it up. 'Cheers,' he said. 'Life with you is never dull.'

'I sort of wanted it to be for a while,' said Miriam, getting back to the food preparation. She took another sip of wine. 'It's a fraught day, and I'm not sure even this is taking the edge off.'

As they were dressing the table in the dining room, Mary jumped in from the hall. 'School's out!' she shouted. Then a bit lower, waving her arms about threateningly. 'School's out ... oh, that's better. Got to practise a bit to get my pitch right.'

Justin began to clap. 'It's as if Alice is in the room!' He laughed as they heard chattering outside the house.

Miriam sighed and closed her eyes. 'Back into Miriam of old,' she said quietly, walking to the door as Mary hid in the kitchen and Justin waited behind her to greet the guests.

'Welcome,' she said, her smile wide, her voice upbeat and professional, whilst her heart began to race uncomfortably again. 'Joanna has taken a last-minute trip, and I'm looking after the house whilst she's gone. She is absolutely fine, I believe.'

'Oh, I hope she's all right,' said the woman at the front. 'We did this last year and it was fabulous.'

'Hope it's as good then,' muttered a man from the back of the group.

Justin touched Miriam's arm. 'Miriam was the owner of a very successful events and catering company until quite recently, so you can rest assured that the quality will be maintained.'

Miriam sighed. Difficult customers were part and parcel of dealing with the public. But she didn't want to deal with the public. That was one of the many things she had been trying to escape from by hiding out in this house. She could feel the anxiety and anger trickling quietly around her body, so she walked into the kitchen and shut the door before they could take her over.

Justin walked in behind her. 'I'll take care of this, boss. Just concentrate on the cooking. I'll do the schmoozing.'

Turning up the music, she fell back into the comfort zone she had been running from and began to assemble the food, fighting with the urge to throw it in a bin, get in the car and drive away. But she had signed a contract, and that picture of Artie Morgan had got into her head again, and she would *not* lower herself to his level.

Justin opened the door. 'Honestly, me and Alice Cooper can look after everything. You look terrible.'

Miriam took the oven gloves off and hung them up. 'Thanks very much!' she said, taking a new bottle of wine from the fridge. 'But, as it's a lovely evening, I'm going to hide outside for a while.'

She could see Alan's frame moving around in the summerhouse as she walked outside, and paused, wanting with every fibre of her body to run over there and cling to him. But … she couldn't trust him. Because, somewhere in the back of her mind, the past was hovering, and it stood like a barrier between them. After a while, he walked into the garden, nodded at her coldly and climbed into the car. She watched him drive away and went back into the house, sneaking up the stairs unnoticed, overwhelmed by sadness.

Chapter Seventeen

In the pitch-black room Miriam sat bolt upright, half awake, the shadows of her dreams not quite gone. She climbed out of bed in a panic and fumbled towards the window, eventually finding the fairy lights on the sill. She switched them on, the tiny pink flowers glowing comfortingly, and she began to calm down. The moon glowed, throwing a triangle of light over the black sea, still and hypnotic. The nightmare slowly ebbed away, swallowed by the new lustre in the room, and she climbed back into bed, sinking into a deep, comfortable sleep.

The alarm woke her that morning as the sun seeped along the floor, climbed up the walls and onto the bed. Miriam rubbed her eyes, pushing away the memories she still carried from the previous night. 'Today,' she said out loud. 'Today is the day we finalise everything for the Look-Alike Festival, and I am a mess. A pure gold, eighteen-carat, top-notch absolute bloody mess. Not for the first time.'

She leaned over and tried unsuccessfully to find her slippers, then gave up, got out of bed and went to the bathroom, where she found them in the shower. Putting them on, Miriam made her way down to the kitchen, hearing the click of a kettle being switched on and the clattering of crockery. Half hoping it was Alan and half hoping it wasn't, she opened the door. Justin was pouring some milk into a mug.

'You could look happier to see me,' he said.

'I am!' Miriam put a tea bag in a cup and threw some boiling water over it. 'Sorry I disappeared last night. I just …' She sat down and looked at the ceiling. '*Ahhhhhh* ... bloody …!'

Justin leaned forward and touched her hand. 'I know,' he said softly.

'You know how I got before. *Please* tell me I'm not getting like that again.'

'Not at all. It's just like …' He thought for a moment. 'An echo, that's right. Of what happened.'

She smiled. 'Good word. It feels like that.' Miriam took a sip of her tea. 'I don't want it to swallow me up like it did then.'

'It didn't,' he said quickly 'You just forget that you're a human being and not a robot.' Justin opened the door to the decking and they sat for a while in silence. Miriam replayed her mental film of the past in her head to a soundtrack of birdsong and distant waves, and the dew lay on the grass like a sea of crystals illuminating the lawn.

'What a mess it was.' She sighed. 'I was going to return to my cooking roots and drive to festivals.' Miriam laughed. '*Me*! I'd got to the stage where I didn't even like picking up a saucepan!'

'We all have our dreams.' Justin stood up. 'Want another cuppa?'

'No thanks.' She put her cup down and folded her arms.

Justin walked into the kitchen, filled the kettle with water and put it on.

'He was so charming. Such fun. So easy … and I thought why not?' Miriam shivered. 'You know when things aren't good, and you get into that mindset, and then you make a bad decision, and then another one and—'

'Very perceptive.' Justin stood in the doorway, waiting for the kettle to boil.

'I've had a lot of counselling … I —' A car door slammed shut outside, and they watched Alan attach a surfboard to the roof.

'He's not him though.'

Miriam stood up. 'No. But he does have an ex-wife who wears his pink dressing-gown.' Stepping inside, she rinsed the mug and put it on the draining board. 'I'm going for a run, then we've got to go through everything for the festival … and, at some point today, I have to tell my solicitor to go ahead and find someone else to do this till Joanna gets back.'

And this time, I mean it, she thought as she closed the kitchen door behind her.

She walked out into the sunlight and put on her headphones, ready to run to a soundtrack beginning with 'Born to Be Wild' to block out her thoughts, and everything and anyone else. Opening the front gate, she turned left towards the village, fighting the urge to run towards the sea and to Alan and his surfboard. The breeze lifted her slightly as she began to move. She followed the gulls swooping high in the sky in the distance, her feet pounding on the ground, pushing all the tension out and sending it towards the ocean to be carried off by the tides till it was nothing but water.

She stopped at the harbour wall for a rest, watching a fisherman unload his catch into a van, the nets piled high on his boat. She took out her phone. Opening her e-mails, she found the message from the solicitors, clicked on reply and typed

Please look for someone to replace me until the end of the tenancy. Terms as discussed.

This is it, Miriam thought. *Once this is done, you are going.* Her finger hovered over the send button as a car drove past and stopped just outside the newsagents on the opposite side of the road. A young woman got out and opened the passenger door. 'Oh, lovely boy, come to Mummy,' she said, picking up a baby who was crying plaintively. 'Come on,' she almost sang, rocking backwards and forwards. 'Mummy's here.' The baby continued to sob, so she started to sing softly.

Miriam could hardly work out what the song was, the sound was so faint, but something about it oozed contentment. She put her phone away, the message still unsent, and listened. '*Que sera sera*,' sang the woman. The film in her head clicked briefly to life. '*Que sera sera,*' sang Miriam's mother, bending down and holding out a spoon covered in thick and creamy cake mix, singing that song and laughing and telling her everything would be all right.

The car door slammed and Miriam realised she wasn't at home but on the harbour wall, watching the mother and baby drive off into the distance. She wanted them to come back and sing again, so she could feel as safe and secure as she had in that kitchen with her mother happily baking and her father poring over astronomy charts at the table.

She sighed, unsure what to do, feeling somehow like the fish caught in the nets piled on the fishing boat.

Justin was putting his suitcase in his car when she arrived back. 'I'm so sorry,' he shouted, waving his phone at her. 'Bit of an emergency with some finance for our new business. I've got to head up to London.'

Miriam sat on the garden wall and smiled, despite the anxious knot taking root in her stomach. 'Oh, goodness, yes. You've got to sort that out. It's your future.'

He sat next to her and put his arm around her. 'Everything is organised for the festival. You just have to do a bit of cooking. And whether you like it or not, you are very good at that.'

She squeezed his hand and lay her head on his shoulder. 'I know. This is the strangest holiday I've ever had though.'

'I wish I could be here for it. Mary, AKA Alice Cooper, is going to be there. Apparently she'll be Jennifer Lopez.'

'Quite the chameleon.' Miriam giggled.

211

'No, that would be Boy George. Her husband and his brothers are going as Culture Club.'

Justin's phone buzzed and he looked at the message. 'Rod's getting a little frantic. I'll call him in the car. Speak to Jim. You'll have all the help you need – and I'll be back, because this is all a bit bonkers and I can't stay away.' He kissed her on the cheek, jumped into the car and switched on the engine. '*Adios*, and until next time,' he shouted. 'Oh, and I've booked that food truck from the beach for the festival. You're welcome.' Then he revved loudly and tore out onto the road.

'The food truck? Why?' Miriam felt the anxiety begin to ooze into her body again. 'I can't get upset every time I have to deal with a food truck at work,' she muttered furiously. She listened as the roar of the engine got quieter and quieter until she could picture Justin at the other end of the village, climbing the hill up to the main road. She was angry with herself for finding excuses not to send the e-mail to her solicitors. She could just go. *No she couldn't. Because she was Miriam Ryan, former MD of her very own successful company, and walking out on her responsibilities was something she never did.* She stood up and pretended to kick the wall just as Alan drove past, misjudged the distance, and accidentally made contact with it. 'Oh, ow,' she screamed, then hopped inside the house to put some ice on her toes. 'Bloody idiot,' she shouted. 'I really am.'

Alan knocked on the kitchen window. 'Are you okay?' he said loudly. Miriam's leg was already propped up on a chair, with a packet of frozen peas she'd discovered at the back of the freezer on her foot.

'Yes,' she shouted, nodding.

'Can I come in?' he mouthed, and something inside Miriam broke a little, longing for the days when he'd use her fridge as if it was his own.

'Of course,' she said brightly and waved her right arm around to indicate he should open the door.

He stepped inside and hovered awkwardly. 'I saw you by the wall, and I wanted to know if you are okay – both physically ... and mentally.'

'Short term answer is no on both counts. I am on the mend though.' She adjusted the peas and moved her leg slightly.

'Justin not around to help?'

'No. There was an emergency.' The hairs on Alan's chest were peeping over the top of his T-shirt again, and Miriam tried not to stare, thankful she wasn't able to move any closer and also glad her rational self was currently in control.

'Oh.' He took a step further into the room. 'Would you like me to order a takeaway?'

Miriam bit her lip, trying to swallow the words "would you like to keep me company?" that were about to jump out. 'That's kind,' she said instead.

'Right, you decide and let me know. I've arranged to meet Jim at the pub in an hour, so I'll get it delivered to the door. If you can't hobble there, just text me and I'll move it before I go.'

'I'll have menu two from the Chinese takeaway. I know it off by heart. It's over there,' she said quickly.

'Great!' he said enthusiastically, picking up the leaflet from the restaurant. 'I'll order it now and ... have it on me, you know ... seeing as you are indisposed.'

'Thank you.' Miriam could feel her voice getting weaker as she spoke.

'Right. I'll be off then. Like I said—'

'I'll let you know if I can't get to the door.' She held up her phone. 'This is within easy reach.'

He nodded then turned and walked into the garden. Miriam watched his back as he went, words ricocheting around her head.

What's the matter with you? Get a grip. She put her head in her hands but the movement dislodged the peas, and she had to stop herself banging the table in frustration. Instead, she sat in silence for five minutes as the clock ticked on the wall.

Deciding she wanted a cup of tea, Miriam tried to stand up, balancing precariously on one leg, but she couldn't reach the worktop to help her move, so sat down again instead then slid slowly onto the floor, shuffling over to the kettle, determinedly pulling herself up to a standing position. Switching the kettle on, she leaned over to open the fridge door to take out the milk, grabbed a mug from the cupboard and took a tea bag from the jar, then made her drink. The cutlery drawer was too far away, so she sloshed the contents of the mug around for a moment and drank it with the tea bag still in.

'Still got it,' she said to the bottle of milk on the counter. 'I remember the day early on in my career. Felix forgot to bring the corkscrew to one of our first events and I ended up having to stab the corks with the wrong end of a fork until they fell into the bottles. Made pouring the wine a bit difficult, and a lot ended up on my T-shirt. But, hey, I did it …'

The doorbell rang and she glanced at the clock. 'That was quick,' she muttered. Her phone lay on the kitchen table, ready to summon Alan's help. But she pulled herself up to her full height, shouted, 'I'll only be a minute,' sank to the floor and shuffled slowly to the front door, still shouting 'A minute, honestly … I'm on my way,' every few seconds. Grabbing the windowsill, she managed to stand up, opened the door and smiled at a confused looking delivery man, who handed her the takeaway and rushed off. 'Sorry,' she said, waving as he got into the car. 'Just a couple of issues I had to deal with.' Closing the door, she sat down and faced the kitchen, contemplating the long journey back. Then she lay the cartons in front of her, took out the wooden knife and fork,

214

ate her meal in the hallway before doing a three-legged crawl to the living room, where she spent the rest of the evening laying on the sofa watching TV.

Chapter Eighteen

'Miriam?' Rhiannon's voice was quiet but stern. Miriam rolled over and almost fell off the sofa.

'Oh God,' she muttered. 'Did I sleep here all night?'

'Yes, you did.' Rhiannon was standing in the doorway. 'Why are there half eaten takeaway cartons in the hall?' she said, with distaste clear in her voice.

'Um … I hurt my foot?' Miriam had no idea why she sounded like she was asking a question. Maybe it was because she couldn't quite believe she had sunk so low.

'Well, *ych a fi* – that means yuck in Welsh.'

They looked at each other for a few moments until Rhiannon burst out laughing. 'I mean, what has Ms High Powered Businesswoman come to?'

Miriam sat up and began to laugh too. 'I know. Honestly …' She felt her foot and tried to stand up on it. 'Oh, not too bad. I accidentally kicked the wall yesterday … no, don't ask.'

'Right, well, I'll clean up this mess.' Rhiannon disappeared into the hallway. 'And then we have to make a plan for this Look-Alike Festival.'

'Are you helping me cook?'

'Yes, but I'm not talking about that. We have to decide who we're going as.' Rhiannon bustled into the kitchen. Miriam followed her slowly, checking the weight on her foot with every step.

'I'm just going as the person who's providing some of the food.' Miriam sank into a kitchen chair and watched Rhiannon throw the cartons into the bin.

'Oh no. I'm going to be *very* visible.' She put the kettle on and took some mugs out of the cupboard. 'Not for Jim, but for me. I intend to have a *very* good time.'

'I think I want to lay low,' Miriam muttered, not wanting to get involved in any kind of drama with Alan and Britta. She just wanted to do the job and get out of the way.

'We can work dressed as look-alikes. We don't have to be in the actual event, just enter into the spirit of it.' Rhiannon sat opposite her and smiled. 'Go on! It'll be fun.'

Miriam sighed. 'Did you have anyone in mind?'

'I love *Grease,* I do, so I thought the Pink Ladies. I've found a website we can hire the costumes from.'

She saw Alan walk across the garden towards the kitchen, and her stomach suddenly filled with butterflies. 'Maybe hiding as a Pink Lady would be a good thing,' she said quietly as Alan knocked on the kitchen door.

'Can I come in?' he said.

Rhiannon stared at her. 'When did he start asking permission to come in here?'

Miriam waved him in. 'Of course.'

'Just wanted to check your foot was okay.' He leaned against a kitchen worktop and folded his arms. 'And you enjoyed the takeaway?'

'All fine here,' Miriam said briskly and stood up slowly. 'Look, almost brand new.' She could see Rhiannon scrutinising them both.

'Good.' He turned to go. 'I'm going to speak to Jim about the festival. And we have to have a meeting about the Stargazing and Sandcastles event. Which is soon. Very soon, indeed.'

'Another event?' The knot re-emerged in Miriam's stomach. 'I'd forgotten about that.'

'Not too much work for you, to be honest. But there will be a marquee in the garden. And a sandcastle competition on the beach.'

'Oh.' Miriam tried to smile. 'Yes, well, let me know when it's convenient to talk about it and we'll get a date in the diary.'

'Right. Then. Okay.' He closed the door behind him and strode back to the summerhouse.

'Something's been going on between you two, hasn't it?' Rhiannon said slowly.

'What do you mean?' Miriam opened the kitchen door and hobbled out. 'I want to sit in the sun,' she said.

'The atmosphere. You could have cut it with a knife. You two have, haven't you?'

'Have what?' Miriam sat down at the patio table and Rhiannon followed.

'Well, I'm not going to spell it out.'

'Okay. Yes, we did sleep together. But it was a mistake.'

'Never!' Rhiannon almost jumped up. 'I knew you would, I did.'

'Well, it turns out it was nothing. He has an ex-wife, and it appears they have unresolved issues.'

'Oh no. Are you okay?'

'Yes. It was just a physical thing.'

'Right …'

Alan walked out of the summerhouse and headed towards his car.

'What a bastard,' Rhiannon said eventually.

Miriam laughed. 'Yes and no. Why don't you show me these costumes? Oh, wait.' The alarm on her phone buzzed. 'I've got an appointment, sorry. Why don't you send me the link?'

'No need. I've actually ordered them already. Yours will be arriving today, I think. Hope I got the size right.' She stood up and hugged Miriam. 'You poor dab. Nasty man. Bye.' Then she disappeared back into the house.

Miriam heard the front door slam and picked up her phone. She messaged Fiona, cancelling the counselling appointment, and shuffled to the kitchen. She was fed up of talking about herself. She just wanted to get everything done, fulfil her responsibilities and get away from all of it.

Making her way to the attic room, she sat for a while gazing at the horizon through the telescope, watching windsurfers skip across the waves in the bay, as two speedboats hummed around the headland and a hang glider hovered like a bird close to the beach. *Oh to be free*, she thought, *of my brain*. Eventually, she stood up and started to go through the boxes of photographs. 'I know you're in here, I know you are.' She scrutinised picture after picture – happy memories of Joanna's life from when she was a child, surrounded by people, laughing and smiling. *Who are you, Joanna?* she wondered, *and why did you leave so suddenly?*

Then she found a photo of Joanna standing by a barbecue wearing an apron and holding a set of meat tongs, and laughed. 'Joanna. I think you are probably like me. You wanted to run away, but you had to make sure everyone was all right before you did!'

The light began to wane as the sun moved west, throwing lines of shadow across the wooden floor. And that's when she saw it. A grainy photocopy of a photograph. A group of people were playing cricket on the beach – her mother, her father, Joanna, a tall, handsome fair man standing next to another younger man, and Miriam.

'I knew it,' she shouted to a seagull perched outside. 'I just knew it.' Then she sat down and pored over it, trying to bring the scene to life. But she couldn't. It was still just a static photograph

219

of her parents that froze them in time. The kind she had hundreds of.

Although, she thought, *there's a connection to this house. Maybe I'm not being haunted. It's just, as they say, my imagination.* Then she tidied everything away, went downstairs, picked up her phone and sat in the garden, scrolling through the videos.

'Right. Let's face this,' she muttered. 'I don't want to be caught in this net any more.'

Pressing play, she forced herself to watch.

Miriam saw the phone being handed to someone. 'Can you record this?' she heard herself say. 'I've pressed the button.' Then she came into view, standing next to Artie in front of the food truck she had just bought from him. He put his arm around her waist and posed for the camera. Miriam felt sick. She was watching herself in the middle of throwing everything that was important to her away.

'This is my new adventure.' She laughed. 'And what better organisation to take over my company than yours.' She dramatically pointed at a large digital clock on the wall behind them. 'In just half an hour, we'll have signed the paperwork and MR Events will belong to Artie Morgan.' She giggled and turned to him. 'That's you.' Then she moved back and kissed the truck and laughed again, just as Justin rushed forward and whispered something in her ear, handing her a piece of paper.

Miriam watched, her heart heavy, as she saw herself read it, then turn to Artie, visibly shocked and angry. She couldn't hear what she was saying, but she knew the words off by heart. 'You're married?'

His expression stayed the same as if this was a well-trodden path. 'It's not that kind of marriage. We're all grown-ups here.'

'And you're going to get rid of all of my staff. Justin's just been sent some paperwork.' Miriam was trying not to shout, her face rigid with a forced smile. Because what the video didn't show was that the rest of the warehouse was full of people attending the high-profile event her company was running.

He smiled, and she repeated his words in her head. '*It's business, Miriam. That's all. It's not personal.*'

She watched herself step back. 'It is personal. To me. To my staff ... they're like my family. No.'

Then Miriam took a breath, bracing herself for what was about to happen.

A woman rushed into shot, pushing Artie against the truck. Her words were muffled but Miriam remembered them, word for word.

'What the hell are you doing now? Another affair? And you couldn't even keep this one quiet. Humiliating me in front of everyone. Who the hell is she anyway?'

The filming stopped and the screen went blank. Miriam looked up at the roses bursting with colour around the garden, the trees heavy with leaves in the summer evening sunlight, and almost gulped in the fresh air. She felt like she was drowning. Because that's what had happened. She'd stopped the sale of the company and got caught up in the kind of legal mess you get into when something is personal.

Scrolling through her photographs, she found one of them both at a networking meeting a few weeks earlier. They were shaking hands: Miriam in her designer power suit, hair sleek and styled, poised and confident. Their time together was brief, but she had clung on to it, her need to escape from the reality of her life overriding everything.

And when she finally got it all back and then handed it over to Felix, she'd had to run away.

And yet, here she was

'I found this on the doorstep.' Alan was walking towards her and stood on the grass, as if there was an invisible barrier between him and the decking. He put a parcel on the table. 'Are you all right? You look exhausted.'

'Oh.' Miriam looked at the floor. 'I was having a bit of a flashback.'

He moved closer. 'I was going to ask if we could talk, but if whatever you're thinking about is making you look like that, maybe we'd better leave it till another day.' He turned and walked quickly back to the summerhouse.

'Oh, thanks,' muttered Miriam to his back as he shut the door behind him. 'You're a great help.' She opened the parcel and pulled out the Pink Lady costume Rhiannon had ordered, then stood up and held it up in front of her. *Maybe I'll be someone else for a while*, she thought and went back into the house to try it on.

Admiring herself in the mirror, Miriam found 'Summer Nights' on her phone and began to play it, putting on lipstick and pouting as she sang along, deciding to spend the evening in the costume just to get used to it.

She was microwaving a ready-made lasagne when Alan knocked on the kitchen door again.

'Come in. You don't have to knock all the time.'

He stood in the doorway and laughed. 'If I'd known it was fancy dress tea-time, I'd have come prepared.'

Miriam sat down and looked at him. 'Is there anything in particular you wanted to talk about? You said you wanted to chat earlier.'

'I don't know how to talk to you,' he said quickly. 'After, you know … we—'

'I don't know how to talk to you either.' Miriam began to cut up her lasagne, a raft of butterflies suddenly flitting around her stomach nervously.

'I just can't cope with this,' he muttered. 'You and your face, and your eyes and your legs and—'

'What about you and your face and your legs and your chest and—' Miriam stood up. 'What am I supposed to do with you being here all the time with—' she pointed at him '—all that?'

They took a step closer to each other, their words hanging in the air. Then another step. 'So,' she whispered.

'So,' he said, taking her hand and pulling her to him.

'Miriam? Miriam!' Rhiannon's voice cut through the music as they lay on the slate floor. Someone was singing 'Look at Me, I'm Sandra Dee', and they had started to giggle like children.

'Oh, bloody hell.' Alan rolled over and began to collect his clothes as Miriam pulled on her costume. 'Don't want to explain this really.'

They could hear her push the front door open. 'You should lock that, you know!' whispered Alan, jumping to his feet, as Miriam pretended to look for something on the floor.

'I'm not sure about the Pink Ladies now. I thought I could go as Britney Spears.'

Miriam bit her lip and tried not to laugh as Rhiannon looked at them both and raised her eyebrows. 'Talking now, are we?'

Alan backed towards the door. 'Got to go. Lovely to see you, Rhi.'

'Alan … Alan?' Britta's voice floated over the garden from outside the summerhouse. 'I know you're in there. We need to talk.'

Miriam looked at Alan and held onto the table, feeling as if the floor was being pulled out from under her. 'No ... I believed you. I *wanted* to believe you.'

'It's not what you think. I told you!'

She stood up, controlling her fury, and pushed him firmly out of the door, closing it behind him. 'Go and deal with your ex-wife.' Then she sat down at the table, head in hands.

Rhiannon sat opposite her and put her phone down. After a moment's silence, it began to play 'Oops! ... I Did It Again'. She paused. 'I think it's wine o-clock,' she said, eventually.

Miriam shook her head and laughed, unable to speak – angry, sad and confused. She wanted to run away. As usual. Instead, she clicked into professional mode, burying her feelings, also as usual. 'None for me,' she said, holding her hand up in front of her. 'It's the festival tomorrow, so we've got an early start.'

Rhiannon poured herself a glass. 'Only one for me then.' She looked out of the window. 'I don't know what they're saying, but it looks like an argument from where I'm sitting.'

'Leave them to it.' Miriam grabbed the festival folder and moved her laptop onto the table. 'I'm going to go through everything to make sure we know what's arriving and when.'

'I got an invitation to go for a walk on the coastal path for tomorrow. It's a work thing – they said there might be a pod of dolphins around. Starting at Solva. I said no, of course. Wouldn't leave you in the lurch.'

'Thank you. I honestly don't know what I'd do if you couldn't come.' Miriam leaned forward and squeezed Rhiannon's hand.

'All that romping with Alan has made you soppy.' She finished her wine. 'Come on, boss. Read me all these food lists then.'

They heard a door bang in the distance. Miriam didn't look up. 'Think they've finished their discussion by the sounds of it,' said Rhiannon.

Chapter Nineteen

The alarm went off at half six, and for a moment Miriam forgot where she was, her mind fuzzy and scrabbling for clues. Pinpricks of sun dotted the floor, lilting birdsong and the roar of the sea slowly bringing her round.

She picked up her phone and checked it, trying to work out why, for the first time in nearly three months, she had decided she needed to get up at a particular time. Then she heard a lorry pull up outside the house and the sound of something being unloaded.

'Oh God, yes. Festival day and deliveries.' She climbed out of bed and opened the window, waving at the delivery driver. 'I'll be down in a minute,' she shouted, then she put on her dressing-gown and ran down the stairs, flung open the door, took the delivery sheet from the driver, checking she had the right fruit and vegetables. She was surprised at how quickly she had slipped into work mode.

The driver helped her carry them into the kitchen and after he'd gone, she made herself a cup of tea and walked outside, drawn to the bench at the end of the garden with Joanna's initials on it. The sky was a clear, cloudless blue, the sun already warming the ground. She kicked off her slippers and brushed her feet along the dewy blades of grass, letting them tickle her toes, and watched as a chaffinch flitted between the branches of a tree.

She closed her eyes and began to meditate, the way she had begun to every day of her working life until last year. When she had lost the focus to do even that, she smiled to herself, glad she was finding something of her old self, even if it was just breathing slowly and thinking about waves.

After a while, Miriam made her way back to the kitchen, glancing at the summerhouse for clues. *Was Britta in there?*

Would Alan really be that *awful? But where did she go last night?*
The pile of crates brought the task ahead into focus, and she
pushed her confusion to the back of her mind, made her breakfast,
had a shower and got to work. She put the radio on in the
background to help her concentrate.

All the deliveries arrived within the hour, so when Rhiannon
walked in and put the kettle on, Miriam was already in full flow.

'Impressive,' she said. 'Just a warning. I'm not a professional.
I'm an amateur. And not even an enthusiastic one.'

Miriam kissed her cheek. 'Enthusiastic enough for me,' she
said. 'Tie your hair back, wash your hands and get to work.'

'Well, you're in a good mood, despite the drama of last
night.'

'Meditation,' said Miriam. 'I've got work to do, and I can't let
someone else's tangled love life interfere with the task in hand.'

'And that is why Miriam Ryan was the MD of a very
successful company, ladies and gentlemen.' Rhiannon passed her
a mug of tea and waved hers in the air. 'Cheers, my dear.'

'Onions are over there. Can you start chopping?' Miriam gave
her a knife and a chopping board.

'Ooh, I feel like I'm on *MasterChef*. What are we making?'

'My special chilli con carne to start off with, then Sri Lankan
style vegetarian curry, rice, Greek salad, and salmon with ginger
and potato wedges.

'All of that?' Rhiannon sat down. 'Tired thinking of it, I am.'

'It's all easy. It's the kind of thing Felix and I used to make
when we toured festivals with our van back in the day.' Miriam
moved the knife and chopping board in front of her. 'There you
are.'

'Do you miss it? The cooking?'

Miriam began to core a red pepper. 'No. It got tangled up with
all the stuff I had to deal with when my mum got ill and died, and

then with trying to make sure the business went to the right person rather than the wrong one.' She sliced through the pepper, then began to chop it up. 'I had to have counselling about it, actually.'

'Did you? That's sad. I'm watching you now, and you can tell it's second nature.' Rhiannon began to peel an onion. 'And if my eyes start to water, it's this. Not your sob story nor nothing.'

Miriam laughed. 'Honestly, I've only been involved with the catering side occasionally over the past few years. Liked to keep my hand in, but the last time I did it … well …' She took a butternut squash and began to peel the skin off.

'Well, what …?'

'I had a panic attack and threw up and … spent the day lying down under a desk in a portacabin at a race course.'

'*Oooh nooo*! Poor dab, you.'

'It was the same day I decided to escape from London and come here. Thanks to Justin.'

'Well, something good came of it.' Rhiannon held up the onion. 'Just chopping it am I? Nothing fancy?'

'No, nothing fancy.' Miriam put the pepper core to one side.

'I managed to cook for Julie and Henry and you without incident though. So that's progress,' she said.

'And Alan. Remember?'

Miriam instinctively turned to the window to see if she could see him in the summerhouse. 'Yes, well,' she muttered, and carried on working. 'I had a lot of counselling to help me get to this stage, and I just feel that somehow I'm going backwards.'

'But not with the cooking, obviously. Have I cut these the right size?'

'Perfect.' Miriam smiled.

'If you're going to throw up, can you give me some fair warning? I'm not good with stuff like that, so I'll make myself scarce.'

Miriam turned up the music and they worked until the kitchen was full of the warm and spicy smells of chilli and curry. They only looked up when the doorbell rang.

'Think that must be Jim with the catering dishes to take all of this down to the pub.' Miriam walked to the door.

'Oh, I don't want him to see me like this,' whispered Rhiannon. 'I'm not interested in him as he asked me out, did nothing about it and flirted with that other woman and stuff. And I don't actually care ... but I do have standards.'

'You can hide if you want to,' said Miriam, holding the door handle. 'Just shout when you've found somewhere.'

Rhiannon rushed off up the stairs. 'Ready,' she yelled eventually.

'Oh, that smells gorgeous, doesn't it, guys?' Three men were waiting by Jim's van as Miriam opened the door.

'Oh, lovely,' they murmured in unison.

'They'll help out serving, they will. Going to dress up as the Rat Pack ... that's Frank Sinatra by there, Sammy Davis Junior and Dean Martin. Or Greg, Martin and Dai.'

'Hi.' Miriam waved. 'Who are you going as?'

Jim leaned forward. 'Las Vegas Elvis. I know I won't be alone, there will be many. But I love the costume. And it's left over from last year.' He laughed and looked up at the sky. 'Great day for it too. Thank God.' They all walked in and loaded the food into the tins, then took it all to the van.

'Right. Thanks, Miriam. I really appreciate it, under the circumstances.' He got in the van and opened the window. 'So, are you okay to serve for the times I sent you? Only a couple of hours, spread out? And you are dressing up, aren't you?'

Miriam winced inwardly, the idea of serving the food to actual members of the public making her stomach knot in a familiar way. 'Yes,' she said, trying to sound confident. 'Rhiannon and I are two of the Pink Ladies from *Grease*.'

'Great.' He switched on the engine. 'I haven't seen her recently. Wondering if she was all right, I was.'

Miriam heard a cough from upstairs and closed the door as he drove off. 'See, Rhiannon. He misses you.'

'He may talk the talk, but he needs to walk the walk with me,' she shouted. 'That's all. Shall we get our stuff on then?'

'Washing up first, I'm afraid,' said Miriam, heading to the kitchen.

'Boring.' Rhiannon walked slowly down the stairs like a petulant teenager. 'If I have to.'

'Yes, and then we can all dress up.' Miriam threw her a towel. 'No gain without pain,' she said and began to fill the dishwasher.

They linked arms and opened the garden gate, giggling at their costumes and their full *Grease* make-up as a Mini drove past. 'Is that a Lady Gaga driving?' shrieked Rhiannon. 'And ... look! I think that's Cyndi Lauper over there.' She pointed at a woman smoking a cigarette on the path opposite. 'Oh, this is going to be so much fun!'

The closer they got to the village, the more people in fancy dress they saw. 'This is a bit like one of those zombie films,' said Miriam. 'Only the world's being taken over by look-alikes.'

'Good one. Very funny.' Rhiannon flicked her ponytail at a John Travolta, and they pushed through a group of David Bowies and into the pub.

'Ladies, welcome,' shouted Jim. 'You look fabulous. What do you think of this?' He spun around, showing off his white outfit and black Elvis wig. 'Hoping I don't get any food on it though. It'll cost a bomb to dry clean off.'

Rhiannon nodded, unsmiling. 'Very good. Now, where's our catering station?'

Jim looked confused. 'It's out in the garden. I'll show you.'

'No, thank you. We'll find it.'

Miriam smiled and followed her outside.

'People have paid for the food with the tickets,' he said to their backs, 'and there's a performance by T-Rox – they're a T-Rex tribute act – by the harbour at one-thirty if you want to go.'

'Okay.' Miriam waved at him. 'Come on, Rhi. I don't think he's seeing anyone.'

Rhiannon grunted as they took their places under the awning where the food was being served, and a queue began to form immediately. Miriam glanced at the table, fighting the urge to lie down under it and hide, then identified the path to the side of the pub as a potential escape route.

'Are you all right?' Rhiannon said quietly. 'You look a bit pale all of a sudden.' Then her eyes widened. 'You aren't going to throw up, are you?'

Miriam picked up a ladle and concentrated on it, breathing slowly to try to combat the panic.

Rhiannon nudged her. 'The queue's getting bigger, we'd better get cracking.'

'Don't know what's in there—' said a Joanna Lumley look-alike '—but it all smells delicious. Doesn't it, darlings? I just can't wait to try it.' The people behind her murmured in agreement. Then Rhiannon kicked Miriam gently in the leg, and she automatically picked up a plate, looked up and said, 'Who's for the Sri Lankan-style curry over here?'

A Liam Gallagher swaggered towards her. 'All right. Got any chutney with that, love?'

'Condiments and dressings are on that table by there,' interrupted Rhiannon, waving her ponytail coquettishly.

'You're not doing this all day, are you?' He took the food from her and then took his sunglasses off.

'No, just for an hour now, and then another hour later on.'

'Cool. I'll catch you later. My band, Dough-asis, are on at four-fifteen in the bar. Which Pink Lady are you?'

'Rizzo,' answered Rhiannon. She giggled and nudged Miriam. 'Who needs Jim?' she said and carried on serving.

Miriam switched into autopilot, and by the time they had finished their first shift, her feet were aching and she longed to sit down. So, she made her way into the bar and found a seat in the corner, where she watched Rhiannon circle around the Liam. Jim placed a beer in front of her. 'She's in a funny mood, isn't she?' he muttered, staring at her as she began to flirt with the band. 'Tell her if she wants a drink, there's a free one at the bar for her.'

Miriam leaned back and sighed, relieved at having managed to prepare and cook vast amounts of food without hyperventilating. The serving of it, however, had been stressful, and she was glad of the break. She picked up her drink, enjoying the feeling of the cool glass in her hands and watched as Alan sidled into the bar. She pushed herself back in her seat and shuffled to hide behind a clutch of Tom Joneses so he wouldn't see her. He was also dressed as Elvis, but he didn't look as comfortable as Jim and stood by the wall for a few minutes before walking out into the beer garden.

An Ed Sheeran look-alike began to sing 'The Shape of You' in the middle of the room, and slowly the whole pub joined in, so by the time he started on 'Castle on the Hill', it felt like a massive, happy karaoke session. Rhiannon sat down as Miriam finished her drink. 'Don't look,' she hissed, glancing behind towards the bar. 'But the woman is here – the one I saw up close and personal with Jim'

'I'm facing the whole pub, so I'm not really looking, I'm seeing,' whispered Miriam back. 'What does she look like?'

'Dressed as the blonde one from Abba.' Rhiannon pointedly looked out of the window so as not to arouse suspicion.

'Ah.' Miriam felt her heart begin to race uncomfortably. 'That would be Britta, actually. Alan's ex. Who looks like the blonde one from Abba even when she's not wearing a blue crocheted hat.'

'What, she's seeing Jim then?'

'I don't think so. I think they probably just know each other. But—' she stood up '—I don't really want to be around for a while. Alan's in the garden, and I don't want to see whatever is going on.'

'Well, the Liam Gallagher said he's going to watch T-Rox. Shall we take a look?'

'Good idea.' Miriam began to shuffle through the bar, looking at the floor and almost jumped out into street, Rhiannon giggling behind her. Then they hurried down to the harbour, passing Julie and Henry as they did who were dressed as Sonny and Cher.

'Hello, ladies,' shouted Henry. 'You look great.'

'Love the hair.' Rhiannon waved at Julie.

'I may keep it on all weekend,' she shouted back. 'We're just off to the pub. See you later probably.'

Rhiannon drank another two bottles of beer before they made their way back to do their next shift and was singing 'Beauty School Dropout' when they saw Jim taking something out of his car.

'You do look lovely, Rhi,' he said. 'You do too.' He nodded at Miriam apologetically. 'But you were made to be a Pink Lady, Rhi.'

Rhiannon flicked her ponytail coquettishly. 'Oh, thank you, Jim. I didn't know you cared.'

The hint of a blush was visible under his beard and he walked back into the pub, past Alan whose wig had gone slightly askew.

'Miriam.'

'Alan ... or should I say Elvis?'

He leaned closer. 'About the other night.'

'Oh, don't worry. It was nothing. Very nice. But nothing.' Miriam walked past him quickly, striding towards the food station and work. Because she was lying and, actually, wanted to ask him very, very loudly what the hell he thought he had been playing at, but she couldn't do that when she had food to serve.

Rhiannon took her place next to her and they picked up some plates. 'Think I've started too quickly with the beers,' she muttered, swaying slightly.

'It's fine. I think I'll join you.' She waved at Jim who was loitering by a nearby table. 'Can I have another beer, please?'

He nodded and went back inside just as Britta walked over. 'Hello. You look very nice. Have you seen Alan? He's being very elusive. I need to speak to him urgently.'

'He was outside a minute a go.' Miriam held up a plate. 'Would you like some food?'

'No, thank you. I've already eaten.' She adjusted her blue hat and pulled down a tassel sleeve. 'But if you see him, can you tell him I'm looking for him?'

'Of course I will.' Miriam smiled sweetly at her, determined to keep out of whatever was going on.

Jim placed a bottle in front of her. 'There you are.' He took a plate out of Rhiannon's hands, brushing her fingers as he did. 'Been busy, have you?'

'Me?' She looked up into his eyes and smiled slowly. 'An ambitious career woman like me is always busy, Jim, and I've been branching out and helping Miriam too.'

They stared at each other for a few moments as a queue formed behind them.

'I just want a curry,' moaned a woman dressed as Madonna. 'Hurry up and decide what you're gonna do.'

'Oh, right.' Jim stepped back. 'Got work to do.' And then he sloped off towards the bar.

Miriam nudged Rhiannon. 'See, I told you.'

'I don't know. I rather like that Liam Gallagher look-alike to be honest. His real name is Harry.'

'Well, nice to have a choice.' Miriam took a swig of her drink. 'Who's next for the chilli?' she asked and began spooning it onto a plate.

Miriam decided to go and see who was performing at the harbour, left Rhiannon flirting with the Liam Gallagher and pushed through the crowds of look-alikes and holidaymakers. Ned Sheeran was dueting with Fred Sheeran, and she listened for a while, buoyed up by the energy of the audience and relieved she had got through the day so far with little anxiety.

Making her way home, she saw Alan and Britta arguing outside the bookshop, and paused for a moment, trying to work out how to get past without them noticing, desperately trying not to listen to their conversation.

'But Britta, I told you. I don't want to do it. It's not me.'

Britta pulled her crocheted hat off and threw it to the ground. 'You are so … you could be so very much more than you are, Alan Thomas.'

His voice rose, irritably. 'I'm quite happy as I am.'

Miriam hurried over to the other side of the road and pushed behind a group of people walking towards the beach.

'Is that why you're running away?' Britta was almost shouting.

'I'm not running away. I'm going travelling. For a year.'

'You are having a mid-life crisis, is what it is.'

'What's wrong with having a mid-life-crisis? I'm enjoying it.'

'You could sell more books if you did more events. You need a higher profile. I don't understand.'

'That's why we're not married any more. Remember?'

The group Miriam was hiding in slowed down. 'Is that Elvis Presley arguing with the blonde one from Abba?' Someone laughed. 'This thing gets better every year.'

Drama, drama, drama. Miriam couldn't get the words out of her mind. *Run away. Don't get involved. Don't*. She darted towards the footpath.

'She's not helping, is she?' Britta had turned around and was pointing towards her.

'It's nothing to do with her. Leave her alone.' Alan took his wig off and began to shake it at Britta angrily. 'Where's your new boyfriend anyway?'

'Working. Hospital consultants do work some weekends, you know?'

Miriam wanted to cover her ears. She didn't want to know about their messy divorce, she didn't want to think of Alan and Britta together. She didn't want any of it.

'If you just tried harder, spoke to more people, you could sell more books and earn more money.'

'I'm going on a break. I'm not going forever. I don't know what this is about.'

'Is she going with you?'

Miriam carried on walking, but Britta's voice just kept following her.

'Why do you keep doing that?' Alan shouted, exasperated.

'When you disappear at the end of the stargazing event that I have spent so long organising, will she be with you? Is she the one distracting you from your commitments?'

Miriam could feel herself almost running. *He was going away. Alan was leaving.* She tried to push the feelings away, to pull the drawbridge up, put on a front like she always did. She didn't care. She *didn't* care. So why was she crying?

The sunset bathed the attic room in an orange glow, the wooden floor warm underfoot. Miriam sat amidst old photographs and paperwork. She was carefully rifling through and examining everything, desperate to find a reason to stay. Another picture of her parents, another familiar recipe, anything to keep her there. But she couldn't find anything.

'I can't do this,' she said to a seagull perched outside. 'I don't want to be involved in any of this any more. It's too hard.' Her phone buzzed and she took it out of her bag.

Are you okay? Off to town with the boys from Dough-asis if you want to join us. R x

Miriam smiled. 'Rhiannon's young and not afraid of anything,' she said to the bird. 'Was I ever like that? '

She opened her e-mails and clicked on the draft folder. The message to the solicitor remained unsent. Her finger hovered over it as she looked out of the window, at the setting sun hanging low over the sea, the sky lilac and pink. 'You were only going to be my view for a while anyway,' she sighed, re-writing the message. *Please contact Joanna's solicitor to negotiate out of the contract. I do not wish to spend my own time or money on employing someone to do this.* She pressed the send button quickly so she couldn't change her mind, then picked up one of Alan's astronomy books.

'So, it's you, me and the stars tonight,' she said, looking at the telescope. Then she hurried downstairs, grabbed some bread sticks, a tub of hummus, a bottle of wine and some water, then ran back up to hide from everyone and everything for a while.

Chapter Twenty

The car park was almost empty when Miriam pulled into it, and she watched a group of friends set off up the hill to the cliff walk whilst she was putting on her walking boots, careful to make sure she kept a distance behind them. She wanted no interaction with anyone today, hoping the emptiness and tranquillity would drive away the demons that had kept her awake the night before. Checking her map, she grabbed her rucksack, locked the car door and set off.

Her solicitor had phoned her that morning in response to her message.

'Are you sure you want to go down this route? Employing someone else quietly would be easier.'

'I don't want anything to do with it. I need to get away,' she said.

'Well, as I said before, strictly off the record, Artie Morgan is known for his litigious nature. He's trying to make drama out of the food truck issue even when there isn't any. And it wouldn't take much for him to start spreading the word that you aren't to be trusted if he found out you had walked away from a legal commitment.'

'That's not fair.' Miriam could feel the anger beginning to pump around her body again.

'No, it isn't. But he doesn't like losing.'

So now she walked, not wanting to think about it any more.

The sea sparkled turquoise below, reflecting the clear, cloudless sky. Miriam moved through the landscape, pink and yellow wildflowers brushing her ankles as she went. She looked towards the horizon, imagining herself on a tiny boat drifting towards land and sleeping for days in a hammock on sandy beach where no one could find her. She stood for a while, scanning the water for signs of dolphins, then she moved on and tried again, eventually sitting down on a rock and staring into the distance, munching on stale breadsticks and slightly warm taramasalata. After that, she stood up and carried on, heading downwards to an isolated empty cove where she took her shoes off and enjoyed leaving her footprints on the sand.

Pulling a towel out of her bag, she stretched it on the ground before lying on it, letting the warm sun lull her to sleep. A loud splash woke her and she sat up suddenly, confused for a moment. She scanned the beach, searching for whoever or whatever had made the noise. A pile of clothes was tucked next to a rucksack close to some rocks, and Miriam could see movement in the water as a swimmer made their way across the bay.

She checked her phone. 'God, I've been here for over an hour,' she muttered and began to gather her things together, keen to regain some solitude by heading for the path again. The swimmer stood up and began to stride through the sea towards the shore. It was Alan. Miriam spun around, shocked, desperately looking for somewhere to hide.

Of all the beaches in all the world, how has he ended up on this one? she thought, almost laughing. Because it was funny. But it wasn't, because she was a grown woman afraid of her own emotions and she didn't like it.

'I can see you,' he shouted. 'It's too late.' Then he walked to his towel and began to dry himself off.

She waved but didn't move. Her feet felt like they were rooted into the sand. 'I didn't know you'd be here,' she shouted. The clear blue sky was now scattered with dark grey clouds and she searched her bag for her waterproof, just in case the rain came when she was standing on an isolated cliff-top path later.

'I didn't know you'd be here either.' Alan moved closer to her. Miriam was busy fighting the urge to rush towards him, so she stood, immobile, watching him as he got nearer.

'Rhiannon mentioned there might be dolphins about, so I thought I'd do a bit of walking and see if I could find any.'

He stopped and smiled. 'I heard that too. I needed a bit of time to myself, so I thought if I'm going to get away from people, this is the beach because the path goes inland away from the cliffs for a bit. You have to know it's here.'

'Oh dear. I read about it online. It said it was beautiful and rarely used.'

'So, what are you hiding from then?'

'Everything. Not seen any dolphins either.' Spots of rain began to land on the towel. 'Oh, excellent. Miles from the car.' Miriam picked up the waterproof.

'Wait …' Alan stepped forward again. 'Why not come for a swim? It's a hot day, and the water is lovely and warm.'

'It's raining!' Miriam laughed.

'So? You're going to get wet anyway.'

'I haven't got my swimming costume with me.'

'Well, I've seen your underwear on more than one occasion.' His eyes twinkled mischievously. 'They could all pass for bikinis.' He turned and headed back towards the sea.

Miriam watched, her eyes on his long, muscular legs, and felt as if someone had flicked a switch. Her feet felt light again, itching to move, and as he got far enough to dive in, she hurriedly took off her clothes and followed as if there was an invisible string pulling her towards him.

'This is not warm!' she shrieked, feeling the water lap over her ankles.

He laughed. 'It is when you're in. Come on. Live a little.'

A wave swept across the bay, splashing her waist. She shrieked again and flung herself in, then jumped up and screamed. 'Is that refreshing?' she said breathlessly. 'Or just cold?'

Alan swam over to her. 'If you moved around a bit, you'd enjoy it more.'

Miriam could feel herself drifting towards him like he was a magnet. *That's what he is*, she thought. A magnet that pulled her to him, and sometimes she just couldn't fight it. Yesterday she could. Today she couldn't.

She lay back and floated, staring up at the sky. The rain was heavier now, pitter-pattering on the sea around her, and she felt her foot brush up against his leg.

'I knew you couldn't leave me alone,' he whispered.

'It's the sea, not me,' she said, closing her eyes, allowing a wave to carry her away from him. He touched her foot, pulled her gently towards him and she opened her eyes. All she could see was him and the sea and the sky. And for a moment, that was all that mattered.

He held her gaze then turned away suddenly. 'Race you to the rocks at the other side of the beach.' He dived down and swam off.

'You cheated,' she shouted, following him and pushing her way through the waves, up and down, until she managed to get to the rocks. Alan was leaning against them with his arms folded.

'Could do better,' he said. 'But nice try.'

'Gee whizz,' Miriam said, out of breath. 'You really know how to motivate.'

'I'm well known for it.' He began to walk back to the beach. 'Sun's out, look. We can dry off now. That way you won't have to walk home in wet undies.'

'I hadn't thought of that.' Miriam watched him as he went, his broad back glistening with seawater and rain drops. 'Where's my

242

self-control when I need it?' she muttered, not moving. 'Right, remember, he's going away. You can't get involved. You can't cope. And he has an ex-wife he sees too much of.' Smiling brightly, she followed him onto the sand, repeating over and over in her mind, *don't stand too close to him, don't get in his orbit, his energy ... or whatever it is that pulls you in so hard you can't do anything about it. Just don't.*

He carried his things over to her towel and set them down. 'Going to get dry in the sun,' he said.

Miriam lay down, closed her eyes and tried not to look at him. 'Shouldn't take too long. It's very hot all of a sudden.'

'I was hoping to see you yesterday but, well, you disappeared very quickly.'

'You were in the middle of an argument.' Miriam kept her eyes firmly shut. 'And Britta seemed keen to get me involved. So I left.'

'Don't blame you.'

'Are you going to tell me what exactly is going on between you two? I mean, you slept with me and yet—'

'Nothing is going on.' She could hear him sigh. 'You can open your eyes, you know? It would help, to be honest – so I can explain.'

Miriam sat up and looked at him. 'Okay, carry on.'

'We work in the same place. Both academics in the same department. So when there's a meeting or a project, we are always there, next to each other, opposite each other. Too close to each other. And it means that sometimes we forget that we're not married any more. We haven't been for five years.' He rolled over and looked at her. 'It's like an echo of another life. I mean, she's in another relationship. We haven't—'

'Had sex,' interrupted Miriam.

'... for over a year.'

243

'Oh, you have a messy few years after your divorce.' Miriam tried to control the irritation in her voice. 'Bad luck for anyone getting in the middle of that.'

'You did say that what we did was only physical though, didn't you? So don't get judgemental please.'

Miriam had said it, but she hadn't meant it. *Shall I tell him? I could tell him. But he is going ... I am going. I can't cope with having something and then losing it. Not again.*

'What was she shouting at you about yesterday? And why was she pointing at me?'

He touched her arm gently. 'I'm sorry. She doesn't normally drink very much, but for some reason yesterday she ...'

Miriam looked down, unable to meet his gaze. Her fingers scratched the sand, drawing jagged lines. She put her energy into the movement, deflecting her thoughts so she wouldn't let her guard down.

'It wasn't very nice. I don't like being sucked into the middle of other people's drama. It's happened before when I was not at my best.' She glanced up. 'It's not fair, you know?'

They fell silent for a few moments, the rhythmic and gentle undulating of the sea filling the void.

'So, you're leaving then?' Miriam didn't look up when she said it.

'Ah, yes. You heard. She wants me to be more visible, do more publicity. We co-wrote a couple of academic books together years ago, so it would help her too. She has this idea I could be on television and radio.' He laughed. 'Then I could sell more books, have more money and help our sons more. But they're adults now, so I think that's another echo of the past. I just want to write my books and work on my projects and that's it …'

'Where are you going?'

'Portugal first. The Alentejo … astronomer's heaven. Eventually Chile. All half formed. I just want to be me for a while. Drift, you know.'

'Yep, I get that. How soon?' She already knew, but she couldn't stop the words coming out of the mouth.'

'Rather dramatically, I announced I would leave straight after the stargazing event.' He laughed. 'Problem is, she helps set it up with Joanna, who is obviously not around. E-mails have not been sent ... I have not been very helpful. In fact, I've been avoiding her, and she told me yesterday,' he glanced at Miriam, 'after you ran away, that she was not going to be available. And I woke up this morning to a torrent of messages detailing everything that hasn't been done yet.' He lay down and stretched. 'And so, in a week, I have my regular event with speakers booked, but no marquee, no sound system ...' He sat up again suddenly. 'Partly my fault. She'd been trying to talk to me but I kept avoiding her.'

Miriam looked at him, angry and sympathetic at the same time. She wanted to put her arms around him, tell him it would be all right, that she could help. Because that's what she did. She ran events. But not any more. It wasn't good for her.

He scratched his chin and gazed into the distance. 'I'll have to cancel all the tickets. Bit embarrassing … but hey-ho …'

She dug her hands in the sand and concentrated on them, as if doing that would stop the words coming out of her mouth. *But ... but ... if she didn't help, Artie Morgan could find out. And she wouldn't let him have the satisfaction of knowing she'd walked out on a big high-profile event. It was nothing to do with wanting to help Alan. Nothing at all.*

'Do you want me to see if I can call in some contacts?' *There it was.* She'd done it. Miriam rolled her eyes at herself.

He looked at her. 'Are you sure? You don't have to. It's my mess. I'm the idiot … but …' He smiled, clearly relieved.

'Technically, it's yours, your ex-wife's and your aunt's,' she said firmly. 'But let's say it'll be my big goodbye too.'

He moved closer, looking surprised. 'You're leaving? I mean I knew you would eventually.'

'Yes. I can't—' she didn't have the words so scrambled to her feet. 'Come on,' she said. 'I've got to walk a few miles back to my car before I can start helping you.'

Alan didn't move. He just stared at her. 'You're leaving ...'

'Are you going to move? We've got a lot to do.'

'Sorry.' He stood up. 'I've parked about four miles that way.' He pointed westward.

'I'm parked about five miles the other way.' She pulled her shorts and T-shirt over her damp underwear and put her rucksack on her back. 'Right ... see you later,' she said, walking towards the cliff path, feeling Alan's gaze on her back as she did.

'You know that wall?' he shouted. 'The one you put up when I get close to you ... what's that all about?'

She turned around and looked at him. But the words wouldn't come, so she waved and carried on up the cliff path, focusing her mind on what she needed to do.

Chapter Twenty-One

Rhiannon was in the kitchen when Miriam arrived home, watching a glass of water fizz.

'Hiya,' she said quietly, then she picked up her drink. 'Just having a couple of headache tablets.'

'That bad, is it?' Miriam turned the kettle on.

'Quite a night, it was. Like a rock and roll tribute act night out.' She sat down and put her head in her hands. 'I only went because I was annoyed with Jim.'

'Cup of tea?' Miriam took the mugs out of the cupboard.

'Go on then. Do you know, I can't remember why I was annoyed with him.'

'I think you thought he was seeing someone else.' Miriam clicked the kettle on. 'But he wasn't because Britta is Alan's ex-wife, and is actually with a doctor.'

'Oh, yes.' Rhiannon looked up, briefly lively. 'She made quite the scene, didn't she!' Then she put her head in her hands again. 'Was he trying to be nice to me yesterday?'

'He was very taken with you. He obviously likes you.'

'Have I ruined it?'

Miriam squeezed her hand. 'Probably not. But then, don't ask me for advice about men. My track record is shocking.'

'Have you got any bread? Breadsticks? If I fill myself with carbs, tablets and tea, I may feel well enough to pop round to the pub just to check.'

'Help yourself. There's plenty in the bread bin. Left over from yesterday.' Miriam saw Alan park his car next to the summerhouse and stood up. 'I've got some work to do as it happens.'

'Oh, what's that? You haven't got a booking today, have you?'

'No … there's a big problem with next week's stargazing event. A void, in fact, and for reasons I want to shout at myself for, I've suggested I try to sort it out.'

'Oh no! Is it going to make you physically sick?'

'I don't know.' Miriam flung her arms in the air. 'And I have to spend more time with *him*.' She glanced out at Alan, who was walking towards them. 'I'm not sure that's a good idea. In fact, it's a terrible idea.'

As he got closer, Miriam could feel her heart begin to race anxiously. She picked up her tea and sipped it, trying to calm herself down, then she sat down at the table. She stood up again and opened the fridge, staring inside as he paused in the doorway.

'I can't thank you enough for this,' he said. 'And I'm sorry for what I said … when you were leaving the beach, you know? It's just …' He stood behind her. 'I'm a grown man acting like a teenager, and it's very childish.'

'But you're right,' she murmured. 'The wall … that's what I do … recently anyway.' Then she closed the door and pulled herself together. 'That's for me to sort out,' she said briskly.

'I am still in the room,' Rhiannon said. 'But I will quickly finish these,' she pointed at the water, tea and breadsticks, 'and be on my way.'

'No rush.' Miriam sat down next to her. 'We've got to go through some logistics, haven't we?' she said to Alan. 'Have you got all the info on your computer?'

'Yep.' He put it on the table and plugged it in, and they all watched it flicker to life. 'There you are.' He clicked on a file. 'This is what we've got … and this is what we need to do. Oh, bloody hell.'

'Right,' said Miriam quietly.

'Ahh ...' gasped Rhiannon. 'All by Saturday? *Next* Saturday?'

'Yes.' Miriam put her phone down next to her, took a pen and pad from the drawer, and began to write, trying to control her breathing. She was about to step back into the world she'd left behind and was trying to keep the wave of the past from overwhelming her.

Alan just stared at the screen. 'Worse than I thought,' he said. 'Much, much worse.'

Rhiannon picked up the breadsticks and put them in her bag. 'I'll leave you to it. I'll have this as a takeaway.' Standing up, she picked up her water and lost her footing, accidentally flinging the dregs of it over Miriam's head. 'Sorry, sorry!'

Miriam looked up. 'It's fine. I need to give it a wash anyway,' she said calmly, but as Rhiannon hurried out of the door, she felt anything but fine. 'Alan.' She nudged him. 'Alan ... right ... let's go through this list, divvy up the work and I'll start making some phone calls.'

He stared at her, a look of mild panic on his face. 'Serves me right this, doesn't it?'

'We'll talk about that another time,' said Miriam briskly. 'Let's just get this done.'

'There's a package at the door,' shouted Rhiannon. 'I've put it in the hallway.'

Miriam went to check what it was, leaving Alan sat staring at his computer screen.

The parcel was addressed to her and as she opened it, a string of golden fairy lights fell onto the floor. Picking them up, she rifled through the packaging to try to find a label or a note, then carried them into the kitchen.

'Have you been sending me these?' she asked. 'I mean, it's kind if you did. But I'm not sure why.'

'Not me, no,' he said, distracted, scrolling through something on the computer screen. 'I should have listened to Britta. She and Aunt Joanna put a lot of work into this. I never realised.'

Miriam picked up her phone. 'Right.' She took a deep breath and placed herself firmly in organisation mode. 'Let's sort out this marquee. With less than a week to go, you've certainly given us a challenge. Where's the number of your usual supplier? I'll give them a call.'

The rest of the day was spent writing lists, ringing people up, calling in favours and making plans. Miriam sat as far away from Alan as she could, desperate not to get caught up in whatever he gave off that made her rational side disappear.

Just as they were about to pack up, Miriam crossed off what she'd done on her list of tasks.

'Where's the health and safety assessment and insurance document?'

Alan looked at her blankly. 'I never got involved with that. It was always Joanna.'

'Okay.' Miriam's heart sank. 'Have you got any previous ones I can look at?'

'She must have sent all the e-mails to Britta before she went, do you think?'

'You may have to swallow your pride and contact your ex.' Miriam had no intention of doing it for him. Britta was not her favourite person after she'd tried to drag her into their argument at the festival. He looked up at her helplessly. 'Oh no. You're not doing that to me, Alan Thomas.' She stepped further away from him.

'Why do you keep doing that?' He closed his computer and stood up.

'Because ... I don't know.' She couldn't tell him why, but she had to keep her distance. When this was over, he would be gone.

She would be bereft and he would be having an adventure. And she was already hurting at the thought of it. 'I'm going for a bath. See you first thing tomorrow.'

'Okay.' He opened the kitchen door. 'I'll nip down the pub then.'

'That's nice.' They stood silently for a few minutes. Words hanging unsaid in the air between them.

'Right then,' he said.

'Enjoy,' muttered Miriam, walking up the stairs, closing the bedroom door firmly shut and running a bath that produced enough steam to power a sauna.

Miriam arranged the fairy lights in the bedroom, next to the others she had been sent and switched them on, then lay in bed with the curtains open. The moon cast its light over the ocean, stars twinkling in their thousands in the sky, and the multicoloured lights around her made it feel like it was all connected. Just like that night with Alan on the hill when the rain cleared.

'Oh, stop it,' she said to herself, and she switched off all the lights and hid herself in the dark under the duvet. The anxiety struck almost immediately, her mind beginning to race, going through lists in her head, memories of the last two years at the company running like a film. *Stress upon stress upon stress.*

Sitting up, she took her journal from her bedside table and rifled through to an empty page. *I haven't written in this for a little while*, she thought. *That's a good thing, isn't it? Now to real life again.*

There's that saying – the definition of insanity is doing the same thing over and over again and expecting different results! Ha ha ha.

She put it down, told Alexa to play whale music and drifted off to a listless sleep.

For the following few days, she threw herself into work, falling back into her old routine of a morning run and evening yoga, finishing with a done and to-do list blue-tacked onto the kitchen wall. Alan spent his time liaising with the guest speakers, occasionally appearing in the kitchen to grab a sandwich and check on Miriam's progress.

By Thursday evening, after many phone calls, e-mails and general begging, the marquee had been arranged, seating, sound system and programmes organised, and Jim had offered to help with the drinks. Miriam had even finished off the health and safety details and insurance information.

But apart from her, Alan and Rhiannon, she had no one to help cook the food or deal with the guests.

And then it came.

She could feel the anxiety running towards her, like a distant patter of feet turning into a gallop, louder and louder and louder, till she had to hold on to the table to stop it knocking her over. Memories of the last event played out in her mind. The people, the noise, the smell of the food, the questions, the responsibility. The sense that she had to do everything. Make it all perfect. Every last detail.

Grabbing her phone and her headphones, she started to practice her breathing. *In ... one ... two ... three ... four ... out ... one ... two ... three ... four.* Then she crawled under the table, closed her eyes and tried to drown out the panic till the sound of birds and waves lulled her into an uncomfortable sleep.

The scene replayed in her dreams again, as it had over and over and over again for the past year. Artie Morgan was standing in front of the food truck. '*It's only business, Miriam. It's only business.*'

252

Miriam looked at him. This man had been her escape from her mother's illness, giving her snatched moments of fun and laughter. Her light at the end of the tunnel for her businesses and her staff.

But he was just a net she'd got caught in. A series of bad decisions made when she was at her lowest.

And then his wife had arrived, trapping her in their stuff. Their angst, their games, their anger.

'Miriam ... Miriam?' She heard Alan's voice but couldn't open her eyes. Britta was shouting, *'Is she going with you? Is she ... ?'*

A hand gently brushed her fingers. 'Miriam?'

'Yes ...?' she felt someone crawl next to her under the table, stroking her hand.

'It's fine ... you were talking in your sleep.'

'I wanted them to leave me alone,' she whispered.

'Yes, you said.' He pulled her to him. 'Whatever it was, it's gone now.'

She felt his breath on her neck, his heart beating slowly as he soothed her and wrapped his warmth around her.

'This is a bit embarrassing,' she said eventually.

'What is?'

'Finding me hiding under a table.'

'You seem to like lying down in places ... on the decking ... on the beach.'

'Thank you.'

He pulled closer. 'For what?'

'For calming me down. Giving me a *cwtch*.'

He laughed softly. 'You're learning the most important Welsh words, I see. Can I ask what drove you under this particular table?'

'The present. And the past. We have no one to help cook the food and no one to help with the public. That's the present. I'd rather not talk about the past.'

'Ah, I see …'

'You sound very measured about it.'

'No. I'm panicking. But quietly.'

Miriam squeezed his hand. 'Shall we get out from under here? The floor is very hard.'

'Okay – I'll roll out of my side and you can roll out of yours. One, two, three, go'

They both clambered to their feet and looked at each other from opposite sides of the table. Miriam stepped back, remembering she was angry with him, and breathed in deeply. 'I don't know where to look for help,' she said eventually.

'Could you contact Justin?'

'It's so last minute. I don't know if he can … I don't know if *I* can.'

'I tell you what, I've got his number. I'll do it. It's my event. Honestly.'

'But I said I'd do it. It's what I do … I'm tying myself in knots here.' Miriam slumped onto the chair.

'You've done so much for me. A problem shared is a problem halved. No one has to do everything on their own.' He put the kettle on and took out his phone. 'We could co-make the tea? I'll just call him and beg for help.'

No one has to do everything on their own. She watched him as he filled the kettle with water and walked out into the garden, her stomach churning with emotions. No one had ever said that to her. Or if they had, she hadn't heard. Or listened. She sat as the kettle boiled and bubbled quietly to a crescendo until steam began to pour out of the spout. *That's me*, she thought and sighed, putting the tea bags in the mugs and pouring the boiling water over them, watching the liquid turn slowly brown. Then she added the milk and carried them out onto the decking where Alan was standing.

'All systems go,' he said, relieved. 'The cavalry's on its way.'

She handed him his drink. 'I thought the same thing when he came down last time.'

'Thank goodness. I mean, I don't care too much about my reputation. But it would have been in tatters if this had all gone wrong. And Joanna's.' He sat down and began to drink his tea.

'Well, the good news is we will get through it somehow. That's you, me, Rhiannon and Justin. It's going to be hard work, but we can do it.'

'When is the food arriving?'

'First thing on Saturday. Oh, I'm beginning to feel funny again.'

He smiled at her. 'You're amazing. Why not think about afterwards? Focus on that.'

When you'll be gone, thought Miriam. She finished her tea and stood up. 'I think I'm going to have a bath and put on some soothing music.'

'I've got to collect some stuff from St David's.' Alan stood up. 'I'll see you tomorrow.'

'Yes.'

He turned and walked briskly to his car, and Miriam almost slammed the kitchen door behind her.

She checked her phone for messages in case she'd missed anything and clicked on a new one from Justin. *Think you need to see this ... here's the link.*

Miriam clicked on it out of curiosity and almost dropped the phone. Artie Morgan had written an article entitled 'In Business, You Can't Always Trust Your Friends'. Her heart flew into her mouth and she scrolled down, looking for the inevitable – and there it was, third paragraph in.

Only a year ago, I was within hours of signing a contract to take over a well-established company. I had spent a lot of time, money and energy on this enterprise, and also felt that the person I was dealing with was a friend. However, at the last minute, for reasons I am still in the dark about, this person decided not to go through with it, leaving my plans for the future in considerable doubt. This person had built up their enterprise with a reputation for being fair, trustworthy and truthful. My advice to anyone is – look beyond what's in front of you. There could be a dark side.

Miriam almost threw the phone across the room. It wasn't libel, it wasn't slander, but anyone who knew him would be able to work out who he was talking about.

And this time, instead of feeling sick and anxious, she rode on a wave of anger, packed an overnight bag, got in the car and drove to London.

Chapter Twenty-Two

Miriam put on the work suit she had brought with her and examined herself in the mirror in the hotel room, pleased with the way she looked, having spent an hour on styling her hair and putting on her make-up. She finally understood what war paint actually was.

This was the Miriam Ryan of old. The one Artie Morgan had never met. And she was very, *very* angry.

She called reception. 'I'd like a cab as soon as possible, please. I'll be down in five minutes. Can you get me one for then?'

Picking up her bag, she glanced out of the window at the bustling city street far below, steeling herself for what she was about to do, then she made her way down to the hotel foyer and straight into the taxi that had been organised for her. The cars and buses and motorbikes weaved past as the cab moved, and she watched them, rehearsing her speech carefully: the one she had been crafting on her journey along the M4, in the hotel, before she went to sleep and as soon as she woke up.

'Can you wait here for me? I'll be fifteen minutes,' she said, climbing out onto the pavement and standing in front of the block housing Artie Morgan's offices.

Taking out her phone, she wrote a message to Jeffrey Goldstock. *I'm about to go and speak to Artie in person about this article. Here is the link. I'll deal with the consequences afterwards. It just has to be done.* She sent it, and then walked down an alleyway to the side of the offices, opening a scruffy door at the back which led to a stairwell.

She looked up, remembering how they'd sneaked down here and out to a waiting car for a quiet meal together at the beginning of their fling. Miriam had decided at the time it was fun and illicit. Now she knew he had been hiding from his wife and that it was a well-worn path with many other women. Taking a breath, she took the first step, then walked up quickly to the first floor, her heart beating fast. She focused on moving forward, not allowing herself to think about anything apart from what she was about to do.

Pushing the glass doors open into the corridor, she hurried to Artie's office, opening the door before slowly walking in front of his desk, relieved there was no one else around to stop her.

He didn't look up, pretending he didn't know anyone was there – his usual power play.

'Hello,' she said. 'I think we should have a chat.' Her voice was steady, but she could feel herself shaking.

Artie stared up at her from his computer, his face confused. He was clearly trying not to look surprised. 'Miriam. You look well.' He stood up. 'What an unexpected pleasure. Take a seat,' he said.

His eyes caught hers and, in that moment, she understood how she had been drawn to him so strongly. But it had gone. And all the blame, guilt and embarrassment she had thrown at herself for what she'd done began to ebb away. 'Haven't got the time.' Miriam stared at him then smiled. 'I read the article. I am very unhappy about the reference you made to the way I do business.'

'What makes you think it was about you?' he said evenly. 'I didn't mention anyone by name.'

'Well, as you're aware, anyone who has had dealings with either of us will know I was going to let you buy my company. I was professional enough not to enlighten our community as to my reasons for changing my mind. You obviously don't have such high standards.'

'You made it personal.' He sat down and began to scroll down the computer screen. 'What exactly have you come here for, Miriam? As you can imagine, I'm very busy.'

'When I met you, I was not fully myself.' She was pleased the words sounded firm and measured, giving her more confidence to carry on with what she had planned to say. 'I simply wanted you to be the answer to my problems. Frankly, you weren't up to the job. I was not going to let you take my years of very hard work and commitment and ruin what I had set out to do. That is why I decided not to let you buy my business. Because of information I had been given about your plans.'

'Like I said – you made it personal.'

'And you are a liar. You have a wife.'

'I didn't say I didn't have a wife.'

'You didn't say you did.' Miriam looked at him, wondering if he ever felt guilty. 'I will not now allow you to sully my reputation by making sniping insinuations about me in print. I have contacted my solicitor. If there is any hint of libel or slander or defamation of my character in that article, I will do something about it.'

'Go ahead.' He smirked. 'My legal team checked it before it went out.'

'It's a bit sad and snipey though, Artie, isn't it? Just because you didn't get your own way. What a waste of your time … I mean, did it make you feel better?'

He began to type, ignoring her.

'I do not like you. I wish I'd never met you. I am glad to have got rid of you. Say anything else about me or the company I used to own, and you *will* be sorry.'

She walked towards the door.

'You assume I didn't feel anything, Miriam. Perhaps you were wrong.'

259

She paused, forcing herself not to respond, and turned into the corridor without looking back, keeping her pace steady and fighting the urge to run out into the road and cry.

Am I supposed to feel better? I feel exhausted. But at least I've done it. Said what I needed to say.

Stepping into the waiting taxi, she leaned back and sighed as it pulled into the traffic. *And now for my next trick*, she thought, *a stargazing event in south west Wales at the drop of a hat. Wonder if anyone noticed I'm not there ...*

Collecting her car from the hotel, she jumped in and set off, counting the miles as she drove, fuelled by adrenaline. The travelling playlists kept her motivated until she arrived home at dusk, climbed into bed, set her alarm, and fell into a deep, comfortable sleep.

Chapter Twenty-Three

The first food delivery arrived at 7 a.m., and Miriam was already in the kitchen going through the list of what needed to be done, half of her mind on the event, the other half focused on Sunday when it would all be over.

'Shall we just put it all over in this corner?' the delivery man asked, wheeling in the boxes of rice, pasta and vegetables.

'Yes, fine, thanks.' Miriam took the order sheet he handed her and checked everything off. 'Perfect,' she said, signing it and giving it back to him.

'Someone was just parking up behind me when I came in.' He smiled. 'Next order, I expect.'

Miriam followed him outside where another man was waiting patiently. 'Ah, great, follow me. Can you just put it in the kitchen?' As she turned, she noticed a jogger running past towards the village. Something about the way he moved made her look again. Her heart stopped. *It looked liked Artie Morgan.* She forced herself to watch him as he went. *It's not him. You know it's not him. It's* not *him. It's stress, Miriam. It's stress. You've dealt with him, remember?* The jogger disappeared around the curve in the road, and with him her anxiety.

Oh, for God's sake, she thought, watching the second delivery man pile the rest of the boxes in the corner of the kitchen. *I can't cope with more phantom sightings. First my mother's voice, then my nemesis jogging.* She almost laughed at herself, then asked Alexa to play whale music once she had the room to herself again. 'I am calm. I will be calm. I *am* calm. I will *not* let this affect me,' she chanted.

For the next two hours, she chopped, sliced, boiled and sautéed, veering from calm focus, to anxiety, anger and frustration depending on what thought arrived in her head every time there was a gap in the music. Even Alexa streaming monks chanting didn't seem to be able to stop it.

I shouldn't even be doing this.

This is someone else's problem.

Why do I always think I have to be responsible?

Why do things keep dropping on my head? It's not a sign. It's not my mother trying to speak to me ... I'm definitely going mad.

Alan. Why am I helping him? I know why I'm helping him ... I'm an idiot.

I haven't got enough onions. Where can I get more onions?

The monk chanting stopped, and what sounded like spa music filled the room. Miriam stood back and took stock of what she had achieved so far: a vegetable chilli bubbling on the range, potatoes chopped and ready to blanche, peppers sliced, garlic pressed and a mound of strawberries washed to decorate several cheesecakes. 'Well done, me,' she said to herself. 'I deserve that well-earned rest I'm supposed to be having.'

She heard an engine rumbling to a stop outside the house and went to check who it was. 'Sound system?' she said, checking the name on the van. 'If you go just down there, there's a little lane leading to a parking space at the end of the garden. Should be easier to unload. Just knock on the door of the summerhouse and Alan will be there to help.' The van driver tooted their horn in acknowledgement and drove off.

Then she checked her list of things to do, took some courgettes from their boxes and began to work again, just as someone knocked on the kitchen window.

'It's us. The sound people ... where do you want us to set up?'

'Um ... Alan can help.'

'No answer from the summerhouse.'

Miriam looked at the clock. 'Right. No idea why. Follow me.' She walked out into the garden and showed them what was needed and where, and then went back to work, glancing at the shut curtains in the summerhouse irritably, but with no time to find out why the event's host was not answering the door.

Rhiannon pushed the kitchen door open dramatically just as Miriam was putting some crumbled biscuit in the food processor.

'I'm late. So sorry. Had a bit of a heavy night. Didn't get in till 2 a.m.!'

Miriam nodded. 'Hi.' Then she carried on chopping.

'Oh, you're not in a mood with me, are you?' Rhiannon went to the downstairs bathroom to wash her hands. 'It's just that Harry – you remember? – the Liam Gallagher look-alike from the festival, asked me out, and I thought why not?'

'Of course.' Miriam glanced at her phone and began to work out the timings for the food in her head.

'You are annoyed, aren't you?' Rhiannon put on an apron and picked up a knife.

'No ... just concentrating. Got a lot to do.' Miriam smiled thinly. 'Can you prepare that mound of spring onions, tomatoes and cucumbers?'

'Sure. What's this music then? Seems a bit, you know, the kind of thing you'd have a facial and a wax to, rather than work.'

'It helps me,' said Miriam, taking the grill pan out. 'I just need to be in the zone.'

'All right.' Rhiannon began to chop in silence for a while. 'Oh no,' she said eventually. 'I think Jim's just arrived with all the drink.'

'Right.' Miriam wasn't really listening.

'It's just ... he saw me last night when I was out. We started at his pub. And he was a bit off, truth be told.'

'Okay.'

'I hope he's not going to make a scene.'

Miriam began to season the courgettes. 'Yes,' she muttered as the door was opened dramatically by Jim, who had shaved off his beard.

'Miriam,' he said, then nodded at Rhiannon. 'Shall I put these in the big fridge in the utility room till we're ready? I've got the beer outside ready to set up.'

'I was right,' breathed Rhiannon quietly. 'He does look like Justin Timberlake ... even without the beard. '

'Yes, of course, there should be plenty of room in there.' Miriam put the pepper mill down and picked the salt up.

'You're not annoyed with me, are you, Jim?' Rhiannon flicked her ponytail at him and smiled.

'Why would I be annoyed with you?' he said curtly, taking the bottles into the other room.

'Oh dear.' Rhiannon went quiet.

Miriam carried on working, her mind still whirring with what needed to be done next and when.

'Do you think I've upset him?' Rhiannon was standing next to her. 'What should I do?'

'I don't know … talk to him about it?' Miriam picked up some olive oil and began to pour it over some vegetables.

'What if that doesn't work?'

Jim reappeared and walked into the garden silently, then came back in. 'So, what exactly are you playing at, Rhi? I thought we were going out for a drink, and then you come in with that ... man.'

'I thought we were too,' Rhiannon almost shouted. 'But you never bothered to get back to me about it.'

'I had the festival and everything. I was going to.'

'Oh, were you now?'

264

'This isn't working!' Alan's voice grew louder as he walked over from the summerhouse. 'I keep getting phone calls from our speakers asking how to get to us. I mean, surely they know!' He burst into the room, staring at his phone. 'What should I do?'

'Give them directions?' Miriam put a tray under the grill, then went to the utility room to wash her hands.

'This is so much work. And I can't find my notes.'

'You must have got them saved on your computer,' she said evenly, checking her timetable again and taking some eggs out of the fridge. 'Where've you been? The sound people were looking for you.'

'I've been looking unsuccessfully for the pieces of paper I have my words on. Why are you so calm? There are many reasons I decided I didn't want to do this any more. It's too stressful for a start.' He poured himself a glass of water and opened the lid of the chilli. 'Are we only having the vegetarian one? That's disappointing.'

'It's what?' Miriam looked up, holding a whisk.

'Um ... I didn't mean to be rude.'

'Oh dear.' Rhiannon concentrated hard on slicing a tomato.

'I've been up since six this morning.' Miriam turned the whisk on and held it in the bowl.

'I know ... honestly, I didn't mean—'

'I am helping you. I don't have to. I *really* don't have to.' She looked up and waved the whisk in front of her. 'I could just go now. I could.'

'I'd rather you didn't point that at me,' he said quietly. 'It looks a bit dangerous.'

'It looks a bit dangerous, does it?' Miriam could feel her focus pouring away. 'It's a whisk – and you promised the cavalry. Where's the cavalry?'

'Lost probably, if Alan's giving them directions,' muttered Rhiannon, picking up a cucumber and cutting through it noisily. 'Sorry.'

Miriam looked at the clock. 'We are open at midday. Your first speakers will be arriving some time after eleven, and you need to check the sound system is working, make sure all the chairs are set up, and here you are complaining about vegetable chilli!' The room was silent for a moment. 'Alexa, play The Sex Pistols, *Greatest Hits*, then anything by Metallica,' said Miriam firmly. 'I can't cope with this relaxing nonsense any more.'

'You're magnificent,' said Alan quietly, then slipped out of the door back into the garden, followed by Jim.

'That told us.' Rhiannon giggled. 'Have never heard the Sex Pistols. Before my time.'

Miriam switched the whisk on again. 'Careful,' she muttered. 'I'm on the brink, as you can probably tell.'

An hour later, they stood back and surveyed what they had done. 'Everything is in order, I think,' said Miriam. She glanced outside to see Alan talking to the sound people and Jim moving chairs around, and suddenly felt very tired. He would be going away in just a few hours. There was so much she wanted to say to him. But she didn't want to say it. She wanted it all to disappear.

And then Britta walked out of the marquee and stood next to him. 'When did she get here?' she said.

'Oh ... no idea. I've had my head down,' mumbled Rhiannon.

'I'm just going to go and freshen up. Take a break, Rhiannon. You've been so helpful. I couldn't have done this without you.'

'Sure. Are you okay?'

'Yes ... just had a very early start.' Miriam climbed the stairs to her bedroom and turned on the shower, setting out a smart sundress to wear that afternoon. Stepping under the hot water, she stumbled a little, dislodging a full bottle of shower gel from the shelf. It fell onto her head, and she froze for a moment as the contents of the bottle oozed down her face.

'If that's you trying to knock some sense into me, Mum, I've no idea why,' she shouted eventually. 'What exactly am I supposed to do? And about what? I'm just trying to get through the day! I've cooked, I've organised. And it's not even my problem. Britta's in the garden too. And I've told Artie Morgan what I think of him. Now *that's* progress.'

Miriam suddenly felt very sick. 'Too soon for that particular memory,' she muttered, quickly getting out of the shower, drying herself off and sitting on the bed. Then she took out the jiffy bag of photographs and spread them out. 'And all I've got left of you, Mum and Dad, is the odd ghostly laugh and constant knocks on the head. Not sure why I thought I'd find something of you here.'

She put the photos away, feeling defeated, but she didn't know what by. She dried her hair, put on her dress and her mother's necklace, and crept up to the attic room, where she lay down under a shelf, as there was no table, and practised her breathing.

'In ... one, two, three, four ... and out, one, two, three, four.'

'Miriam ...' there was a tap on the door. 'Miriam?'

'Justin?' she said, surprised.

'Yes. The cavalry's arrived. We're all looking for you, and Alan said you could be hiding under a table somewhere, so we're searching in all the rooms with tables.' He pushed open the door and sat down next to her. 'Here we go again,' he said quietly. 'It looks weirdly comfortable down there. Can I join you?'

'Sure.'

'Is she in there?' Rhiannon said softly from the landing.

'Yes.'

She pushed the door open. 'Oh, Miriam. Poor dab. Hyperventilating on the floor? Can I come down too?'

She lay down next to Justin without waiting for an answer. 'There's someone to see you. Well, some people to see you.'

They heard two male voices muttering outside. 'Come in,' said Justin. 'It's fine.'

Alan and Jim almost tiptoed in. 'So this is ... what? Meditating or something?' asked Jim, lying down next to Rhiannon.

'It's one of Miriam's coping strategies,' whispered Alan, who crawled next to Miriam and put his arm around her. 'I hope you don't mind,' he said. 'But I find this strangely comforting.'

'Are we all supposed to count our breathing or something?' Jim stretched and must have accidentally touched Rhiannon's arm. 'Sorry about that.'

'No problem,' she whispered.

Miriam smiled, her eyes still closed. She felt different. She didn't feel alone.

'Are you all in there?' Julie's voice pierced through the silence. 'I haven't been in this room for years. Come on, Henry. Let's give her the news—what on *earth* is going on here?'

Miriam opened her eyes as Henry sat down next to her and handed her a photograph.

'Here it is. I just had to go back and check. I've been thinking about it for ages and finally put it all together.'

Julie joined him on the floor. 'We've just been back for an unscheduled visit home to get it. This was definitely not in our diary, but we couldn't wait.'

'What is it?' Miriam examined the photograph.

'I think you'll find it's you,' said Henry gently.

There was a group of people on the beach playing cricket. Miriam's mother, father, Joanna and the fair man. Miriam was at

268

the front holding a plastic bat and looking up at the sky, a little boy was scowling behind the wicket, and there was also a young man with a wispy beard. It was similar to the one Miriam had found.

'That's me,' said Henry.

Miriam sat up. 'You?'

'Yes. I came here a few of times before I met Julie with some friends. And that particular year, somehow, I found myself on the beach when you were playing cricket and got involved in the game. You'd had terrible dreams the night before. Terrified of the dark, you were, and your parents were trying to keep you occupied to stop you thinking about it.'

Miriam ran her hand along the photograph and tried to replay the scene in her mind.

'You'd just been hit on the head by the cricket ball. It was plastic, thankfully. But we were all holding our breath, hoping you wouldn't cry. One of my friends took the picture.'

Miriam looked at him. 'Did I cry?'

'No … you laughed, you did, and chucked it back at the person who threw it in the first place – him.' Henry pointed at the little boy. 'Alan.'

'Oh, I *knew* you were here for a reason,' squealed Rhiannon. 'I told you, didn't I? You didn't believe me though.'

Alan sat up. 'Me? Let me see.'

Miriam handed him the photograph. 'We seem to have already met,' she said more calmly than she felt. 'You were winding me up, even then.'

She closed her eyes and remembered. She could hear her parents laughing, the sound of the sea, people chattering around them, her father scooping her up and dancing around with her. *'Miriam,'* she could hear her mother's voice, young and light and vibrant. *'When we've finished playing we can go for a swim …'*

'*And then we can go and look at the stars later. Would you like that? There's a telescope at Joanna's house, and we can see them all shining really brightly.*'

'*Yes, please,*' she heard herself say. '*Can I play more cricket now?*' Her mother almost skipped barefoot over the sand and laughed. '*Yes we can, Miriam, my gorgeous girl. Yes we can.*'

Alan squeezed her hand. 'I'm sorry I threw a ball at your head.'

'You're forgiven.' Miriam sat up, not sure what to say or do. 'I'm overwhelmed. I'm just …'

'Henry, don't forget the lights.' Julie nudged her husband.

'Oh, yes.' He gave her a box. 'We used to have a lighting shop. A few, actually. And supplied events and such. Still have a stash in our garage, don't we?'

Miriam picked out a string of orange lanterns. 'You've been sending me the fairy lights?'

'The first time I saw you, I felt you needed some light in your life. You seemed lonely and, even when there were people around you, you'd just make yourself alone again. Every time we met, I thought you seemed so familiar to me. I kept saying it, didn't I, Julie?'

'He did.' Julie squeezed her hand. 'But he couldn't work out why.'

'It gradually all began to fall into place.' Henry pointed at the photograph. 'That necklace you're wearing – look, your mother is wearing it – and the fact you look just like her. I didn't really know your parents – I don't think I even know their names – but I'd been sorting out our old photographs recently, you see, before we came here, and finally it all clicked.'

Miriam leaned over and hugged him. 'That's so kind. *So* kind … confusing – but kind.'

'Your dad kept talking about the stars to you that day, to stop you being afraid of the dark.'

'Oh, I don't remember.'

'You were very, very young,' he said.

An alarm buzzed on someone's phone. 'Sorry to dampen the mood, but we've got work to do,' said Justin briskly. 'Don't look at me like that. You asked for my help.'

They all clambered slowly to their feet. 'I don't believe in all this spiritual, mystical stuff,' said Miriam. 'But, well, I'm trying to find an explanation.'

'Just go with it,' said Alan softly. 'Don't overthink.' He held her gaze for a moment until Justin's alarm buzzed again. 'Where were you yesterday, by the way? I couldn't find you anywhere, and you didn't answer my texts.'

'Just had something to sort out,' she said, watching everyone walk down the stairs. She took a deep breath and followed them. The garden was full of people in smart uniforms, and the food had already been transferred to the catering dishes, ready to be taken out to the garden.

'Ta dah!' said Justin. 'We're all here.' He pulled her outside. 'It's Miriam, everyone.'

Every single person in the garden turned and waved. 'They're ...' she muttered, unable to finish the sentence.

'Say hi to your former employees,' whispered Justin, 'who, actually, are also your friends.'

'Hmmmm ...' she said, then took a deep breath and shouted. 'Hello, everyone. And thank you, thank you, thank you!' Then she rushed back into to the house, smoothed down her dress, counted to ten and walked back outside. 'Right, what do I need to do?'

'Well, you've done virtually everything. Come back in an hour or so.' Justin picked up a clipboard from a chair and walked over to Alan.

Miriam stood for a moment, confused, then caught a glimpse of the sea in the distance. 'Right. I'll go then,' she muttered, opening the garden gate and walking towards the village past a sign that said, "Stargazing and Sandcastles event, parking 300 metres". *I sorted out that sign and confirmed with the farmer in less than a week*, she thought. *Amongst other things, I did that.*

Taking the steps to the beach, she sat on the rocks and stared at the sea for a while, oblivious to what was going on around her, her mind racing, trying to understand what had just happened. Justin finding the house online at the last minute, the mistake that got her here – because, had she known, she would have run a mile in another direction – Julie and Henry, the fairy lights, the events, the food, Alan ... *Alan.*

A plastic ball hit her on the head.

'Oh, I'm so sorry.' A woman rushed over to her. 'My son gets a bit carried away.'

Miriam saw a little boy staring at her. 'Is the lady all right, Mummy?'

'I'm fine.' Miriam laughed. 'It didn't hurt at all.'

'Do you want to play? Can the lady play, Mummy?'

The woman touched her arm. 'Actually, there's only me and him. We could do with an extra person to make it a bit more exciting.'

Miriam looked at them. 'Of course, I'd love to. I haven't played cricket on the beach for a very long time. It *was* on this beach ... actually.'

'Thank you, lady,' said the little boy. 'You can be the wicket keeper.'

'Whatever you say.' Miriam smiled, taking her place.

'Do you need any more players?' Julie and Henry were walking towards them, with another couple following.

'Goodness,' said the woman. 'That would be lovely. It's usually just us, so a few more people would make it much more fun.'

'I love playing cricket on the beach,' Henry said to the little boy. 'You will be gentle with me though, won't you?'

The little boy giggled. 'I'll try!'

'Before we start, we'd like to introduce you to someone, Miriam.' Julie beckoned the couple behind her to come forward. 'This is Joanna and Horst. We just found them outside the house. It was such a surprise.'

Miriam stood, unable to speak, but held out her hand.

The woman took it. 'Miriam Ryan. I am *so* pleased to meet you.'

'Joanna …?' Miriam said eventually.

'I got the e-mail from my solicitor, and I felt guilty about leaving organising this bloody event in such a mess, so I thought I'd better come back. Although I didn't tell anyone in case I got cold feet on the way and changed my mind.'

'It's all fine now – the event, I mean.'

'I was hoping I'd meet you at the end of the lease anyway. I remember your parents fondly. Your mother was the one who got me into cooking.'

'Did she?'

'Your parents used to rent a cottage close to mine – it's not there any more – and your mother was always creating the most wonderful things. It's a pity they stopped coming, but you know, that's life.'

'My mother …' Miriam trailed off, not knowing what to say.

'And your dad was always talking about astronomy to my father. They'd spend ages in the attic room, just staring at the sky.'

'My dad …'

'And you! When you applied for the job, I was thrilled. It was such short notice and to know someone of your calibre was taking over made it so much easier to go.'

'Me?' Miriam said, confused.

'In the events and catering world, you are very well regarded. You know that, don't you?'

Miriam smiled at her. *I suppose I am*, she thought. *For a while there, I forgot…*

'Can I ask why you disappeared so suddenly?' she said eventually.

'Ah, well ... Horst—' Joanna pulled him to her and put her arms around his waist '—came back into my life. We had a fling when I was young, and he asked me to go away with him, but family stuff got in the way and so I said no. I regretted it every single day.' She gazed up at him adoringly. 'And then I started cooking for everyone, and it became my life for a while. I wanted to go and find him but always found a reason not to. I was always caring about everyone else!'

'But why go so suddenly?'

'I just had a bit of an epiphany. I wanted something for me for once. I'm seventy years old – I've waited long enough! He found me on Facebook and we started messaging, and one day I decided to go to Australia and see him without anyone talking me out of it. So I did. And cut everyone off for a while ... and, actually, I was relieved not to be involved in this stargazing event. Alan and Britta are a complete pain!'

Miriam laughed. 'I can confirm that. So, you just decided not to worry about everyone else for a while?'

274

'And just worry about me, yes. But not before I made sure everyone else was all right.'

'Same as ever,' said Horst, kissing her on the cheek. 'But that's why I love her.'

Joanna smiled up at him again.' We had flown back anyway and were enjoying ourselves in London when I got the message about you wanting to leave. So, it's all worked out in the end. Horst will stay with me until the end of the summer and then we'll head off on another adventure.'

'Mum, when are we going to play the game?' the little boy shouted irritably.

Miriam hugged Joanna. 'It's so lovely to meet you, but I think he's waited long enough. Shall we all play cricket?'

Joanna picked up the ball. 'I'll bowl, shall I? And how about building a sandcastle with your mum afterwards? Further down the beach is a sandcastle competition, and I'm the judge!'

'Cool,' shouted the little boy. 'But can you throw the ball? I still want to play cricket!'

Miriam lingered in the village after the others had made their way back to the event and meandered down to the harbour, reluctant to watch Alan do his talk and then drive away out of her life.

The sight of a food truck selling cockles and mussels parked next to the bookshop sent the familiar surge of anxiety through Miriam. A man stood with his back to her, his hair the same colour as Artie Morgan's, his stance, even his clothes. And suddenly she was angry. *I've already told him*, she thought. *He already knows. Surely I shouldn't feel like this now? I'm not going to revisit my past every time I see a food truck or a stocky middle-aged man*, she thought. *Take responsibility for your bad decisions, finally forgive yourself, Miriam Ryan, and move on. Or you'll be bouncing around your life permanently on edge.*

She almost laughed. Then she stepped forward and waited behind him in the queue. He bought his food and turned round, smiling at her as he did. Miriam smiled back. He looked like Artie Morgan from the front too, but she didn't care. The spell she'd put herself under had gone, and she ate her carton of cockles on the way back to the house, feeling much lighter than she had done for a while.

A queue of people snaked onto the road waiting to be let into the garden, and she watched Justin stand with a clipboard checking them in one by one. Taking her keys out of her bag, she let herself in through the front door and walked into the kitchen. Everything had been cleared up and there was nothing for her to do. She looked out of the window and saw a Porsche parked where Alan's blue Datsun had been.

He stepped out of the summerhouse, looking uncomfortable in a suit and tie. Then he noticed her and waved, looking relieved, and began to walk over. She smiled and went into the garden to meet him halfway but as she did, Britta came out of the marquee and stood in front of him, holding some books.

Miriam stopped, not wanting to get caught in the middle of their conversation, weary again of other people.

'You've done well with this,' she heard Britta say. 'I'm pleasantly surprised.'

'Thank you. Or, actually, thank Miriam.'

Britta turned and nodded in her direction. 'He's very frustrating, isn't he?'

Miriam smiled but didn't say anything. *Don't get involved*, she thought.

'So. Here are the books we co-wrote. It would help me if you mentioned them.' She gave them to him and looked at him expectantly.

276

'I will.' He held them up in front of him. 'They are good books. You know, you are an excellent writer on your own, Britta? You really don't need me any more. Just have confidence in yourself and go for it.' He held out his hand and took hers. 'Are we okay?'

She nodded. 'We're okay.' Then she turned and walked towards the marquee. 'I'm just going to listen to this speaker. Good luck.'

A group of people surrounded him, asking for his autograph, wanting to talk about his books, so Miriam walked to the bench in the orchard and sat, watching everyone work through the tiny gap in the trees until Justin appeared and beckoned to her.

'Felix is here by the way.'

'Felix?'

'Yes, he wanted to help too.'

'Where is he?'

'Got swallowed up in the crowds somewhere. I'm sure he'll find you.' He checked his clipboard. 'I'd better get back to my super-organising. You can honestly just relax now. You've done all the hard work and we can all take over.'

'I can do that, can't I?'

'Yes, you can. Are you going to listen to any of the speakers?'

Alan had managed to break away from the people around him and was walking over to her.

'I can't thank you enough,' he said. 'Really.'

Justin smiled and walked back towards the marquee.

'I'm glad it's going well.' Miriam looked around her. 'When are you doing your talk?'

'Soon. I'm very nervous. I hate doing them, to be honest. At least this is the last one.'

'Yes … and then you're off on your adventure. In your Porsche, I see. When did you get that? Your last car was a Datsun.'

'I'm driving it as a favour to Dewi … don't ask. It will look good as I drive off into the distance though.'

Miriam smiled. 'You must be very excited.'

'You could come with me,' Alan said quietly. 'Have an adventure. Travel the world. Look at the stars. Aunt Joanna's back. You don't *have* to stay.'

Miriam felt her heart pull her towards him, but her feet remained firmly on the ground as if they were made of lead. She held her arm out, hoping that would make them move, and touched his cheek, unable to say the word. *Yes*, she wanted to say. *Yes*. But she couldn't do it. She just smiled.

'Miriam!' Felix shouted, running over and grabbing her before swinging her into a hug. 'I've been trying to get hold of you, but you haven't been answering my e-mails.' She watched Alan move away, swallowed by the pockets of people gathered in the garden, and then saw the summerhouse door shut behind him.

'I'm sorry. I've been trying not to get involved with the business so haven't been opening most of my messages,' she said, untangling herself.

Felix laughed. 'So, this isn't work?' He pointed at the tables full of trays of food, waiting staff, an orderly queue into the next event in the marquee, and Justin standing by the PA system with a list, ready to start issuing orders again.

'This was an accident.' Miriam smiled. 'I got drawn into it.'

'It's what you do and who you are.'

'Not sure about that any more to be honest, Felix.'

'Well, the messages I sent are about a proposition I have for you.' He squeezed her hand. 'This company – you built it up. When you bought me out, you took it and it flew. And the people

278

that work for you love you. They know you stayed on longer than you should have to sort out that mess with Artie Morgan so they could keep their jobs.'

Miriam looked around. *They had dropped everything to come and rescue Alan's event.* 'I do miss them,' she said quietly. 'I don't miss the job though. I just don't. I stepped back and let them take over. It made me quite anxious.'

'You trained them very well.' He squeezed her hand again. 'I want you to come back as a consultant. You can pick your hours. I want to expand over into Europe and Australia, and you'd be perfect to help me do that.'

'Oh.' For a moment Miriam clicked back into her past. Her mind automatically began to rifle through ideas and strategies. *Could I do it?* she wondered.

'There you are. You're interested, aren't you?'

She saw Alan come out of the summerhouse and walk towards the marquee, notes in hand, ready for the big event. She could feel her heart flutter, and she tried to move but remained rooted to the spot.

Felix looked her in the eyes. 'And you like him, don't you?'

She hesitated, then looked at the floor. 'Yes, yes I do.'

'Well, why aren't you with him, then? Miriam? Look at me.'

She sighed. 'I think it's because it's important, Felix. And I don't know if I can cope with having something like that and losing it … maybe it's better not to have that. Protection and all that …' she trailed off.

Justin tapped the mic, and the high squeal of feedback rang around the garden. 'Sorry about that. The Alan Thomas event is starting in five minutes, this is the last call. Please take your seats.'

Miriam looked around and saw Alan nervously pacing backwards and forwards near the Porsche, before turning and walking swiftly into the marquee, to be greeted by enthusiastic applause and cheering.

'Well, you have a think about my offer. And don't forget, I've still got your food truck. That could be part of your job … going off to festivals and such to fly the flag. Anyway, I'm going to have a listen to him, see if he can enthuse me about the planets.' He joined the last-minute stragglers as they headed towards their chairs, and Miriam walked into the kitchen, picked up her phone, then went to her bedroom and called Fiona.

'Please be there, please be there,' she muttered. 'I know I haven't got an appointment. Please be there.'

The phone clicked. 'Hello, Miriam. Is everything all right?' Fiona's voice oozed calmness and tranquillity.

'No.' Miriam could feel herself wanting to burst into tears. 'Have you got five minutes?'

'I've got more than that. I hadn't heard from you for a while, so I assumed everything was going well.'

'It was. It is …'

'Has anything happened?'

Miriam breathed in. 'I've fallen in love, and I'm frightened.'

'Okay.' Fiona's tone was measured. 'Why do you think you're frightened?'

'Because. I don't know … over the past few months, I realise I lost everything that was important to me and it all got tangled up. And I've managed to pull myself together at last. I'm not sure I can risk loving anyone or anything again in case I lose it.' She took a long breath. 'I'm not sure I can cope with that.'

'You've said that you've fallen in love.'

'Yes.'

'Well, you've already done it.'

Miriam grabbed a pair of tights from the drawer and wiped her eyes and nose with them. 'He asked me to go away with him,'

280

she said. 'And I couldn't say yes. I couldn't even move. My feet wouldn't move.'

'Do you want to go away with him?'

'What if it goes wrong?'

'What if you don't try?'

'It'll have gone wrong already.' Miriam almost smiled. 'Although. Felix – my ex-husband – has just offered me a consultancy job with my company—I mean his company. I mean the company my former employees own.'

'Okay. How do you feel about that?'

'Panicked. Grateful. Not sure I want it. Maybe I do.'

'What do you want to do?'

'I don't know. But I don't want to do it yet. I want to ...' Miriam stood up and looked out of the window. Sailing boats glided across the bay under a bright blue sky dotted with cotton-wool clouds, and the cliffs glistened under the sunlight in the distance. 'I want to see the world again,' she said.

'Sounds like a plan.' Even over the phone, Miriam could tell Fiona was smiling.

'I've got to go. Thank you for picking up the phone.'

'My pleasure. I'm here when you need me. Miriam ... before you go ... thank you for supporting me when I first started.'

She paused. 'I knew you'd be good, and you've made a real difference to me so I was right.'

'Based on what – a week as an intern in the company six years ago?'

'I could see something in you even then.'

'But not in events management.'

Miriam smiled. 'You obviously had other talents. And when Justin handed me your card when you first started out, I instinctively knew that if I needed help, you'd be the one to go to. And I like to support talented people.'

'Instinct.'

Miriam thought for a moment. 'Instinct. Yes …'

'You should trust yourself more often. Good luck with everything, Miriam.'

'Thank you, Fiona. You too.'

She put the phone down and looked at the view again as a windsurfer disappeared around the headland. Then she rushed downstairs and out into the garden, her legs suddenly light, the heaviness gone.

'Justin.' She ran up behind him as he was leaning against a tree, drinking a bottle of water.

'Miriam! You frightened me.'

'Sorry.' She hugged him. 'Can you take over completely? I need to go on adventure, and I think it's starting in about an hour.'

He glanced at the marquee. 'Is the adventure hosting a talk in there?' He smiled.

'Yes.'

'Leave it all to me. Joanna's in there anyway, and it's her house and her event so easy peasy. I'll sort your car – now, go.'

She hugged him tightly again, then ran back up to her bedroom and began to pack, throwing her clothes into her suitcase and flinging everything else into her rucksack. Going through the bedside cabinet, she placed the jiffy bag containing her family photographs inside the journal and put them in her case. 'I'm rubbish at writing what I'm feeling,' she said out loud. 'But maybe I can write about the food I taste along the way.' Then she gathered the fairy lights and packed them too.

Taking her phone out of her bag, she stood at the window and took a photograph of the view. 'I will never, ever forget you,' she whispered, then dragged her bags down the stairs to the hallway. Jim and Rhiannon were talking quietly in the kitchen, and she paused for a moment, wanting to run in and hug her friends goodbye. She smiled as Jim gently pulled Rhiannon towards him and decided to leave them be. She put her rucksack on her back and pulled her suitcase along quietly, then stepped through the door and closed it softly behind her.

Sitting on the wall, she watched the sea in the distance for a while, enjoying the sound of the far-off tumbling of the waves on the sand and the familiar birdsong. The sound of a car engine brought her back to reality, and she felt a lump in her throat. *What if he changes his mind?* she thought. *Why didn't I say yes as soon as he asked me?* Taking a deep breath, she stood up and watched the road, her heart beating faster and faster. When the Porsche nudged its way out of the lane, she almost winced with fear.

She watched Alan check the road for traffic and smiled, ready to hitch a lift with him to her future. Then she let go of her suitcase as he drove off in the opposite direction.

'Oh,' she said. 'Oh ...' The car disappeared from view, the sound of the engine getting fainter and fainter until she couldn't hear it any more. Miriam sat down, unsure what to do, too surprised to cry and too embarrassed to go back into the house.

'Oh,' she said, suddenly overwhelmed. 'What do I do next? Without him? I feel sick.'

She stared into the distance for a few minutes, her mind racing.

'Right,' she muttered eventually. 'If you don't want me, I'm not hanging around. I'll have an adventure on my own, thank you very much, Alan Thomas.' She put her headphones on and found 'Gonna Get Along Without You Now' to drown out everything and everyone. Then she began to search the internet for local taxi companies ... so she didn't notice the sound of a car pulling up next to her.

'Oi!' The driver beeped his horn. 'Need a lift?'

She looked up. Alan's arm hung nonchalantly out of the open window. 'I said, did you need a lift?' He opened the door, got out and picked up her case. 'That's a yes, then.'

Miriam laughed with relief. Or was it joy? She didn't know. She just climbed in and did up her seatbelt without looking at him.

'Ready?' he said, revving the engine.

'Where did you go?' Miriam adjusted her sunglasses.

'I was just winding you up,' he said, unsmiling.

'You …'

He revved the engine again and laughed. 'I know … I am.'

She smiled and hit his arm, then leaned back in the seat.

'I promise you won't have to cook anything ever again.' He began to pull away from the house. 'We can live off wine and crisps and ready meals forever and ever and ever.'

'That is the most romantic thing anyone has ever said to me.'

'Wherever we go, I'll make sure there's a table you can lie under …'

'It just keeps getting better and better, *and* I never thought I would ever literally get to drive off into the sunset.'

'Well, technically, we aren't. Although I've got to turn left to go to the petrol station, so for five minutes we will.'

'Now you've ruined the mood.'

'First overnight is Bristol, so that's east. Then we drive south-east to Guildford to hand over this car.'

'Is it not your car?'

He laughed. 'This? I'm delivering it for Dewi.'

'I only decided to come away with you because you have a Porsche.'

'At Guildford your carriage turns into a pumpkin, I'm afraid. I think it's a blue camper van.'

'Oh, it gets worse.' She leaned her head on his shoulder.

'Thank you,' he said, 'for joining me in my mid-life crisis.'

'It's going to be wonderful.' She sighed as they sped past the petrol station. 'Did you mean to do that?'

'Your wish, Miriam Ryan, is my command. Let's look at the stars over the Welsh sea for one last time.'

'Oh, how lovely. I can see the sky turning orange over there already.'

'And I know a great place where we can get fish and chips and a can of Fanta.'

'Once again, you old romantic.'

'Get used to it, baby. I've got a playlist all ready.' He clicked a button, and the car filled with music.

'Is this Happiness?' Miriam laughed.

'Indeed. One of McFly's finest,' said Alan. 'I'm glad you decided to come. I took a long time putting this particular group of songs together.'

Miriam leaned over and kissed him on the cheek. 'I haven't had an adventure for so long,' she whispered. 'What do I do?'

'You'll learn.' He laughed. 'As will I! I think we make it up as we go along. To infinity and beyond!''

He revved the engine again as they drove towards the horizon, beckoned by the stars slowly appearing in the darkening sky as they did, shining and glimmering with life and hope.

* The End *

Thank You

Dear Reader,

Thank you for choosing *Finding Summer Happiness*. I really hope you enjoyed it.

It's set in a fictional village in Pembrokeshire in south west Wales, and the idea of how to tell the story came to me whilst walking a stretch of the glorious coastal path between Manorbier and Bosherston with friends.

I'm a lover of beaches and always happy to carry out research, and south Wales has some wonderful stretches of sand to visit. I was born in Neath in west Glamorgan, so was lucky enough to be close to the Gower, Rest Bay in Porthcawl, Southerndown and every single piece of the coast in Pembrokeshire. I hope I've done them all justice in this book.

If you've enjoyed *Finding Summer Happiness*, please leave a review for on Amazon, Goodreads or the website where you bought the book.

If you want to find out more about my writing I'm on Twitter, Facebook and Instagram – you can find the details at the bottom on the next page at the end of 'About the Author'.

About the Author

Chris Penhall is an author, freelance writer and radio producer.
Born in South Wales, she has also lived in London and in Portugal,
which is where her first two novels, *The House That Alice Built* and
New Beginnings at the Little House in the Sun are set. It was whilst
living in Cascais near Lisbon that she began to dabble in writing
fiction, but it was many years later that she was confident enough to
start writing her first novel, and many years after that she finally
finished it!
Now she's finished her third book, *Finding Summer Happiness*, set
on the south Wales coast, and his busily writing her fourth.
Chris has worked in BBC local radio for many years, written articles
and features for local papers and magazines, and produces podcasts.
A lover of books, music and cats, she is also an enthusiastic salsa
dancer, a keen cook and loves to travel. She is never happier than
when she is gazing at the sea.
Chris has two grown-up daughters and lives in the Essex countryside.

Follow Chris:
Website: www.chrispenhall.co.uk
Twitter: www.twitter.com/ChrisPenhall
Facebook: www.facebook.com/ChrisPenhallBroadcasterWriter/
Instagram: wwww.instagram.com/christinepenhall

More Ruby Fiction
from
Chris Penhall

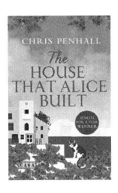

The House That Alice Built
Portuguese Paradise Book 1

Home is where the heart is ...

Alice Dorothy Matthews is sensible. Whilst her best friend Kathy is living it up in Portugal and her insufferable ex Adam is travelling the world, Alice is working hard to pay for the beloved London house she has put her heart and soul into renovating.

But then a postcard from Buenos Aires turns Alice's life upside down. One very unsensible decision later and she is in Cascais, Portugal, and so begins her lesson in 'going with the flow'; a lesson that sees her cat-sitting, paddle boarding, dancing on top of bars and rediscovering her artistic talents.

But perhaps the most important part of the lesson for Alice is that you don't always need a house to be at home.
Visit: www.rubyfiction.com for more details.

New Beginnings at the Little House in the Sun
Portuguese Paradise Book 2

Follow your yellow brick road ....

Alice Dorothy Matthews is on the road to paradise! She's sold her house in London, got rid of her nasty ex and arranged her move to Portugal where friendship and romance awaits. All that's left to do is find a place to call home.

But Alice's dreams are called into question when complications with friends, work and new relationships make her Portuguese paradise feel far too much like reality.

Will Alice's dream of a new home in the sun come true?

Visit: www.rubyfiction.com for more details.

Introducing Ruby Fiction

Ruby Fiction is in imprint of Choc Lit Publishing.
We're an award-winning independent publisher, creating a
delicious selection of fiction.
See our selection here:
www.rubyfiction.com
Ruby Fiction brings you stories that inspire emotions.

We would love to hear how you enjoyed *Finding Summer
Happiness.* Please visit www.rubyfiction.com and give your
feedback or leave a review where you purchased this novel.

Ruby novels are selected by genuine readers like yourself. We
only publish stories our Tasting Panel want to see in print. Our
reviews and awards speak for themselves.

Could you be a Star Selector and join our Tasting Panel?
Would you like to play a role in choosing which novels we decide
to publish? Do you enjoy reading women's fiction? Then you
could be perfect for our Tasting Panel.
Visit: www.choc-lit.com/join-the-choc-lit-tasting-panel for
more details.

Keep in touch:
Sign up for our monthly newsletter Spread for all the latest news
and offers: www.spread.choc-lit.com
Follow us on Twitter: @RubyFiction and Facebook: RubyFiction.

Stories that inspire emotions!

Printed in Poland
by Amazon Fulfillment
Poland Sp. z o.o., Wrocław

76565238R00176